"Outside! She heads for the courtyard!" the Dragon-Blooded warrior called over his shoulder.

Taking a deep breath, Arianna flipped backward toward the ground, falling headfirst from her perch like a cliff diver. Tucking her knees toward her chest, she rolled in the air, unfolding upright just before her feet struck the flat slate roof of the castle's entryway. The Dragon-Blooded warrior matched her leap, sweeping down the stone wall like a typhoon. Arianna marveled as he fell with equal grace and greater speed than she had. Behind him, he left a blazing comet tail of blue and white lightning bolts. Even in the reflected light of the low clouds, his jade blade gleamed fiercely, crackling with energy as he plunged toward her.

He landed on the small crenellated wall encircling the entryway's rooftop. Balancing there, he spun toward her. His attack came at her like a tornado, the long blade of his sword spinning faster than thought. She threw herself to the left, bending nearly in half, and for a moment, it seemed her efforts would take her out of harm's way. Then, the cruel north wind caught the blade, and it sliced faster than sight could follow, sundering her magic's armor and leaving its pitiless bite across her face.

"You will not escape me!" he roared. Arianna feared he might be right.

EXALTED FICTION
FROM WHITE WOLF

CURRENT SERIES

THE TRILOGY OF THE SECOND AGE

For all these titles and more, visit
www.white-wolf.com/fiction

Jess Hartley

ISBN 1-58846-861-5
First Edition: November 2004
Printed in Canada

White Wolf Publishing
1554 Litton Drive
Stone Mountain, GA 30083
www.white-wolf.com/fiction

IT IS THE SECOND AGE OF MAN

Long ago, in the First Age, mortals became Exalted by the Unconquered Sun and other celestial gods. These demi-gods were Princes of the Earth and presided over a golden age of unparalleled wonder. But like all utopias, the age ended in tears and bloodshed.

The officials histories say that the Solar Exalted went mad and had to be put down lest they destroy all Creation. Those who had been enlightened rulers became despots and anathema. Some whisper the Sun's Chosen were betrayed by the very companions and lieutenants they had loved: the less powerful Exalts who traced their lineage to the Five Elemental Dragons. Either way, the First Age ended and gave way to an era of chaos and warfare, when the civilized world faced invasion by the mad Fair Folk and the devastation of the Great Contagion. This harsh time only ended with the rise of the Scarlet Empress, a powerful Dragon-Blood who fought back all enemies and founded a great empire.

For a time, all was well—at least for those who toed the Empress's line.

But times are changing again. The Scarlet Empress has either gone missing or retreated into seclusion. The dark forces of the undead and the Fair Folk are stirring again. And, most cataclysmic of all, the Solar Exalted have returned. Across Creation, men and women find themselves imbued with the power of the Unconquered Sun and awaken to memories from a long-ago golden age. The Sun's Chosen, the Anathema, have been reborn.

Two of these Exalts—the assassin Harmonious Jade and the soldier Dace—have already crossed paths in the lands around the great Eastern trade city of Nexus. But the lines of destiny know no geographical boundaries. Other Solar Exalted are returning in other lands, ones whose fates are intertwined with Jade's and Dace's.

This is their story.

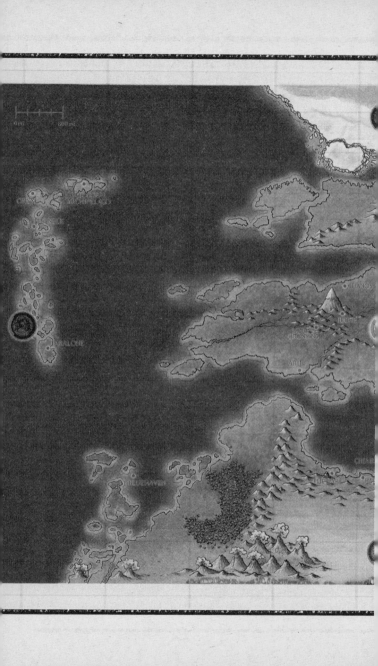

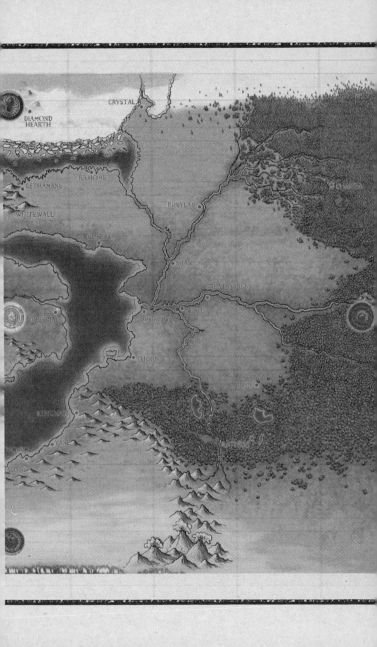

PROLOGUE

Samea drew a long breath, exhausted from her efforts, and stared into the sacred circle. Around her, the great stone room was once again silent and still. Here, hidden deep within the mountain, beyond miles of twisting corridors, behind solid granite doors, even the air was now at rest.

The stone floor beneath her feet was perfectly smooth, save for at its center. There, ageless arcane symbols cast in orichalcum were inlaid in a circle that glowed warm gold against the cold gray stone of the granite floor. On each side of the ring of runes ran a deeply etched channel full of clean sea salt. Abhorrent to most spirits, these conduits ensured that hungry ghosts could neither enter nor exit the center area. Within the protected ring, the inner circle would have taken ten strides to cross and was, again, seamless. Centuries of devoted attention had left it polished smooth as obsidian.

Directly in the center of the circle were two metal lions, crafted of rare orichalcum. Each stood higher at the shoulder than the tallest man in Samea's tribe, and between them, the pair contained enough of the precious metal to bring tears to the richest merchant's eye. The lions' features glowed in the unwavering light of the room's oil lamps, echoing the golden gleam from the ward-runes. Every detail of the first statue was perfectly matched in the second. Each hair and whisker of the pair was identical. Samea gazed upon them without breathing, and for long moments, the room was frozen in timeless stillness as the lions stared back at her in golden stolidity.

She jumped as one of the metal lions yawned, breaking the silence. His jaws stretched enormously, metallic tongue curling past golden teeth that were as long and sharp as daggers.

The muscular feline stepped forward, shaking his great mane. Each step echoed with a metallic ring against the stone floor. The lion sat, looking down with disdain at the rune-scribed border, then he returned his indignant gaze to the woman who had summoned him and his companion from their rest in the Celestial City of Yu-Shan. Wisely, the woman stood just outside of his reach beyond the binding rings. Looking past her, the lion surveyed the rest of the cavernous room.

Things were much as they had been since time beyond time. But here and there, changes had been wrought. Bookcases still lined two of the walls, carved directly into the stone. The lion remembered them from long ago. Back then, they had been filled with great leather-bound tomes and woven baskets of scrolls, herbs and other sacred items. Now, more than half of the shelves lay empty. At least the dust of the long darkness had been cleared away.

The farthest wall still held the enormous altar shelf, also hewn from the granite of the mountain itself. In the time of beginnings, the long open lamps that were carved into the altar had never lacked for oil. Supplicants would arrive, heavily laden with tribute. Among their gifts was oil from the immense seals found on the Inland Sea coastline several days distant. In the earliest times, the lamps had glowed constantly, but then had come centuries of disuse and darkness. Now, once again, the lamps had been filled with sacred oil and glowed warmly. The room shone, illuminated as it had not been for hundreds of years.

Opposite the altar, behind the dark woman who had called forth the lions, two great stone doors still stood. The lion wondered how many thousands of times he had watched those gates swing wide, clearing the winding passage upward and outward to the rest of the temple. They had been crafted so masterfully that even the slightest touch could open them. The intricate carvings that decorated their sturdy locks now gleamed, polished after centuries of tarnished inattention. Someone had attended to this temple as it had not been for centuries.

The huge lion returned his attention to the dark-haired woman standing before him, looking at her while his counterpart stretched languidly behind him.

"You have called us from our slumber, human," the lion rumbled. "Why have you disturbed us?"

Samea straightened, donning an air of authority as tangible as the mountain stone around them. She was no longer a young woman, but her body was straight and lean, and her muscles were strong. Her dress was made of the felted wool of tundra sheep and was plain cut and unadorned, a stark contrast to her fluid and ornate words. Her voice filled the huge granite chamber almost as richly as the lion's had.

"You have slumbered, honored guardian spirit, because this place, once great and glorious, is no longer so. What once stood proud fell so long ago that even its ruins no longer needed protection. The glories of the First Age are gone, swept from the memories of the people of Creation as surely as if they had never been. And gone with them is your purpose for being."

With her bare feet planted against the cool, gray floor, the woman was as deeply grounded as if she had been born of that rock herself.

"Long have I have studied the tomes, Celestial Lion," she said. "I know as few others do that there was a time when this place was not what it is now. I know its purpose, and yours, and I offer you a bargain."

The lions watched her intensely as she addressed them, and Samea suddenly realized how a lemming must feel under the gaze of an owl. The golden spirit farthest from her was indiscernible from its partner save in body language. He moved with an air of slinking stealth, where his companion was brusque and forceful. The quiet spirit stole back and forth, pacing the furthest arc of the salt binding circle as if instinctively trying to flank Samea, watching her with a crafty gleam in his eye. The tuft of metallic fur at the tip of his tail twitched impatiently.

Samea hesitated, studying the lions intently. Dealing with spirits was a tricky business, and she knew that much of her agenda relied on being able to recruit this pair as she had the demon Florivet. Florivet's inherent desire to travel and explore the unknown had given Samea a firm path to approaching him, but these two celestial lions were a less known quantity. She continued addressing the closest spirit as an honored equal, her words chosen with the same care a seasoned icewalker would put into traversing the snows at spring thaw.

"Neglect has taken this place from its former purpose. Its secrets are now stored away in volumes written in languages few can remember ever existing, let alone decipher. What has not been stolen by rodents or raitons to line their nests had been rendered useless by time and deception. Your former purpose may be restored to you, honored guardian, if that be your desire. It is within the power of my Circle to do so."

Samea watched the lions for a reaction, ready to send them back to the Celestial City she had called them from if they appeared hostile. She knew that some guardians fell to madness when denied their purpose. These two had been so long in the spirit world, away from this former temple, that it might have affected their sanity. Seeing no reaction yet, she continued.

"Twilight is falling," Samea said, her voice rising with an air of prophecy. "The time of the Terrestrial's reign is coming to a close. A new Age is upon us, and the new Dawn of the Solars is inevitable. The lies told by the Dragon-Blooded will be burned away, and the truth will shine forth like the Unconquered Sun himself!"

The brusque, dominant lion yawned again, imperiously putting an end to Samea's visionary proclamation with the gesture. "Enough," he growled. "You will drive us back to slumber before you have finished."

Samea nodded, continuing more succinctly. "What I wish is simple, honored guardians. Your aid in returning Creation to rightness. Your strength, your cunning, your wisdom."

The celestial lion regarded her thoughtfully for a long moment, his orichalcum eyes gleaming in the lamplight. "And in return?" he asked, leaning down as close to Samea as he could, within the confines of the binding circle. "What do you offer us?"

"In return for your aid, when all is as it should be— when the Solar Exalted are no longer Anathema, but are returned to their rightful place as leaders of Creation— then I will see that this temple is returned to its former glory as a bastion of sacred knowledge and worship and that seekers again attend these halls to understand the mysteries and wonders of the five winds."

The lion glanced over his shoulder at his companion for a long moment, exchanging some silent communication that was beyond Samea's comprehension. He then turned his attention back to the waiting witch. His slitted yellow eyes took her in, drilling intensely into her own. Samea felt his gaze tunnel deeply, as if he could see not only all that was within her, but all that she had ever been and all that she would ever be. Though only seconds passed, it was an eternity for Samea. At length, the lion straightened to his full height and then nodded regally.

Samea relaxed in relief. Perhaps this would not be as difficult a task as she'd feared.

"We will require one thing further," the lion purred, ending Samea's moment of respite. Behind him, the other groomed himself lazily. He spread one golden paw, worrying between the toes at some imperceptible imperfection, and then rubbed the wet paw from the golden mane at his forehead down over his muzzle. The gesture was remarkably like that of a domesticated cat, despite the beast's size. Samea was once again struck with the impression of being rodent prey in the presence of these feline hunters. She nodded, waiting to hear the lions' demand.

"The life of a child."

"I…" Samea hesitated. "You ask a heavy price."

The nearest lion tilted his head, regarding her coolly. "You ask a heavy bargain. Not for one act do you call us forth. We have been set to guard, to kill, to protect. One service for a year and a day, that is the way. But you ask for our service on many levels and offer only the *chance* of success in return."

Samea nodded, knowing she was pushing the limits of the summoning spell beyond their traditional usage. She wanted not only the obedience of these spirits, but their cunning and aid. She needed them as allies rather than imprisoned slaves.

She hesitated for only a moment and then nodded. Her tribe had existed since its beginning on the edge between life and death. Most of the Northlands were too cold and hostile to farm. Instead, the Blackwater Mammoth tribe followed the great herds as they traveled through the tundra. Sometimes, a winter would come that stretched longer than usual, where the winds' bite was crueler than the tribe remembered it to be. At times such as those, even bountiful stores ran empty, and the summer season's gathering of food lapsed to a bitter memory. In winters such as those, it was not unheard of for unwanted children to be left to the snows. Too many mouths meant everyone starved, and the tribe must go on. Now, in war, just as in harsh winter, difficult times brought the need for difficult actions. The sacrifice of one life to save many more was a regrettable, but acceptable, loss.

"It will be done."

"Then, we will do as you ask," the lion agreed. His promise hung in the air, almost tangible in its enormity.

Samea bowed deeply, her long black hair veiling her face. When she raised her gaze, the stone circle was empty once more.

Three days out of Cherak, a small stone outpost stood at the top of a high craggy mountain. The road up to the outpost had once been lavishly paved with basalt cobbles, uniformly carved so that each was exactly like the other, interlocking to form an almost seamless surface. Now, it lay in ruin, the remaining cobbles providing stumbling blocks for mounted visitors and making arrival by wheeled transportation an impossibility. The outpost itself was built of the same stones, perfect and dark. From any of its half a dozen windows, approach to the outpost could be seen for miles virtually unobstructed.

If one knew where to look, four other outposts were in sight, though several days ride away in each direction. Barely visible on the clearest of days, the outposts could communicate basic messages via mirrors during the day or signal fires at night. More elaborate messages came by trained bird or, sometimes, by runner or rider, though the ruined road made passage slow and treacherous.

Sesus Adish had watched the roads and skies each day for the past few weeks. Likewise, his sentinels had watched each night, anticipating the arrival of orders that were long overdue. His group, like most Wyld Hunts, worked best when on a mission. Given too much time to idle, they grated against each other like bones in a bag, instead of working like the finely muscled beast of destruction they were trained to be.

Fortunately, today was the day. Word arrived in the form of an ornately carved ivory tube, inlaid with red jade. The seal marked it as coming directly from the office of the Immaculate Order. Adish had woken at dawn to find it sitting on his bedside table with no sign of the method of delivery. The sentries had seen no one come or go, and there were no signs of intrusion other than the mysterious appearance of the orders themselves. It was as if the tube had appeared directly from the beyond, which, considering its origin, was not impossible. The ways of the Immaculate Order never ceased to surprise Adish. He'd taken the scroll tube with him downstairs still sealed, waiting for witnesses before reading its contents.

When he entered, he found one member of the Hunt already present. Perched on one of the massive stone window ledges, Otieno watched his leader descend the stairs through glittering dark eyes. Dressed as always in black silk from head to toe, Otieno was rarely seen and heard even less often. But his ability to scout and sneak had saved the group more than once since he'd been assigned a few months ago. Not one of them particularly trusted him, but Adish knew that, so long as Otieno thought serving the Hunt was in his own best interests, he could count on him to do so to the best of his ability.

The rest of the Hunt drifted in from around the building as if drawn by each other's curiosity. When they saw the scroll case with its distinctive seal in Adish's hands, they inevitably found a seat, watching their burly leader. A Fire-aspected Dragon-Blood, Adish's skin was crimson, and his eyes glistened like backlit topaz. He kept the long scarlet mane that was his pride and joy carefully plaited down his back. When he lost tight rein on his temper, his skin glowed ember-hot, a sure sign to his Hunt that they should be elsewhere until he cooled, literally and figuratively. He had firm control of his fiery nature at the moment, witnessed by the fact that the wax seal had not yet melted in his hands.

"Come on, Adish, don't keep us waitin' now," Tepet Ciro crooned plaintively in a heavy Southern Isle accent. She peered up at the Hunt leader through her unruly hair as Adish opened the scroll case. The dark strands had an unnerving way of writhing gently around her face even indoors. She sat on the stone floor, knees pulled up to her chin, arms wrapped around them, back resting against a rough-hewn bench. "Where are we headin'? Back to the Isle? North, maybe? Maybe they'll give us a shot at that Kaneko fellow... Wouldn't that be somethin', us takin' out the Bull of the North! Wouldn't that just frost them back home?" As always, Ciro's bright gray eyes glowed with a surreal light. Mortal observers often attributed the luminosity to madness. She claimed, to anyone who'd listen, that far in her distant past one of her ancestors had dallied with the Fair Folk and returned just a bit changed. When she'd first joined the Hunt, Adish thought the glow was just a sign of her strong ties to the element of Air. After getting to know her, however, he had come to believe that perhaps the mortals had been correct.

Ciro's passion for fighting wasn't uncommon among Dragon-Blooded, especially not those who'd advanced enough in the imperial military to be assigned to a Wyld Hunt. But she'd shown a startling propensity for rushing in where wise men feared to tread, regardless of the odds. If there was blood to be spilled and risks to be taken, Ciro was in the thick of it. Her maniacal laughter, known to turn even brave opponents to flight, was just a bit too wild to be completely sane. More than once, covered in gore, gray eyes glowing like foxfire, the petite woman had spooked men twice her size, who feared she'd followed just a bit too closely in her fey ancestors' footsteps.

"Shut your damn hole, Cir, and maybe we'll find out," suggested Tepet Dalit, lounging along the length of the bench against which Ciro was leaning. Long and lanky, Dalit was half again as tall as his companion. He and Ciro had known each other for decades. Both had attended the House of Bells in their youth, honing their martial skills. Dark and somber to her stormy caprice, Dalit never ceased to harass Ciro for her lack of forethought or berate her for the results of her impatience. When one of her mad adventures went awry, however, as they often did, he was always the first at her side. And woe be unto the individual outside of their Hunt who gave Ciro any grief. While she was as likely to ignore outside insults as to take umbrage, Dalit had more than once sent those who spoke ill of her to an early grave. It seemed no one was allowed to give Ciro a hard time but him, at least in his mind. Adish had used that bit of information to the advantage of the Hunt more than once.

Across the room, Cathak Savin leaned with his back against the wall, feigning disinterest in the proceedings. His steel-gray eyes focused on the knife he was sharpening. Over and over, he guided the blade in a meticulous arc against the whetstone, pausing occasionally to check the edge against the flat of his thumb. Savin had served in the Hunt under Adish longer than any of the others had. He liked to play the role of the cool, experienced soldier, but Adish knew him well enough to tell that he was just as anxious to hear about their long-awaited assignment as any of the rest were.

"We're heading north." Adish resealed the scroll case and sat it gently on the nearby table. Then he turned his attention once more to the sheaf of delicate parchment that had come from within it.

Ciro gave a whoop of delight. "We're gonna bag us the Bull!" Her tiny form virtually vibrated in place. "I'm gonna run him through! I'm gonna—"

Adish shook his head. "No. We're not after Kaneko, although the order stands to destroy him if he's encountered, of course."

Around Ciro's face lanky wisps of hair had been flailing in excitement as if buoyed on a frantic wind. At Adish's words, they sank limply in disappointment. "Well, what then?"

Dalit nudged Ciro with the toe of his boot. "If you'd just shut your damn trap, maybe we'd find out what the assignment is."

Ciro answered by way of a subtle gesture. There was a loud *thunk!* and Dalit looked down to find the toe of his boot skewered to the surface of the bench. The dragon-headed hilt of Ciro's favorite dagger looked at him, standing upright through the heavy leather.

"Damn it, Cir, now they're going to leak. Don't you ever think?" Dalit plucked the dagger out of his boot, wiping the blood from its tip against Ciro's shirt sleeve. "I should just keep the damned blade, if you can't be more careful with it."

"Give it back, or I swear I'll slit you in your sleep and leave you bleedin' in your bed." Ciro leapt for her knife, and the bench rocked precariously. Dalit rolled onto his feet with catlike grace, holding the knife out of her reach above his head. A slow grin slipped across his face, white teeth highlighting the aqua tint to his skin.

"Enough!" Adish's bellow shook the stone building, filling it with the scent of brimstone and smoke.

Dalit dropped the dagger into Ciro's hand and reached down to examine the damage done to his boot.

Ciro grinned smugly. "Yeah, Dalit... Adish don't want us fightin' among ourselves when there's other stuff to be killin'. Don't you remember anythin' he tells ya?"

The wiry woman made the mistake of carrying on her taunting a bit too long, and Adish's wrath was upon her like a lightning strike.

One fiery hand lashed out, slapping her across the back of the head with such force that she crumpled to the floor. Dalit looked up from his boot and a moment of silent communication passed between him and the leader of the Wyld Hunt.

I let you do that only because you're in charge, Dalit's emerald eyes said.

And don't forget that I am. Adish's topaz gaze answered back, before he turned his back on Dalit and walked over to the long table laden with maps.

Dalit watched him for a long tense moment and then reached down to pick Ciro's stirring form up with one hand. "Wake up, ya damn fool." He hauled the wiry woman up by the scruff of her shirt and carried her off like a puppy.

Knife sharpened to his satisfaction, Savin slipped it back into its sheath at his waist and set the whetstone on the stone fireplace mantle. He crossed the room, looming over Adish's shoulder.

"They're sending out another group to reinforce us." Adish said to the table and anyone who happened to be listening.

"That seems... unnecessary." Savin bristled, his ego bruised at the idea that their Hunt couldn't handle anything thrown against it. Together, he and Adish had taken down more than a dozen Anathema in the past few years. The rest of the Hunt had been added almost a year ago, after a particularly difficult assignment had thinned the ranks of their previous group, but they'd never come close to failing. The idea that they would need back up was insulting.

Adish responded without raising his gaze from the maps. "Seems like they're coming out a bit stronger, these past few months… not that it's slowed us down. But orders are to meet up with the other group and take out the objective together. We can operate on our own; we're not under their command. But they want both of us there."

Savin nodded, slowly. "As long as they don't get in the way."

Adish glanced up at Savin, his eyes sparking. "I guess we just won't let that happen, will we?"

The pair continued to lay out plans for their Hunt.

From the windowsill, Otieno watched, his dark eyes glittering.

CHAPTER ONE

Dawn had just begun to pass the frozen horizon as the horse-drawn cart rattled its way up the hill to the stone castle. The old bay plodded up the incline, stiffly shuffling one hoof in front of the other. Its breath formed steamy clouds from its nostrils with each step, although the cart was lightly loaded. Anton glanced up from the frost-slicked cobbles and was not surprised to see the girl there beside the castle's kitchen door, despite the cold.

He never saw her arrive. She seemed to appear as the door came into view as if she'd waited there all night. She'd been there, waiting, every morning for more years than he could remember. Impeccable dark robes and veils covered her from head to toe, leaving only her eyes and hands bare. What skin was exposed was ghostly pale, timeless and perfect. Her eyes were the dark blue of summer twilight, fringed with the palest lashes he'd ever seen. As he did every morning, Anton wondered what she looked like behind those mysterious veils. But her demeanor was as cold as the crack of dawn and left little opening for small talk, let alone exploration beyond conversation.

Anton knew that most of the unmarried women in the town behind him would have gone out of their way for the opportunity to spend a few warm moments with him. His swarthy good looks and charming smile were a winning combination. His early inheritance of The Journey's End, one of the more profitable inns in Glassport, only helped matters along. Business had been picking up of late, as had the attention he'd been receiving from myriad young women in town. Anton had little time or inclination to change things at the moment.

As he unloaded the wooden boxes into the kitchen, the veiled woman examined the day's bill with a sharp eye. Experience had taught him that any discrepancy between what was on paper and what he unloaded would be brought to his attention promptly. While haggling and good-hearted arguments over a bill might have been a jovial part of the transaction with his other customers, Anton did not look forward to a conflict with this young woman over her order.

For one thing, he had yet to catch her in a mistake. Unlike his other clients, the first error she had brought to his attention had actually been his fault, not an effort to get a better deal. But her accuracy wasn't nearly as disturbing as the discomfort of squirming to explain the inconsistencies while under her dark and somber gaze. Although it had happened long ago when he was a younger lad, still under his father's tutelage, the memory always sent a chill down his spine. That one time had been enough for Anton to adopt the habit of double- and triple-checking the castle's paperwork every morning before he left to make his delivery.

Not that the order was difficult. Every day, he delivered enough food for the morning and midday meals of the two dozen students who studied at the library here in the castle. The menu changed as seasonal foods became more available from the lands to the south in the harvest months or as delicate fruits and vegetables became rarer in the winter and his cooks had to rely more on preserved meats, fish and dried grains. But as long as food of sufficient quality was delivered on time, and as long as the receipts were in order, there was never a complaint or comment from this mysterious caretaker.

The wagon now emptied, he turned to the woman and nervously asked, "All in order?" His voice, normally booming, broke on the question, and he frowned. Something about her left him uncertain, and he didn't like the feeling.

She looked up at the innkeeper. Her dark blue gaze held his for a moment before she slowly nodded and handed him back the receipt. He glanced at the paper after taking it from her. It had looked dingy compared to the pallor of her flesh but stark white in contrast to his own. Beginning to turn back to the wagon, he jumped in surprise when she spoke.

"We will need a dozen more cups and a half dozen each of plates and bowls." Her crisp tone cut each word into the stark morning air, every syllable given precise emphasis. As a young man, he'd thought she was an old woman hidden behind her dark veils, until she had spoken the first time. But her voice, when she used it, was sweet and clear. He had to admit that, on the rare occasions she'd spoken since then, he'd found it quite pleasant.

Turning to face her with a blush that he didn't quite understand and hoped was not as blatant as it felt, he nodded. "A dozen cups and a half dozen plates and bowls," he repeated back, dazed. "I'll get them ordered straight away, miss. If they're in stock, I can bring them tomorrow morning. If not, we should be able to have them in before the end of the month."

She nodded, curtly. "That is acceptable."

He turned back to the wagon, grateful for the conversation to be over. He used more care than strictly necessary when filing the bill with the rest of the papers for this month's deliveries to the library in the leather satchel he kept under the seat of the wagon. With a quick glance at the doorway, he made a careful note to himself as to the crockery order. He knew the payments for this would be made promptly, as they always were. Delivered by servants of the castle's lords through the Guild, there was never so much as a penny off in reckoning, and Anton was grateful for the regular income.

Years ago, while his father still ran The Journey's End, there were seasons where the money from the castle had made the difference between success and starvation. Times were much better now, but Anton didn't have any intention of ending the arrangement. A sure thing was a sure thing.

Still blushing, Anton made one final trip into the kitchen to gather the boxes he'd delivered yesterday. They were now emptied of food but filled with soiled table linens from the previous day's meals. The library used the same laundress as his inn did. She ran the only professional laundry in town, and one of the services he provided was transporting the linens back and forth from her shop each day. The laundress herself was an old woman and could hardly be expected to make the trip up the hill to the library to pick up her work. And, as far as Anton knew, no one had ever seen the library's caretaker down off the hill.

Anton carried the boxes out, past the robed woman. She stepped lightly out of his way, holding open the heavy wooden kitchen door. Pushing the boxes into the back of the cart, he tied them down lightly to prevent them from slipping out on the journey home. He finished, turning just in time to see the hem of the young woman's robes disappear back into the kitchen. She didn't stick around, once the work was done. He had never heard her utter a word that wasn't strictly necessary. To the best of his knowledge, no one else in Glassport had ever spoken to her at all.

The majority of the students at the library rented rooms at The Journey's End or spent evenings engaged in rowdy discourse in the inn's tavern. He'd heard them ramble on many times about activities up here at the castle. From time to time, they'd rant to each other about the "ice maiden." Once in a while, they'd challenge one of the newer students to try to thaw her out. But the stories never lasted long, and none of them ever bothered claiming to have held a conversation with her, let alone any other type of intercourse. Strangely enough, the few words he'd exchanged with her in the past years seemed as if they might be the only interaction she'd had with anyone from town.

The idea made him a bit sad. Briefly, he pondered the idea of marching back up to the kitchen and attempting to strike up a conversation with her. Then, he looked at the firmly shut kitchen door and remembered her cool gaze and clipped words. He clambered back up onto the wagon seat.

"Maybe next time, eh, Red?" he asked his mare. Her only answer was to continue leveling the patch of dried grass struggling between the cobbles in front of her.

Turning the cart around and heading it slowly back down the frozen hill, Anton looked over his shoulder at the intimidating stone wall.

"Or… maybe not."

Night fell, the day's chores were almost done, and the library was hers once more. The last of the official scholars had left their studies hours ago, and the halls were once again empty of their inane humor and egotistical voices. As Arianna wiped the last candelabra and placed it carefully in the center of the long table, her mind was already upstairs planning her evening's studies. Before the sun had risen that morning, she'd finished the last in a book of short poems exploring the experience of lost love. Penned by a writer using the pseudonym "Kuronuma," the poetess claimed to have been left behind in shame when her noble husband answered "The Empress' Call" some 700 years previously in the first decades of the Scarlet Empress' reign.

"A child's smile, a cherry blossom and love's faithfulness," Kuronuma wrote. "Loveliest are the things that surely must end. Dawn is hope, but true beauty is found only in twilight, when all that is fades away."

It was beyond Arianna's understanding. How could anyone possibly pen more than 300 pages of verse without having some purpose beyond bemoaning a fate that she apparently was doing nothing to change? It was difficult to believe that there was not some meaning beyond the obvious in the woman's words.

Her duties finished, Arianna leapt up the steps two by two. There were two steep flights of stairs between herself and her precious tomes, but her long stride made short work of them. She was grateful for the freedom of movement granted in leaving behind the robes and veils she wore during the day. Throughout the day, this castle, and specifically this library, was the territory of others, twenty-some scholars whose families had negotiated for their access to this ancient collection with funds or favors. Some were young men, expanding their knowledge past the teachings of their private tutors. Others were nominally researchers tied to wealthy mortal families or obscure Dragon-Blooded lines. Having been found unsuited for the political machinations of the Blessed Isle itself, they were exiled to the far corners of Creation in hopes that their literary explorations would reveal some previously undiscovered (or not-as-yet-exploited) tidbit of information that would aid their familial position in the Realm. All were male, and she, of course, was not. This fact, as well as her low birth, was a handicap that Arianna apparently could not overcome, despite her intellect and intuition. Had it not been for her father's former position as groundsman and caretaker of the castle, she'd have never had access to its mysteries at all. Now, left as its keeper out of respect for her father's lifetime of dedicated work—or more likely through some Dragon-Blood's inattention—she could take advantage of the library's wealth of knowledge as a clandestine student, although she would never be accepted as a legitimate one.

After nightfall, however, the library was hers and hers alone.

She paused at the landing halfway up the stairs. From here, she could survey almost the entirety of the building. The castle itself was three stories tall, enormous by local standards. On the main floor, the great kitchen alone boasted three fireplaces tall enough for her to stand upright in them without striking her head on the arched stone chimneys. Bread ovens large enough to walk into stood gaping and unused. Once, they were heated not by fires, but by some long-forgotten technology, lost after the fall of the golden days of the First Age. Likewise lost was the means for transporting mass quantities of water for the once-bustling kitchens. The huge stone washbasins had been fitted with hand-pumps that, despite their antiquity, were still obviously hundreds and hundreds of years newer than the original stonework. Now, many years after her father's passing, she carried water from the courtyard well by the bucketful. Without his constant tinkering, the last of the hand-pumps had long since fallen to disrepair, and the massive ovens were home to generation upon generation of twittering sparrows who found the chimneys an easy respite from the outdoors despite her vigilant efforts to keep the kitchens pristine. She could keep the dust away, but more than any other place in the castle, the kitchens stood in silent testament to the passing of a once brighter and busier Age.

On the north side of the building, where she now stood, steep stairs led up out of the great hall to the main library on the second floor and then zigzagged back again up to the third floor, which consisted mostly of storage rooms and long-unused quarters. Arianna made her home there, by herself, in a room that had once housed four students. Many, many decades had passed since the castle's library was popular enough to draw those who would board here for months or years at a time to study its wealth of knowledge. Now, students took advantage of one of the inns in town, traveling up the hill from town each morning and returning each evening, leaving the once sumptuous furnishings draped in dust covers and locked away. The arrangement suited Arianna well.

Across from her, the south side of the castle was open from the great hall to the third-floor ceiling, more than 50 feet high. Tonight, moonlight shone silver through the great cathedral window, splitting into innumerable beams that illuminated the interior with a gleaming twilight. Stretching the entire height of the south wall, the cathedral window was a masterpiece of glaziery. Many of the panes had been replaced over the castle's history, the colors varying over the centuries. Here and there, a shard still shone with emerald or ruby fire, perhaps dating to the castle's creation, and these ancient panes put the more recently replaced ones to shame, still vibrant and gleaming beside their pale modern cousins.

Where Arianna stood on the second floor landing, the balcony opened like a loft over the great hall. Below, ancient oak flooring gleamed in the pale moonlight, a testament to her handiwork that day. In exchange for her own presence being tolerated in the library, Arianna kept this shrine to knowledge pristine, despite the apathetic daily invasion by the rest of the scholars. Millennia ago, Arianna imagined, citadels such as these were commonplace. Bustling staff would have populated every room, vital to the everyday functioning of a massive population of nobles, scholars and alchemists. Now, food was brought up from town each morning, and the laundry was farmed out to local citizens who had been handling such matters as their parents and grandparents had, back since the building had fallen from full use centuries ago. All other upkeep on the building's interior was her job, one that she had perfected to a science to allow her the maximum possible freedom to her own studies.

Her calm expression tightened. The childish scholars who came here for a few short hours of "study" each day never appreciated the wonder that surrounded them. They played at learning like babes with baubles. Few understood a fraction of what they read, and fewer still hungered to look beyond the main library with its tomes in the more commonly known dialects of the Realm. Like cows, contentedly ruminating over their cud, none of the legitimate scholars here possessed the slightest drive or passion for their work, a fact that made her own segregation from their company both maddening and yet tolerable. Had she been allowed to work among them, rather than relegated to the background, had her studies not been limited to candle- and moonlight, had she been allowed full run of the library every day, rather than only when the "real" scholars took holidays, vacations and sabbaticals… things might have been different. She might never have been led to investigate further, to probe so deeply into the texts and tomes that they led her to where she was today. And yet, it could not be said that the years of segregation had not had their effect upon her. One did not endure years of being considered a nonperson of less import than the building's chairs and tables, of being recognized for nothing but one's suitability as the butt of others amusements, without effect.

Long ago, she had realized that any kindness shown to her was only the honey to lure her into some cruel joke. While her father was still alive, her early attempts to be recognized as their scholarly equal had left her open to ridicule and scorn, both from the illiterate craftsman himself and the students whose families could afford to pay for their studies here. In the years since her father's death, she'd found great pleasure in realizing that she was truly faster in wit, more adept in research and capable of fluid translation of far more languages than any of those "legitimate" students with their years of mentors and teachers. Her bitterness had become its own armor, proof against those who were not worthy of her attention. The legitimate students here were merely a distraction, a weight to endure that would only make her own studies stronger. Wrapping herself in that knowledge as she wrapped herself daily in the loose robes and veils, she had become a discrete fixture in the castle. She had become as much a part of it as the brooms or buckets, relegated away into closets and dark corners so as not to distract the male scholars from their studies.

Taking a deep breath , Arianna looked up the stairs to the main library. She smiled to herself, savoring the silence, drinking it in like a connoisseur might delight in the bouquet of a fine vintage. Slowly, deliberately, she took the stairs to the library one by one, each tread its own part in her private ritual. She left the daytime world behind her, step by step, reclaiming the sanctuary of her own role as a researcher and a scholar. By the time she'd reached the huge wooden doors of the main library, she had no thoughts save for the wonders she would find within.

She entered the room, crossing to the section of shelves that had been her focus for the past few months. While she found little of import directly in the collection of historic love poetry, there was, as always, the possibility that some of the text held meaning beyond the obvious.

She would not allow herself to be daunted by the inane babbling of a thousand mynas, if it would keep her from discovering one seed of true understanding. While Kuronuma had seemed, at first, quite a disappointment, she would not give up hope that somewhere in another night's studies she might find the key that would turn what seemed to be endless pages of emotional drivel into something of true merit.

Arianna was intent upon consuming the library tome by tome, forcing herself through page after page written by sailors and herdsmen, merchants and princes, sages and servants. She drove herself relentlessly through hours upon hours of repetitive translation when necessary, to make sure that she had not missed a single nuance of what might be gleaned from the tomes there. Tonight, Kuronuma's work finished, she went on to the next book, a collection of poems by Bernlak, translated hundreds of years ago from its original script. Arianna frowned, hungering for a copy of the original, never completely content to accept the rendition of some unknown scribe with his own agenda and objective. A cursory search of the nearby shelves revealed no original copy, however, and once again, Arianna found herself bitterly contemplating the difference between her role here at the castle and that of those who studied here during the day.

Should they wake themselves out of their lackadaisical stupor long enough to develop a desire for anything more than wine, they could send word to other centers of learning, asking to visit long enough to study the original works. With sufficient monetary lubrication in the right locations, they could even obtain handwritten copies of those works for themselves. Instead, although she was the only scholar here who might consider requisitioning more than a particularly bawdy collection of poems or prose, she had neither the authority nor the financial wherewithal to do so.

Refusing to be defeated by the bitterness of her own thoughts, Arianna took the small leather-bound tome, marking its place on the shelf so that she could return it before the other scholars arrived the next morning. She moved downstairs to her favorite reading spot, the seat below the cathedral window in the great hall. It was here that she spent most of her nights.

On the Fall of the Silver City rolled beneath her vigilant gaze, the words painting the ancient tale of the grand and glorious warrior Suzake and the conflict between her sworn lord and her beloved husband's family. The heroine's honor required she follow her liegelord's orders and lead a war against her in-laws, while her husband's love of her family and their children's love for their grandparents seemed surely destined to drive her family to madness, should she do so. The climax of the book centered on a scene wherein the warrior and her husband said their farewells, a ritual fivefold repetition, followed by seven words of love. Arianna placed the small leather tome on her lap, leaning back against the stone wall to contemplate the meaning behind the wording chosen by the author.

Arianna's pale eyelids dropped slowly as she mulled over the poet's words. She often alternated between studying and lightly dozing, using the short cat naps as time to allow her mind to wander across the meanings of the passages she had previously studied. Many times when it seemed that she would never truly understand the meaning behind a particularly obscure passage, such dozing would allow her mind to make intuitive leaps that were the key to connecting aspects of the literature in such a way as to unlock its true meaning.

Drifting, she pictured the scene in her mind's eye. The warrior stood tall and armored in gleaming black, her charger at her side. In the clear light of the rising sun, her husband and children stand formally gowned in white and solemn with the import of this farewell. They bowed deeply in respect to their beloved wife and mother. Knowing that she would probably never see him again in this life, she charged her husband to remember their times of love beneath the lilac trees.

"Nothing can destroy this." The warrior's words, whispered to her husband, tickled at Arianna's ears as if spoken for her alone. "We are one."

Arianna could almost smell the blossoms herself. She tilted her face into the dream dawn's glow, feeling it warm against her face. The sky grew brighter and warmer, as the sun rose fully over the dream horizon. In a few heartbeats, it shone so bright that the landscape and its occupants fell from sight. Arianna found she could not look away.

The sun flared. Its brilliance burned her eyes, her skin, her hair, stripping it away like dust. She tried to scream, but the light filled her mouth, her nose, her lungs, searing them away. It scoured her, charring away all that she was, and she was unable to move to fight it. Within seconds, she was destroyed, consumed until there was no Arianna. There was no woman, no scholar, nothing but the sun in its glory, blazing like an inferno. She couldn't breathe, couldn't think, couldn't feel anything but the clear light that was both within her and all around the nothingness that had once been her.

After an eternity, the sun began moving slowly back down toward the horizon. As it fell, it cleansed her, healed her and remade her as the colorless light took on shades of twilight. Somewhere in the cobalt and rose, she found herself again, whole and unharmed, Arianna once more.

The sun released its hold on her, and Arianna gasped for breath, clutching at the cushions under her hands like a drowning woman grasping for solid ground. Heart racing, she struggled to separate dream from reality. Around her, the great hall blazed with light, flickering coral and lapis and bronze. Light, as from her dream, but this light was real and emanated not from the cathedral window nor from her own small candle, but from her body.

For a long moment, Arianna stared in wonder at her hands, outlined in blue-gold flame, and then, understanding struck her, leaving her stunned. Her skin tingled, remembering the sun's blazing flame, its welcome, its promise. The light of her spirit shone unbound, and the air around her crackled with energy. It was as if her own spirit had split open, an eggshell turning outward on itself to reveal more than it could have contained while whole. She did not need to see the golden half circle gleaming from her forehead to know that she had been chosen. She felt it in her soul, and when she closed her eyes, she saw it branded on the darkness of her eyelids. Her understanding in that one moment had broadened, and the bits and pieces she had read about the Solars, the "Anathema," the "Unclean," all became stunningly clear to her. Text upon text written by the Dragon-Blooded rulers of the Blessed Isle labeled ones such as her as demon-possessed, power-mad horrors of ancient legend. The Unconquered Sun's flames had burned enlightenment deeply into her being and left her to know those self-serving lies for what they were.

She knew then, without a doubt, that she had been chosen by the Unconquered Sun. She knew that her quest for knowledge would drive her not only to learn, but to burn away ignorance and to destroy the wickedness of those who would enslave others like her with its chains.

With a start, she also realized that the night had passed far quicker than she had thought. "I cannot lose this place now," she said to herself, thinking of all the tomes that might hold clues to her new destiny. If the others knew, if word spread, she would be hunted. Or even worse, forced to leave those precious manuscripts. That could not be allowed.

The dawn's light was brightening, pink and gold. Arianna concentrated and quelled the fires within her to deep glowing embers. She dampened the rich golden glow, a light that would proclaimed her Exalted nature to any who might see it. For now, the spiritual flag would have to remain hidden if she was to remain at her studies. Drawing her robes and veils around herself once more, she picked up the small volume of poetry, which had slid off of her lap during the night, and went back upstairs to replace it carefully on the shelf, removing all traces of the night's experience.

CHAPTER TWO

For some things, the handsome young diplomat thought, looking across the dining hall at his companion for the evening, *there is simply not enough wine in the world.*

DiBello Batilda was pretty enough, as far as that went. Her ebon hair was knotted and piled in complicated braids and ringlets that he supposed were designed to titillate and intrigue. Somehow, it left Swan with the rather disturbing impression that a cliff-weaver had chosen her head for a nesting ground.

Her features were delicately highlighted with cosmetics, bringing out the bronzed tones of her skin, her dark almond eyes and her pouting lips. Her beauty was undeniable.

And certainly, one could make no complaint about her figure. Her outfit for the evening had been painstakingly designed to accent every feminine attribute the girl possessed. Tailored in the latest style from the Blessed Isle, the long crimson sleeves came to a point at the back of each wrist, lending her fingers an almost alien illusion of length. While they technically covered her arms completely, the sleeves clung as tightly as a second skin. The neckline likewise was technically a modest scoop, more than presentable for this evening's setting. The bodice, however, was fashioned in the style of the Blessed Isle, inset with panels of a fabric so sheer as to be virtually undetectable, leaving great expanses of skin along her torso and back available for effortless perusal. The skirt was constructed of similar stuff, flowing almost to the floor in ethereal layers that barely obscured one's vision. Only her black pants, so tight and sheer that they could be classified as hose, gave the outfit the slightest definition of modesty, but that definition could have easily been argued out of court by a half-witted lawyer.

Batilda was unquestionably a national treasure, a stunning beauty and would doubtlessly make a perfect wife... as long as one had no desire to ever carry on a conversation with one's spouse.

What must my mother have been thinking?

"And so, I said, 'Why would they even bother with the green, if scarlet was available?'" Batilda's covey of friends perched around her, cooing in response to her ever-so-witty observation.

Thus far, the conversation had covered fashion, food, fashion, the weather, fashion, infidelity and then taken a brief return to the topic of fashion. Any subject of import stood no chance in the shark-filled depths of gossip on clothing styles, local social intrigue and long-distant rumors of Dragon-Blood court ploys. All of which might have been bearable, or even entertaining, had any of their social information been half-way accurate or even partially feasible.

Instead, it seemed that one Dragon-Blooded noble was rumored to have begun an illicit affair on the Isle with an imperial officer who Swan personally knew had been assigned to duty in the Far South for at least a year. Another was supposedly the Scarlet Empress's newest favorite despite Swan having heard of his assassination more than a season ago. Swan wasn't sure where the clucking hens and crowing roosters gathered around these tables were getting their news, but it was outdated at best, if not made up whole cloth as grist for the always-ravenous rumor mill.

Here, many months' sail across the Great Western Ocean from the "civilization" of the Blessed Isle, many of the high-society Western islanders' desire to emulate the styles of the Dragon-Blooded exceeded their need for comfort, as well as their common sense. This fact was proven by the current position of this dinner party's guests, propped on piles of pillows around a knee-high table, which Batilda's mother had heard was all the fashion on the Blessed Isle. None of the guests, including the hostess, looked in the least bit comfortable. Most of them wore semi-pained expressions, and Swan himself found the whole gathering suddenly overwhelming. In his training and experience serving first his family and then the entire Coral Archipelago as a diplomat, he had endured exercises to prepare him to wait through hours of complex negotiations in antagonistic environments. He was adroit in parrying both physical and verbal assaults, and he had once stayed both awake and alert through the drafting of a peace treaty between two minor islands that had taken more than four days and nights to formalize. And yet, at the moment, Swan found himself incapable of withstanding another second of the inanities before him. Instead, he opted for a hasty diplomatic withdrawal. Unfolding his lissome form from the miniscule table with grace born of years of martial-arts training, Swan caught sight of another escapee slipping out of the room. Admiral DiBello, Batilda's father, disappeared swiftly down the main hallway, providing Swan with an inarguable excuse to depart as well. Swan flashed a smile at Batilda.

"You will excuse me for a moment? I really must speak with the Admiral."

Swan knew suddenly, from the spark in his companion's eyes, that she'd taken entirely the wrong impression about the nature of the conversation he was seeking with her father.

Batilda exchanged sly glances with the buxom redhead beside her. The two women seemed to share a hasty nonverbal exchange.

Swan knew from the rumor mills that he was considered quite a catch. And since he and Batilda had been partnered as dinner companions several times in past months when his schedule allowed, in many books they'd already been penciled in as the next couple to formalize their relationship. For weeks, everyone had been speculating when he might ask her father for her hand in marriage. He'd even overheard one of the local matrons predicting that, with Batilda's blue eyes and his soft violet ones, their children would be beautiful! Unfortunately, Swan's interest had more to do with who Batilda's father was than in long-term plans with her, and despite his attempts to make this clear to her, she seemed intent on misinterpreting his intentions.

She leaned over to whisper quietly to her companion, behind her fan. "What do you think he's talking to Father about?"

The redhead smiled slyly, hissing back under her breath just loudly enough for Swan to hear. "Well, maybe he's asking for a reduction in your bride price, since that dress is so tacky."

Batilda flushed, snapping a scowl at her catty companion, then she beamed a sweet smile at Swan. "Of course, my dear," she crooned, while attempting to put on a demure expression of innocence. Considering the large expanses of flesh she was currently displaying, the gesture was difficult to accomplish. "You take your time speaking with Father. I'll be right here."

Swan fought his instinct to bolt for the nearest exit. Instead, he forced himself to saunter after the Admiral who had disappeared through an ornate archway inlaid with a coral and jet mosaic of a sea battle. The short corridor he found himself in opened onto a raised veranda that overlooked the sea, and as he strolled toward it, the occupants' boisterous conversation was carried to him on the night wind.

"I don't care if he's *Chosen* by the Empress herself!" a masculine voice reverberated in the basalt hallway. "I've got too much riding on this, and no fur-wearing barbarian is going to interfere!"

Swan paused in the hallway, trying to link identities to the voices as a second answered the first, speaking too quietly to be understood clearly.

"If Balan can't handle it, I'll put someone more effective on it!" the first voice boomed again, clearing any doubt as to the identity of its owner. "Those trade agreements must be renewed!"

DiBello Gerarde, Dictator Elect of the Coral Archipelago, Admiral of the Coral Navy and, by default, head of the Coral Archipelago's trade council, was well known for both demanding and achieving his own way. While he preferred sheer intimidation and volume, he was reportedly not above other, less straightforward methods of persuasion, should they prove necessary. Swan had argued both with and against him at the negotiating table at various times. Over all, he found that he preferred to be on DiBello's good side. The man might be loud, but generally speaking, he was well informed and had an excellent head for tactics.

During DiBello's tenure as leader of the Coral Archipelago, Northern trade routes had been established for the first time in history. Stretching from the northern tip of the Western islands, across the Western Ocean to the frozen Northlands of Creation's main continent, these routes required months of hard sea travel. The new trade had been so successful, however, that wealth had trickled down throughout the Coral economy, raising the majority of the Coral Archipelago's population from subsistence living to relative luxury in the past decade.

Sitting like a bloated spider in the middle of a web that stretched to the far corners of Creation, the Dragon-Blooded nobles of the Blessed Isle had not failed to notice this rise in fortune. Born to inherit a legacy of more-than-human powers that derived from the five elements, the Dragon-Blooded had ruled Creation virtually unchallenged for hundreds of years, establishing a Realm rivaled only by mythic tales from the First Age. Only at the outskirts of their Realm, in the Southern wastelands and the furthest fringes of the world did a handful of rebellious barbarians and scruffy self-proclaimed tyrants still hold fast against the domination of Creation's rightful rulers. Or so the Dragon-Blooded propaganda would have one believe. In fact, here in the Western islands, there were varying degrees of loyalty to the Blessed Isle, and some pockets of outright independence, as there were throughout Creation. Certainly, the Dragon-Blooded held the majority of wealth and power in Creation, but their Realm was neither as stable nor as all-powerful as they would like to believe.

The Coral Archipelago gave respect to the Realm, from its position many months across the Great Western Ocean. This distance served the islanders well. Under DiBello's tight military control, the Coral navy had perfected the delicate art of privateering on the other nations in the Western island kingdoms just enough to prevent formal action from the Realm fleets that occupied their waters. The Coral economy was soaring, which pleased both the Dragon-Blooded, who benefited from their increased taxes, and those who dwelled in the islands themselves. Using this newly acquired national wealth, DiBello kept the majority of the Coral population, including his daughter and wife, distracted with the lavish Dragon-Blooded style festivals and parties they desired while he pursued his own agendas. The people of the Coral Archipelago were, for the most part, ignorant and happy.

As if pushed out of the room by DiBello's thunderous demand, a dapper young fellow in a long wig plaited into a queue scampered backward into the hallway while making apologetic but not entirely coherent noises toward the doorway he'd just exited. He shuffled frantically back toward Swan, unaware of the diplomat's presence until Swan stepped nimbly to one side to avoid the imminent impact.

"Oh!" The black wig slipped forward, stopping crookedly low across the anxious young man's forehead. He began cooling his flushed face with a delicately carved sandalwood fan, kowtowing his way backward away from Swan as if Swan were now a threat. "I'm so sorry, Diplomat. Forgive me, it's just that…" The young aide made a series of nervous motions indicating the veranda and its intimidating occupant.

"Courage, my good man," Swan said, with a reassuring smile. He reached over, straightening the wig, and clapped the young man's shoulder soundly. "I'll go talk to Admiral DiBello. Would you do me an immense favor? Make sure his daughter isn't wanting for company?"

Relieved at his apparent rescue, the handsome young man clasped Swan's hands between his own, shaking them fervently in thanks while almost crushing his fan. "Oh, thank you, Diplomat Swan... I just... thank you!" He backed away toward the door, smacking firmly into a tall porcelain vase filled with an ornate flower arrangement. The urn threatened to topple over, rocking for a long moment before settling back onto its base.

Swan smiled, shooing the young man back to the banquet room. "No... thank you. She's a lovely girl. Tell her I might not be able to return this evening." The retreating figure grinned and agreed as he hurried down the hallway.

Swan turned his attention to the veranda and its daunting inhabitant. Clearing his throat to announce his presence, he waited in the doorway.

"Come." DiBello's voice was as rich as the white silk of his long tunic. He turned slowly, the leather soles of his formal dinner slippers scraping softly on the granite cobbles of the veranda as he glancing over his shoulder toward the doorway.

"Swan! I was hoping perhaps we'd talk tonight. How are you?" The Admiral crossed the space between them in a few steps, sweeping one strong arm around the diplomat's shoulder while the other shook his hand firmly. The sheer confidence of the older man swept over Swan, enveloping him like a warm wave. If Batilda had half the charisma of her father, dinners as her escort would have held a great deal more merit. But unfortunately, the girl seemed to have inherited her mother's insipid personality along with her striking looks.

"I'm doing well, Admiral, thank you for asking. I hope I'm not interrupting?" Swan glanced around the empty veranda, pausing a moment to admire the breathtaking view of Azure Bay and the ocean beyond. Rank truly did have its privileges, though there were few places in the archipelago that didn't have at least some view of the Western Ocean that surrounded them.

DiBello took a step back, smiling over at Swan. "Of course not... Was there..." The Admiral followed Swan's gaze out over the ocean with a small, smug smile. "Was there something in particular we needed to discuss? Something you wanted to ask me?"

Swan sighed. Not the Admiral too. The time had obviously come to set the record straight. "Actually, yes, Admiral." His voice was dour. "I hope you will understand. I have greatly enjoyed escorting Batilda these past months, but I really feel that she deserves more… companionship… than I can truly offer."

This was obviously not the message that DiBello expected to hear. He turned toward Swan, nodding slowly. "Go on."

"There's not much more to say, Admiral. I am honored to have been allowed to escort your daughter, but I feel that the time has come for me to return my attention to my duties more single-mindedly, and a lady such as Batilda can only serve as a distraction. She deserves someone more suited to her interests, someone whose obligations will keep him closer to Azure."

The Admiral nodded, sagely. "I see. Well, Swan, I certainly respect your honesty. My daughter will be… disappointed… but…" He chuckled deeply as his solemn expression lightened. "I suppose she'll just have to turn her sights elsewhere, won't she?"

Relieved, Swan nodded. "Thank you for understanding, sir."

"Oh, I understand. She's her mother's daughter, that's for certain." He winked at Swan conspiratorially. "Why do you think my duties take me so often out to sea? There are only so many dinner parties a man can stand."

Swan's laughter joined with DiBello's.

"Speaking of duties, Diplomat… There's a matter I'd like to consult with you on." Like the ocean currents, the change in the Admiral's mood came deep and swift. "I'm not certain what you've heard about our situation in the North…"

"Not a great deal, sir. Last I'd heard, trade had slowed a bit, but… "

"Cut in half, Swan. More than half, if you count the shipments that are still pending payment. This could be disastrous to the Coral economy."

"Half? But… why?"

DiBello frowned out at the ocean, as if his enemy could be seen from the veranda. "It's that damned Bull of the North. He's got the Northern councils scared, and what money they're not stockpiling, they're spending on weapons and fortifications, rather than luxury items. And you can't build swords out of pearls… More's the pity."

"But, at last report, the Bull's forces were nowhere near the White Sea ports we're trading with, and Crystal's far out of his path as well. His focus is far to the Northeast. Why are the Northerners reacting as if he's on their doorsteps?"

DiBello turned to Swan, taking the measure of the younger man with his eyes. "It's not just the threat of war that has the Northern cities spooked. It's the Bull himself. The idea that a force led by an Anathema could defy the Scarlet Empress's rule, in an area that's been Realm-held for hundreds of years. Rumors are flying. They're saying he's amassing an army of Anathema. Some say that he's stood toe to toe with the Dragon-Blooded's Wyld Hunts without taking a scratch. They say he's turned his attention from the small tribes and is tackling Linowan proper. I've even heard that some believe he's angling to depose the Scarlet Empress herself."

DiBello shook his head at the idea. "As if a flea-ridden, fur-wearing barbarian had a chance of unseating the ruler of the Realm, the leader of the Dragon-Blooded nobility and the heart of the Blessed Isle's domination. I don't know exactly what's happening. Our trade ships have been more focused on business than on gathering information. But that has to change. If our economy is going to stay strong, then the Northern cities have to renew their trade alliances and be assured that this upstart of a barbarian is not going to bring about the fall of society as we know it."

Swan nodded, his mind racing over the implications.

"I need someone who can deal with those councils, someone who can negotiate firmly, someone who can come home with the proper signatures on the proper treaties, but most of all, someone who can reassure the councils that all will be right in Creation if they simply avoid panicking." DiBello's gaze held Swan's, refusing to release his eyes. "What do you say, Swan? Will you take it on?"

Swan took a deep breath. Taking on this mission would obligate him to at least a year's harsh travel, round trip, across treacherous oceans, frozen tundra and brutal wildernesses, far from the comforts of home. It would require all of his training to successfully renegotiate these delicate treaties with the Northerners and to restore their confidence in not only the Coral Archipelago, but ultimately, in the stability of the Realm itself. He could easily end up drowned, frozen, beset by beasts or bandits or simply return home a failure.

Of course, the alternative likely included more dinner parties hosted by Batilda and her mother.

"I'm your man, Admiral DiBello. You have my word."

CHAPTER THREE

A few moments of covert observation sometimes can reveal more about a situation than a hundred pages of second-hand reports.

At a table in Glassport's most popular inn, a young man with violet eyes glanced across the room, then back at his meal. His clothing suggested that he might have come in on one of the recent ships to port, and his bronzed skin and violet hair marked him as a Westerner. In a city with as much water trade as Glassport, none of these things was remarkable, and neither the city council gathered on the far side of the room nor the inn's staff paid a great deal of attention to him. More than two months at sea had Swan's mouth watering for the stew and fresh bread before him, but years of training allowed him to split his attention without handicap, to fully enjoy his meal while concentrating on the conversations going on across the room. He'd watched members of the city council separately and in pairs over the past few days since arriving in Glassport, but this informal meeting was the first opportunity he'd had to observe them as a group.

"It just doesn't matter whether it comes or not, that's all I'm saying," a wiry, red-haired drunk declared. "What happens to Linowan is Linowan's problem. If the Bull and his barbarians take over, that's fine. We'll sell our stuff to them. If the Foresters hold them off? Wonderful, we already have trade set up with them… If the Isle sends troops to help them? That's great, too. More people means more hungry mouths, more worn-out clothing and more soldiers taking home gifties to their loved ones back home. As long as someone's fighting someone and it's far enough away not to be our houses they're burning, then we have a chance to sell to both sides. I don't see a problem." The redhead struggled with drunken boldness to make himself heard over his companion's voices, but the conversations around him barely slowed when he spoke. With a shrug designed to show his own nonchalance toward the fate of the Eastern nation as well as his companion's apathetic response to his words, he finished his drink in a single gulp and shoved his glass into the path of a passing waitress for a refill.

Swan forced himself to control his reaction to the man's drunken impoliteness. Marta, the serving girl, had shown herself to be efficient and considerate during his stay at the inn, a combination that rarely lasted long when faced with such clientele. She frowned at the glass thrust into her face by the less-than-sober patron but filled the cup before returning to the bar to speak with her employer.

"Caleb's rambling, Anton. He's about two cups away from a brawl," the pretty server said softly to the innkeeper, setting her tray on the counter and wiping her hands on her apron in frustration.

The innkeeper looked up from the accounts he was tallying. It wouldn't be the first time that particular customer had caused problems in The Journey's End, even during Swan's brief stay, and Anton looked like he was used to hearing Marta's assessment of the man. It wasn't unusual that Caleb was the most inebriated customer in the inn. He was a surly drunk, often to the embarrassment of the small group of merchants, shopkeepers and tradesmen who made up the city council gathered informally that evening. He was one of the newest members of the council, as well as one of the least influential.

"The rest of the council's better off. They'll keep him in line." The more established, and more sober, members of the council could be trusted to rein Caleb in before he got disastrously drunk. And since the rest of the inn was almost empty, it seemed that trouble would most likely be averted for the evening, despite Caleb's efforts.

"Gentlemen, allow me to reiterate," a gray-haired man who stood at the head of the council's table said. His discretely cut tunic and trousers seemed out of place among his companions, who advertised their prosperity with clothing adorned with wide strips of fur trimming and embroidery of precious metals. Where most wore multiple amber necklaces, ornate brooches and heavy gold and bronze wristbands, the only ostentation on his person was a dark metal gleam at the end of the handle of the dagger hanging from his belt. The heavy silver hilt cap had been cast in the shape of a ring of jagged inward-stretching teeth that represented the jaws of an open animal trap.

The rest of the table grew quiet, listening to the head of the council. Kallio Johan's family had begun in the trapping industry, but in the past seven generations, it had expanded to control at least partial interest in virtually every shipping company that brought goods in to or out of town by water— and many of the overland companies as well. Kallio had strengthened his family's already well-established holdings until there was not a member of the council who did not, in some way, rely on him for some irreplaceable portion of their industry. But his political savvy contributed as much toward his leadership of the council as the favors the rest of the council owed him. Swan had been continually impressed by the information his research had revealed on the head of the Kallio family.

"Linowan is too far away to be of concern to us here in Glassport, I'm hearing some of you say. Win or lose, their cities will need our trade, and we're out of reach of the Northern forces ourselves." Kallio paused, waiting for a response. The rest of the council nodded, with varying degrees of enthusiasm.

"Exactly what I was saying," a disgruntled Caleb slurred into his wine cup. "Exactly my point."

"But," Kallio continued, playing on Caleb's retort, "there is a larger issue here, gentlemen. An issue you seem to have overlooked." He paused, taking a sip from his own cup to give the rest of his companions a chance to look at each other in confusion.

"This... Bull of the North as they're calling him. This barbarian warlord, he himself is the issue." Kallio looked from one confused face to another before going on. "The issue is simply this. He is not human." The council leader paused for effect. "He is, in the vernacular of the Immaculate priests, 'Anathema.' 'Unclean.' Corrupted by the dark spirits, his soul lost to evil."

Kallio's wry tone gave witness to the sarcasm inherent in his statement. The noble Dragon-Bloods of the Blessed Isle might mindlessly follow the doctrine of the religion of state, which lauded them as the next great step in humans' spiritual evolution, a step that regular humans could only hope to reincarnate into. (Not a difficult theory for the egotistical aristocracy to buy into.) Likewise, it was easy for them to profess that all Exalted souls other than their own were unclean and should be destroyed. It was a self-perpetuating philosophy, which worked well for the Dragon-Blooded and their allies and kept everyone else in their "proper" place. But even Swan knew that here, on the threshold of the great ice lands, survival was of more concern than religion. Here, a man was more likely to pray to his ancestor spirits than to the Scarlet Empress on her throne in the Imperial City or the gods of the state religion as dictated by the Immaculate priests. The Empress was a long journey away, and the spirits were a part of everyday life.

"This fact, gentlemen, raises two separate issues for us. The first is that we cannot predict whether or not to expect a threat from him. Had a human warlord sent his troops to attack the tribes near Linowan, even Linowan herself, it would be of little concern to us. Our goods would be required by whoever won the battle, and one client is little different from another, so long as the accounts are paid up."

Caleb shook his head heavily, staring into his near-empty cup. "Exactly what I said. Isn't that exactly what I said?" The cup did not answer.

"However, if a human war leader grew too powerful, we could count on the Empress' forces to focus on him and winnow him down," Kallio said, drawing chuckles. "She doesn't much like competition for her sovereignty, and expanding one's holdings that greatly would certainly draw her attention. Hence, we would not need to fear that a human warmonger would set his sights on our city from that distance, as she would deal with him, quickly and effectively, before he could do so."

The councilmen gathered around the table nodded. The Empress was renowned for her ability to weave a political tapestry so convoluted that at no time in the past 600 years had the line of succession to the Scarlet Throne been in any way clear. She played one bloodline against the others in endless games of manipulation and brooked no possible threats to her sovereignty either on or off the Blessed Isle. So, while the Northlands received little in the way of support from the Realm in exchange for their yearly tributes, they could definitely count on the Empress' unending desire to remain in control.

"However, rumors have it that this 'Bull' has already withstood three Wyld Hunts. Funeral services were held in secret for the failed hunters, to reduce their families' shame."

Kallio paused to let the information sink in, along with the ramifications thereof. Swan watched for the impact this revelation would have on the members of Glassport's council. Wyld Hunts were the Empress' way of dealing with the return of Anathema to Creation. When one of the Unclean "awoke"—changing from normal human to demonic monster—a Wyld Hunt led by members of the Empress's own holy Dragon-Blooded warriors swept down upon them, wiping the scourge from the face of Creation. Stories were sometimes told of Wyld Hunts who pursued their prey for weeks or months before destroying the unnatural creatures. For a Wyld Hunt to fail was unheard of. For *three* to have failed after pursuing the same creature was world-shaking news.

All in all, Swan was surprised by the degree of accuracy of Kallio's words. It was rare for anyone this far from the Isle to have access to more than shaky rumor, but Kallio's words thus far agreed with the pre-mission briefing that Swan himself had been given.

Silencing the rest of the council's concerned cross talk with a glance, Kallio continued. "The second issue at hand is a decision we will have to make, assuming that the Wyld Hunts continue to fail and Yurgen Kaneko continues to take Eastern lands. What if he takes Linowan cities that we currently trade with? We will then be faced with a quandary. Do we trade with his barbarian icewalkers and their newly claimed cities, risking the censure of the Scarlet Empress falling directly on us? Or do we abandon those trade routes altogether?"

Caleb stood shakily, slamming his cup down on the lacquered table with a ferocity that threatened to shatter the heavy glass tumbler. "What? We can't abandon the Eastern routes!" Caleb's own business centered around importing ocean fish products from the multitude of fishermen who harvested the White Sea, trading them to the East for exotic woods and seasonal foods that couldn't be grown at the edge of the frozen Northern wastelands near Glassport. If the Eastern trade routes were shut down, the majority of destinations for Caleb's exports would disappear with them.

Kallio stepped to Caleb's side, a heavy hand firmly pressing the smaller man back into his seat, while his smooth words reached out to calm the tradesman. "Certainly, closing the Eastern routes would have strong impact on our city. But so would having the Empress focus her attention here." The other council members nodded, talking quietly among themselves.

"Neither course is without its cost," he said, clearing his throat with a significant glance at Caleb, "which is why I recommend we call a formal meeting of the council to discuss the situation and plan for whatever eventuality may arise. We can no longer ignore the possibility that Yurgen Kaneko's actions will affect Glassport."

Shaken at the idea of the loss of his future trade, Caleb's transformation from opponent to ally was immediate. "Of course, Johan! It has to be discussed! We have to call a formal meeting. Right away. Tomorrow night! The Eastern trade routes cannot be closed." He stood, wobbling from the alcohol he'd consumed.

Swan smiled down into his bowl, admiring the council head's expert manipulations. With a few sentences, his staunchest adversary had been transformed into an adamant collaborator.

The council quickly settled on a meeting time, and by ones and twos, they began drifting out of the inn's main room into what passed for a mild spring night here. It was still colder than temperatures ever reached in the Western islands, but nothing short of blizzard deserved the title "cold" here in Glassport. Swan watched Johan wrap himself in a light woolen coat and leave the inn. The young diplomat got to his feet and handed the waitress a generous payment for his evening's meal. "Thank you, Marta," he said, violet eyes twinkling as she smiled. The waitress blushed deeply, twisting the coins into her bar towel. Swan grinned over at the innkeeper, his affable disposition chasing away any thoughts of jealousy between the two men. "And thank you, Anton. I'll need the room for another night or two, if it's not a bother?"

"Of course not, Master Swan," the innkeeper said, wiping down the counter. "I'll send up Marta to lay the fire, if you'd like?"

"Don't bother," the young diplomat replied. "I'm not sure when I'll be back. I'll be fine."

Anton nodded. "As you wish, then." He smiled at the still-blushing waitress. "Guess you're getting off early tonight then, Marta."

The waitress scurried off to clear Swan's table, and with a final glance of admiration at the view, and a conspiratorial wink to Anton, Swan bundled himself into his heavy cloak and hurried out of the inn after Kallio.

Past the warm glow emanating from the lanterns on either side of The Journey's End's front door, darkness fell across the town like a velvet blanket. Fortunately, Kallio hadn't gotten far ahead, his tall gray silhouette still visible in the darkness ahead. Swan's long legs ate up the distance between them in short order, although there were only a few blocks between The Journey's End and the conservative stone building in which Kallio's family dwelled.

"Councilor Kallio, may I have a moment of your time?"

Glassport was a small town with a strong city watch, but even so, Kallio's hand slipped beneath his coat to rest lightly on the handle of his dagger as he turned to face Swan at the gate. He paused, sizing up the younger man and then relaxed after a quick glance around for other possible assailants. "Yes? How may I help you?"

Swan bowed politely, extending a small coral scroll case sealed with Admiral DiBello's signet. "My name is Swan. I've come from the Coral Archipelago to discuss the trade treaties with you."

The councilman's expression swung closed. "DiBello works quickly. We did not expect to have word from him for several weeks yet. Had I realized that our audience at the inn was working for him…" His gaze flickered down to the scroll case, but he did not reach for it.

"Is there somewhere we could talk, sir? I'd offer to buy you a drink at The Journey's End, but we both know that public conversations may reach ears that could misunderstand them, and perhaps a more private location would be… simpler… for both of us?"

Kallio nodded and hesitated only a moment before nodding and opening the gate to allow Swan to pass into the courtyard that surrounded his home.

Once inside, Kallio himself showed Swan to a room that obviously doubled as office and parlor, turning to a subtly carved side table upon which rested a glass liquor service. "Drink?" He looked from Swan to the liquor and back.

"No thank you, Councilor," Swan smiled warmly. "I'm not used to your local vintages yet, and I'd hate to duplicate your red-haired associate's performance earlier this evening."

"Little chance of that. Caleb's had years of experience to perfect his foolishness. No layman could match it without training." Kallio's wry smile returned as he poured himself a glass of amber liquor. Seating himself behind a modest wooden table, the council leader turned his attention back to Swan. "So, you've come from DiBello?"

Swan placed the coral scroll tube on the table in front of Kallio. "He understood that there's some concern about the impact the Anathema's attacks on Linowan may have on Glassport's trade routes to the East. Especially if they manage to gain a foothold there and establish a semipermanent presence."

Kallio nodded. "He understands correctly."

"I'm here, Councilor Kallio, to assure you that the threat of the Bull of the North has been noted by the proper authorities and is being attended to."

One craggy pewter eyebrow quirked upward, the only outward sign of Kallio's skepticism. "Go on."

"Linowan has officially requested aid from the Blessed Isle. And I have it on the strongest authority that the Scarlet Empress will be granting their request."

"More Hunts? So far, reports are that they've proved ineffective."

Swan turned half away from Kallio, studying a tapestry that covered the entirety of one wall of the room. After a long pause, pregnant with possibility, he shook his head. "No. No more Hunts."

Kallio frowned, staring intently at Swan's profile as if to summon the information from him by visual force.

The young diplomat turned his violet gaze on the older man. "To say that your discretion in this matter is important is an understatement, Councilor Kallio. To have this information pass out of this room and possibly into barbarian ears would be a disaster, not only for the Realm, but for Northeastern trade as well."

Kallio nodded, impatiently scowling. "Get on with it."

"Within the next few months, some of the Realm's finest fighting forces will be arriving in Linowan to halt the Anathema's advance and drive his forces back. We have it from reliable sources that the Empress is committing a major army to the effort. Two dragons worth, as well as a strong special force that includes a full unit of warstriders."

Kallio blinked, surprise slipping past his cool demeanor. Legendary weapons of the First Age, warstriders were exceedingly rare. Modern craftsman had long since lost the ability to create the most intricate of these machines, and only the Realm possessed the resources to create even the simplest of the giant suits of armor. It required a masterful sorcerer to pilot such a creation and a magical power source of unbelievable strength to keep one mobile. They were rarely used in modern times, and an entire unit formed of the twenty-foot-tall war machines would be unthinkably powerful.

"With the eminent arrival of hundreds... thousands... of Realm troops, along with their support, surely Glassport can see that this would be a... financially disadvantageous time to reduce imports of luxury materials such as those Glassport receives from the Western islands. Not to mention the continued information resources possible through a continued venture. While your resources seem surprisingly accurate, it seems ours are perhaps more... up to date, and that could prove vital in the upcoming seasons. War is, after all, often won by those with the best information."

Kallio steepled his fingertips, leaning his elbows heavily on the desk in front of him. For a long moment, he was lost in silent thought, though Swan could practically hear the mental processes occurring behind his eyes.

Suddenly, his attention snapped back upon Swan. "We'll sign. Same terms as last time, a five-year contract. But I want an additional provision made. A formal protection. If Kaneko's troops cut off our major trade route to the East, I want a reduction in quotas and a parlay to renegotiate numbers. I can't afford to bankrupt Glassport in pearls and coral if we don't have a market for them."

"Agreed. If Kaneko's troops take control of the road between Glassport and Rubylak for more than the turn of one season, the treaty may be renegotiated. I'll draw the papers up this evening and bring them to you tomorrow for signatures."

Kallio nodded, slowly. "Make it the day after. Tomorrow, I'll meet with the rest of the council and explain our situation—without, of course, mentioning the Realm's troops."

"Thank you, Councilor Kallio." Swan bowed respectfully and then turned to go.

"And Swan?"

The diplomat paused, turning back toward Kallio at the door to the study.

"Yes, Councilor?"

"It goes without saying that... should additional information become available... Well, what strengthens one side of our treaty strengthens the other, yes?"

Swan smiled, with a brief nod. "Of course, Councilor Kallio. I'll make certain that Admiral DiBello knows you'd welcome correspondence from him when possible."

"Thank you, Diplomat."

Slipping his jacket back on, Swan returned to the street outside, smiling to himself at the thought of a job well done—and so quickly—as well as the possibility of another bowl of Anton's stew before bed.

CHAPTER FOUR

"That's ridiculous, Lethe. You might as well base your theory on 'The Horse of the Sea' or 'The Ice Maid.' Brigid's tale is obviously a derivation of the tale of Hesiesh. It's a hacked together colloquial derivative designed to make the Dragon-Blooded and other true sorcerers feel indebted to mortals for their powers. The tales are identical. It's so obvious, I can't believe even you could miss it."

Ronal's voice carried out of the great hall and into the foyer where Arianna was sweeping up the dried mud the debaters had dragged in. Lethe and Ronal had entered the castle more than an hour ago, arguing over the fabled origin of sorcery in Creation, a topic that had apparently sprung up during their afternoon ride. Never known for moderation, Ronal's temper was beginning to flare. Lethe's patience with his companion was obviously starting to wear thin as well, and his voice had grown lean and sharp.

"Don't use that tone with me, Ronal. 'The Tale of Brigid' may not be entirely documentable, but it's certainly more than a wet-nurse's tale. And as for Hesiesh, I'm well aware that the main points of the two stories are similar, but that doesn't mean that the translation we found is a bastardization of Hesiesh's tale. Many cultures have similar but unrelated creation myths or tales of explanation for why Creation works the way it does. It is entirely possible the two tales are just coincidentally similar."

From the hallway, Arianna gritted her teeth. Her patience with the inanities of the students at the library had waned over the months since her Exaltation. The more she gleaned from the tomes of knowledge here, the more she realized what they were not learning, and their insistence on remaining mired in their own ignorance ate away at her patience. Having no one with whom to discuss the wonders she was finding did not ease her frustration in the slightest.

Sweeping finished, she hurried to the kitchen for a tray of sweet cakes she'd set aside for her own evening meal and carried it into the great hall thinking to offer it as a snack, as an excuse to listen further on the conversation. She set it on a table near the entryway but didn't leave immediately, instead stationing herself at the doorway to listen.

A handful of students were lounging on the low couches that formed a half-ring near the fireplace. This late in the afternoon, most had already returned down the hill to Glassport, but apparently, the debate held enough interest to make Ronal and Lethe and their companions not mind being late for their evening meal. Lethe stood by the fireplace, the last bits of the day's glow filtering down from the cathedral window to catch in his gold-red hair.

Ronal sat on the upholstered arm of one of the chairs, boots on the dark crimson seat cushion, as if the extra height would somehow make him more commanding. The fifth son of a minor Dragon-Blooded family line in House Cynis, Ronal's absolute inability to empathize with others or to see things from any perspective of his own had likely contributed to his being sent to study far from the machinations of the Blessed Isle. Here, however, his status as Dragon-Blooded, his striking cobalt hair and handsome features and his unflagging confidence had done much to add to his role as ringleader of the scholar group.

Lethe, Ronal's constant companion and second, had come from a wealthy noble family in Sion. His line was not of the Dragon-Blooded, but it had enough holdings and history to make itself useful to the Empress' court. Slim and tall to Ronal's squat stockiness, Lethe nonetheless had started his studies here in Ronal's shadow, playing the perfect toady to Ronal's role as visiting royalty. Over the passing months, however, the two had come to harsh words more than once. It seemed that perhaps even Lethe's patience had its limits, and Ronal was quickly on his way to crossing them.

"Of course," Ronal admitted, "it's possible." He waited long enough for Lethe to nod and relax in the face of his companion's apparent concession.

"Of course, it's also possible you'll be called back to the Isle to marry the Empress. But I'm not betting my pocket cash on it." A snigger of amusement rolled forth from the pair's audience, and Lethe's freckled skin burned painfully red in embarrassment at Ronal's cruel barb.

From the back of the room, Arianna spoke, her clear voice carrying over the chuckles of ridicule that cut off sharply as the occupants of the room turned as one in surprise.

"Considering the tome you're describing is actually a translation of a much older text—one that predates the earliest known extant copy of 'The Tale of Hesiesh'—it seems to me that the Hesiesh story is actually a derivative of 'The Tale of Brigid,' rather than the other way around."

The room was silent for a long moment, and more than one jaw slowly fell open in astonishment at the voice coming from beneath Arianna's normally silent veils.

Ronal was the first to recover, his surprise turning quickly to haughty disdain. He hopped to his feet, rolling his eyes in a gesture of overblown forbearance.

"I suppose that's possible," he said, drawing out the statement dramatically. His voice turned cold. "And it's also possible that if we wanted the input of the cleaning help, we'd have asked the broom."

"Goodness knows you haven't shown an ability to use it for anything else," Arianna said quietly, her veils unable to mask the wry sarcasm in her voice.

Around the small circle, chuckles of amusement sprung up, and Ronal fairly swaggered across the room toward her. He pulled himself up to his full height, still shorter than Arianna by several inches and sneered boldly up at her, inches from her veiled face.

"Stick to what you're good at, girl," he snorted, "and leave the thinking for those capable of it." He reached out, as he headed for the doorway, and deliberately upset the tray of cakes, sending them scattering down Arianna's dark robes and into a pile on the carpet beneath the table. With a smug backward glance, he gestured for the rest of the students to follow. "Let's finish this conversation over wine, shall we? The Journey's End, anyone?"

Arianna's fingers itched with the desire to throw a physical answer at his back. One of the tomes she'd been studying had described a magical attack that sent a huge flock of sharp-winged insects after one's enemies, and in her mind's eye, Arianna could see the buzzing cloud tearing Ronal apart as he begged for mercy. Or perhaps, she mused, simplicity was better. The two silvered knives she'd discovered in her exploration of the castle's unused rooms were not perfectly weighted for throwing, but she'd taught herself to compensate for their imperfections in the past few weeks. Ronal's back seemed a broad target, compared to the abandoned bedpost she'd been practicing against.

Instead, she clenched her hands into tight fists, unwilling to gamble the loss of the use of the library and the knowledge still hidden in the tomes therein against the satisfaction of this smart-mouthed pup's permanent silence.

In a great herd of feet, the room cleared, leaving Arianna alone in the silent castle, trampled cakes at her feet, robes dusted with spoiled crumbs and sugar dust. Slowly, she shook her head. "From lies, they curse the truth; from the night, they curse the dawn." The ancient proverb echoed in the empty hall.

Since her Exaltation two seasons before, many things had become much clearer to Arianna. Among the tomes in the library upstairs were ancient texts, rumored to have been translations of those written in the First Age and tomes that had been long since forgotten by human scholars. Their languages were all but lost, as were the stories within them. Mixed in with the tales of Fair Folk and monsters, they spoke of the Solar Exalted. Arianna had become fascinated by the stories of individuals like herself, who had found themselves to be chosen by the Unconquered Sun and marked as his heroes. The earliest books told of a time before the current Age, when the Solars and their loved ones, the blessed beast-heroes of Luna, had ruled justly, in peace and harmony. They had been aided by their Terrestrial cousins, the Dragon-Blooded who were the heroes of the Five Elemental Dragons. Although the tales grew confusing, Arianna had been able to glean that there had been a great discord between the Terrestrial Dragon-Blooded and the Celestial Lunar and Solar Exalted, and somewhere in that discord, the end of the First Age came about. With its end, the Celestials came to their present state, labeled "Anathema" by the Dragon-Blooded and hunted and exterminated as soon as they manifested. For most who lived in Creation, however, there were only the modern tales. All Exalted spirits who were not Dragon-Blooded were tainted, demon-spawn, evil, and must be exterminated before they were able to learn enough to fully utilize their powers. The Scarlet Empress' propaganda had done its job, and her Wyld Hunts were quite efficient.

Obviously, being a Solar was not something that was broadly advertised. It was essentially a death sentence for a young man or woman to Exalt. Even those who struggled, as she had, to keep their nature a secret would eventually be found out. The Wyld Hunts would track them down and destroy them. It was only due to the treasure trove of knowledge still hidden deep within the library's texts and the smug stupidity of the scholar Dragon-Blooded here that she dared to remain so long. After finishing each book, she promised herself she would leave and find a safer place to avoid their gaze. But no sooner had one closed than the call of the next tempted her, and she could imagine herself many years from now, still hiding behind her veils in these hallways.

After the destroyed sweet cakes had been cleared and evening began to fall, Arianna climbed the stairs to the highest point in the castle. She shook the last of the crumbs off of the rug from the top of the castle wall. In the chill evening's twilight, a crisp wind rose, tugging hungrily at her hair, whipping a few bright white strands loose from her tidy braid. It was an uncommon sensation. For years, she'd worn the veils whenever she was likely to see others, in an attempt to prevent claims that she'd attempted to use feminine whiles to win or keep her place here at the castle and, later, to avert unwanted attention from the scholars studying here. At night, alone at last, she shrugged them off, but she spent so few evenings outside of her beloved library that the feeling of the night wind against her skin was almost forgotten.

As she looked out over the countryside that swept down from the tall hill beneath the castle, an amber light caught her eye. It was barely visible, glowing from over the top of the small hill that hid Glassport from sight. The sun had sunk below the horizon behind her, and the orange glow over the hill grew brighter as the sky darkened fully into night. A thick white line of smoke crept up from hill to sky, joining in with the low clouds.

Arianna supposed that that smoke could be coming from a holiday bonfire, but she could not bring to mind any harvest festivals near this time of year. She continued to watch the horizon, as a group of chariots accompanied by a handful of mounted riders emerged across the crest of the hill, silhouetted against the fire's glow.

The horsemen, all heavy with armor, wove in and out of the chariot formation like a course of hunting hounds speeding around their master's mounts. Lit by the town's glow, they raced down the road that struck out from Glassport, a radiant river that disappeared behind one hill and emerged from the behind the next. Their weapons, spear tips and swords, reflected like fire and ice in the night air. A pageant of banners flapped above them, a flock of brightly colored carrion crows snapping at the party's shoulders as they quickly covered the ground between the town and the castle.

Why would a noble party be heading this direction? Arianna thought. She continued to watch, the rug forgotten across the stone embattlement. As the party left the town's light and still shone in the night air, its otherworldly glow gave no doubt to its Dragon-Blooded nature. But it was almost unheard of for those of the Blessed Isle to travel to this area on leisure. Hunting for the deep arctic beasts took place much further inland, in the great frozen lands, and the only prey of note to be found near Glassport were herbivores and other food animals, not much challenge to a noble hunting party.

The armed band cut across the open hills beyond Glassport, chariot wheels and hooves tearing at the earth. Flares of crimson and sapphire lashed out from the group, tearing at the darkening sky with hungry tendrils. From one jade spear point, a flash of lightning lanced out, striking a passing boulder with an earthshaking clap that echoed throughout the night. The rock exploded, raining granite shrapnel around the speeding party, the stone rain seeming only to goad them to greater speed.

Near the center of the group, one figure let out a howl. His crimson war chariot flared, gleaming with infernal fire. At the rear of the chariot, a banner pole struggled to remain upright as the massive standard of House Sesus fought against the chariot's speed. Living flames danced along the figure's outline, framing him in demonic light. As Arianna watched with growing horror, the fire-skinned war leader turned his attention up to the castle, and the flame in his topaz eyes reached out directly for her, burning with a blazing hatred that could not be mistaken.

They do not hunt deer this night. Arianna stood, frozen on the rooftop, unable to draw breath.

Spurred on by their leader's orders, the hunters picked up speed, their eerie war cries reaching out for the castle and its sole occupant.

Arianna did not wait for their arrival. As the first of the horses clattered into the courtyard of the castle, she was already halfway down the stairs, rug abandoned on the rooftop.

How could I not have been ready for this? Arianna chided herself, racing down the stairs and slamming the heavy bolt on her bedroom door behind her. She had known this day would come, known it was as inevitable as the dawn. And yet, as she threw together a bundle of the books she could not bear to leave without and a few necessary supplies, she was still incredulous that the Wyld Hunt had arrived for her. For one irrational second, as she buckled her belt and daggers around her waist, she regretted having not dealt with Ronal when she'd had the opportunity.

Heavy boots echoed up the stone staircase, and angry shouts carried even through the solid oaken door.

"Sivan! This way! I know I saw someone up above! She's probably hidin' up on the roof!" The woman's voice was drawing nearer, and Arianna knew she only had a few moments at best.

Escape down the already occupied hallway was obviously not an option. Arianna turned toward the only other escape route. Jumping out the small third-story window was not a pleasant prospect, but it was still a better option than facing the fate that was rushing up the stairs to meet her.

"Unconquered Sun, you did not create me to be snuffed out so quickly! Give me strength!"

Arianna concentrated, asking for protection, and her plea was answered as her skin began to glint a metallic bronze. Slinging the bundle of supplies onto her back, she grabbed the first piece of furniture at hand, a heavy oak chair, and flung it up through the western window. The resulting crash made Arianna cringe. There was no way her pursuers could have missed that sound. It was immediately echoed by the sound of pounding as heavy iron gauntlets began beating on the thick wooden door to her room, attempting to force entry into her chambers.

Betting on the door's strength to hold, she shut her eyes, gulping the cool night air as it swirled down around her through the broken window's gaping maw. With a moment's focus, Arianna summoned forth all of her strength and agility. In one dexterous leap, she was on the window's edge, landing light as a peregrine. Broken glass crunched beneath her soft slippers. She glanced down.

Beneath her, several outcroppings of stone emerged from the stone wall, window frames or projections whose original uses were long forgotten. It was easily 60 feet to the ground, and a misstep would give her no chance to recover between there and the unforgiving cobbles of the courtyard below. For a second, she could see herself, sprawled and broken on the stone as the Hunt descended upon her, but she shook the image away. She could not chance a broken leg at this point. Behind her, the door exploded inward, forcing her decision. Heralded on a maelstrom of shrieking wind, the doorway was suddenly filled by a gray-haired warrior who did not hesitate to launch himself toward her. His armor gleamed in the room's firelight, as did the wickedly sharp daiklave in his hand.

"Unclean! I am Cathak Sivan, and I shall purify your taint!" came his arrogant shout. Arianna was certain it was as much a rallying cry for the rest of the Hunt as it was a prideful proclamation of his intent to destroy her.

She leapt, arms outstretched, cloak and scarf billowing behind her. Borne lightly on the night wind, she sailed from the window ledge to the nearest outcropping. She landed lightly on one foot, the other raised at the knee to give her balance.

Broken glass scattered upon her like a cruel hail from above as the Dragon-Blooded warrior leapt up into the broken window she had just left. "Outside! She heads for the courtyard!" he called over his shoulder. The wind outside surged around the castle walls, as if answering his call.

Taking a deep breath, Arianna flipped backward. She plummeted toward the ground, falling headfirst from the stone like a cliff diver. Tucking her knees toward her chest, she rolled in the air, unfolding upright just before her feet struck the flat slate roof of the castle's entryway. Still twenty feet above the courtyard floor, Arianna spared a glance above her, as the Dragon-Blooded warrior matched her leap, sweeping down the stone wall like a typhoon. Arianna marveled as he fell with equal grace and greater speed than she had. Behind him, he left a blazing comet tail of blue and white lightning bolts. Even in the reflected light of the low clouds, his jade blade gleamed fiercely, crackling with energy as he plunged toward her.

"You will not escape me!" he roared. Arianna feared he might be right.

She ducked, rolling to the right. She was on her feet faster than she believed possible, but Sivan was faster still. As she checked over her shoulder, he landed on the small crenellated wall encircling the entryway's rooftop. Balancing there, he spun toward her. His attack came at her like a tornado, the long blade spinning faster than thought. His daiklave sliced the air above her. The sword hummed with power, hurtling like a jade lightning bolt arcing directly for her head. She threw herself to the left, bending nearly in half, and for a moment, it seemed her efforts would take her out of harm's way. Then, the cruel north wind caught the blade, and it sliced faster than sight could follow, sundering her magic's armor and leaving its pitiless bite across her face.

Arianna screamed as the blade bit home and a salty torrent of blood blinded her. Her wrath peaked, and she leapt toward her assailant in a murderous fury. The unexpected gesture drove her blindly past his defenses, slamming her face hard against his metal breastplate. The metallic tang of blood swept across her tongue, as the impact split her lip.

Her momentum drove her assailant off balance, and she found herself falling on top of him as they tumbled from their perilous perch. The blood cleared from her eyes as they crashed down toward the cobbles. He called out in a tongue she did not understand, and their fall slowed as a gust of wind buoyed them from below.

With an eerie howl that surpassed even the Dragon-Blood's pet storm, Arianna ripped one of her long knives from its sheath at her waist and plunged it underhand into his ribcage. Its point split his leather armor like parchment and sank into his body to the hilt. The hunter's face distorted in shock and pain as her blade twisted into his heart. Before they struck bottom, all knowing had left his eyes. She rolled shakily to her feet, her impact broken by her hunter's corpse.

"Down there! She's gettin' away!" The winds picked up again and a single flash of lightning illuminated the armored woman who now crouched in Arianna's window.

The sound of pursuit began to emerge from the entryway. Arianna took no time to consider her options. There was no way she could outrun the Wyld Hunt on foot, and their steeds eyed her with hatred across the courtyard. Raising her fingertips to her lips, she sounded an ethereal whistle that pierced shrilly out into the night air, cutting through the darkness and distance of reality itself. The undulating shriek, fueled by need and formed by will, called out to summon a steed of the spirit world. Suddenly, the evenings she had spent poring over the words written by a nomadic Southern herdsman extolling the graces of these phantom horses seemed incredibly worthwhile.

In a blaze of golden flame, the horse leapt into the courtyard, trailing a sparkling aura of energy. Arianna's bloodstained hands shook as she tangled them into the horse's mane and pulled herself onto its back.

From the entryway rang the sound of hurried footfalls. "Sivan? Damn! I think she's out here!" A man's voice echoed in the stone foyer, and Arianna knew he was not but a few steps from the door.

Her mount barely slowed as it streaked across the courtyard, past the Hunt's horses and chariots and out into the hilly countryside.

CHAPTER FIVE

Swan was saddling his mare when he first smelled the smoke. The smell was… off somehow. Something about it caught his attention among the normal cook fires of the city, but just enough to niggle at the back of his mind.

By the time he had loaded his gear into Eldy's saddlebags and turned to lead her out of the stable, the smell of burning wood was noticeably stronger. Swinging up into the saddle, he could see the pillar of smoke reaching from the north quarter of town. He nudged her into a gentle trot, heading that direction. Although the sun was setting and the markets were closed, the streets were crowded with village folk who'd stopped to peer at the smoke column as well.

"Looks like The End," someone said as he passed. Swan nudged Eldy gently in the ribs and hurried her through the crowded intersection.

As he turned the corner, he could see that it was indeed The Journey's End that was ablaze. The little brown mare shied at the acrid scent of smoke, whinnying her strident objection to the fire. Swan leapt off her back, pulling her to a side street out of sight of the blaze. He left her there with her reins tied tightly to a post and ran back toward the inn.

On the near side of the inn, Kallio Johan had taken charge of fire-fighting efforts. The gray-haired council leader directed a line of neighbors who formed a line from the nearest well to the inn, passing sloshing wooden buckets of water forward at a frenzied pace. As Swan ran up, he watched the man at the head of the line throw a bucketful of water directly onto the side wall nearest the well. The flames did not so much as sputter. The water hit the burning wall and exploded into steam as if it had never been liquid. Again and again they tried to douse the flames with no effect. Shaking his head, Kallio called out over the fire's roar.

"Try the outbuildings! They haven't caught yet. Douse them down! Maybe they can be saved. Wet down the grounds and anything nearby. Nothing we can do for the inn."

The bucket brigade scattered, dousing anything that was not already in flames.

Sharp smoke filled the air, burning Swan's eyes. The inferno crackled as it consumed the sap-filled beams that supported the building, snapping and popping above the roar of the flames. As he continued around the corner at the front of the inn, he was almost floored by the smell of burning human flesh. The cloying stench swept over him, like overly sweet meat left on the spit too long. It clung to the nose, the mouth, the skin as if it would never fade. He'd smelled it, once before, on a sea journey. One of the ship's holds had caught fire, and the oakum used to caulk cracks in the hull had exploded. Its pitchy tar went everywhere, carrying flame with it. It had coated the skin and hair of the carpenter who'd been down tending a leak, and the woman was so badly burned that it had been a relief when she'd died the next day. The smell was unlike anything else, and Swan had hoped never to smell it again.

In front of the inn, the street was no less crowded. Village folk had gathered, milling in small clusters. Swan recognized several of the men from the council earlier that week. They stood in a tightly packed circle, shouting to each other to be heard over the chaos in the street.

In another small group, a dozen or so well-dressed youths gathered, comparing small injuries. Marta, the young serving girl from the inn stood near the center of the group of young men, as if they'd clustered around her. She seemed in shock, eyes fixed to the blazing inn. She might have been alone in the street, for all the attention she paid the boys, but that didn't stop them from vying for her nonexistent notice. A stocky blue-haired boy with an arrogant demeanor complained loudly enough to be heard over the noise from the fire.

"I told you we shouldn't have come here tonight. But no, you insisted. Now look! Look at my face! I'm burned half to death, and it's all your fault!"

Beside him, a lanky redhead dabbed at his companion's forehead, treating a tiny burn that marred the pale skin there. "It's okay, Ronal. It's really not that bad of a burn. You're going to be just fine."

"Ow! Get that thing away from me! By the Five Dragons, Lethe, are you trying to kill me? Leave it alone!" The first boy slapped away his friend's hand, knocking his clean handkerchief into the dirt road.

The redhead sighed deeply and shook his head in resignation. He picked up the cloth and went to douse it in a nearby horse trough.

Swan ran over, putting himself in the path of Marta's glazed stare.

"Marta! What happened?"

She blinked as he stood between her and the blaze. Her eyes were glassy, wet with tears. Soot stained her clothing, and her face was flushed from the heat of the blaze. For a moment, it seemed she wouldn't recognize him. Then, she took a few stumbling steps forward, falling sobbing into his arms. Swan was startled to find himself in possession of double armful of crying Marta, but he held her gently, patting her back as he asked again. "What happened?"

Face pressed against his shirt, she gasped for breath around her tears. "Anton was out front in the courtyard, working on the horse trough. I was inside. I was just heading to talk to him when I heard them. There must have been twenty of them, in chariots and on horses." She sobbed, barely able to continue. "They asked him which road led up to the castle." She pointed into the hills outside of town. "He wanted to know why they were looking for the castle, and all of the sudden, one of them was on fire! It sounded like the forge when Smithy's making a sword, all roaring and thunder. We looked out, and his skin was glowing, red as a flame, and smoke was coming out of his mouth. It smelled foul and we could see the flames from inside. He yelled something about Anton being impure, and then... then... he just... and I..."

Marta broke into tears again, pressing her wet face back against Swan's chest, and gestured toward the front of the inn.

"I came out and... and he... he just fell in two. I didn't even see the spear move until after he was... he was dead! And then, the red man pointed it at the inn, and I ducked back, and all his fire just flew at the building, and we all ran out the side! One of the boys couldn't get out, and we couldn't get him out, and the flames were so hot... And they... they just laughed! They stood there in the street and laughed while he burned! And now, it's all gone."

As if on cue, with a loud groan, the burning ruin of The Journey's End crashed in upon itself, sending sparks up into the twilight sky.

Swan looked back over his shoulder. The crowd had backed away as the building fell in, leaving the Widow Maressa kneeling alone in the street before the inn. Her body wracked in soundless sobs. Before her lay her son, Anton. He'd been split at the waist, but there was no blood on the road beneath him. Swan could see the charred flesh, blackened where the attacker's fiery weapon had seared him in two. Anton's clothing still smoldered in the cool evening air, singed along the wound line. Swan found he was grateful that the innkeeper's face was turned away from him, sparing him and Marta the burden of his death gaze.

"That's what he gets," Swan heard the injured boy say, after a few moments. "Interfering with a Wyld Hunt is dangerous business. Not aiding them is like aiding the Anathema. He got what he deserved."

Swan glanced over. "The young lady doesn't need to hear that right now, kind sir. Nor does the man's mother.

Perhaps you'd give the ladies a respite for their grief?" His tone was unarguably respectful.

The young man seemed to want to press the point, but his lanky friend distracted him. "Ignore him, Ronal. Let's find a place to get some wine, instead, and then you can tell us about how you almost rode with a Hunt." Happily ensconced as the center of attention once more, the blue-haired boy led his pack of companions off, trailing jealous glances Swan's direction.

Swan nodded gratefully to the red-haired boy, and the young man nodded and hurried off after his companions.

Further up the street, Kallio gestured for the town council to join him, and they disappeared toward another inn a few blocks away. The bucket brigade worked for a while longer, each person using water from the well near the inn to wet down the surrounding area, but the Wyld Hunt had done its work efficiently. To each side, although their roofs almost touched, the nearby buildings stood unharmed. Even the dry grass beside the next building had not succumbed to the flames. Only magic flames burned so selectively. Realizing their efforts were superfluous, the brigade drifted away, its members returning to their own homes and businesses, thankful to have escaped mostly unscathed.

Around them, the town grew eerily quiet, except for the crackle and roar of the ruined building. Swan held Marta, allowing her to cry out her anger and loss. At length, their only company in the empty street was the unmoving figure of Maressa, still kneeling before her murdered son.

Swan rode past the ruin of the inn, his recovered mare picking her way gingerly along the cobblestones, skittish at the smell of fire and burnt flesh. He didn't want to pass by again, but the road out of town ran right by the inn. The prominent location of The Journey's End had worked against Anton, as the hunters sought directions to the castle and their prey. Perhaps if the inn had been on the opposite side of town, he'd still be alive.

Swan had given Marta what comfort he could before sending her off toward her parent's farm. He'd attempted to aid Maressa, but the older woman was catatonic. A neighboring merchant's wife had agreed to look after her as best she could. There seemed little else he could do for the town. The fire was in no danger of spreading and inflicting the Dragon-Blood's ire on any other buildings. In fact, it had consumed the inn with such intensity that there was almost nothing left of the building to burn. He thanked the fates that he'd finished his treaty dealings here this afternoon. Papers signed, he'd been anxious to be on his way and decided not to wait for dawn before heading on to the next stop in his trade negotiations. As it was, his traveling equipment and possessions were all intact. Even the precious signed agreements had been loaded into Eldy's saddlebags before he'd smelled the first traces of smoke.

From horseback, Swan could see no accompanying fires from the direction Marta had indicated the attackers had set off in. But fortunately, that road was to the southeast and his to the northeast, branching a short distance from town. Swan shook his head sadly. It was terrible that Anton had come between the Hunt and its quarry just by doing his job, but there was nothing for it now. Swan had a job of his own to do, and the welfare of the Coral islands hinged upon him doing it successfully. The trade treaties between the islands and these Northern cities had turned Coral from a barely self-sustaining kingdom to one of moderate wealth. While Coral paid token tribute to the Blessed Isle and the Realm of the Scarlet Empress, it was mostly ignored. If the Empress suspected that the Coral Archipelago was on the verge of becoming financially independent, it was likely that the wrong sorts of attention would become focused on the islands. The appearance of a Wyld Hunt here was an unexpected complication, and one best for him to avoid if possible. One thing his mission did not need was to attract the attention of the Empress in a negative manner.

As Glassport disappeared slowly behind him, low clouds that had been threatening snow all afternoon lazily fulfilled their promise. Swan rode through the wood, marveling at the silent hush the soft dusting of flakes gradually put on the world. In Coral, as in most of the Western kingdoms, snow was virtually unknown save for at the summit of some of the highest mountains. To see it drifting casually was a pleasure that had not yet faded on his journeys here in the Northlands.

A rhythmic thumping began, almost imperceptibly, behind him as he rode, and it took a few moments for the sound to sink in, playing counterpoint as it did with Eldy's gentle jog. Swan turned in the saddle, glancing back down the road, surprised to see a glow in the direction of the long dark horizon. Straining to see more, the gleam grew brighter. Swan blinked, clearing his eyes as the shine slowly resolved into a sight no more probable than the reemergence of the now-set sun.

A horse thundered toward him, but it was no ordinary horse. Nor was it a mounted Dragon-Blood. The mount was like no other Swan had ever seen. It shone, not with sweat, but radiantly gold in the growing night. It glowed clear and bright like a miniature comet flying down the roadway. The rider, though dressed in black, trailed a brilliant radiance of its own. All the colors of the sunset danced in the horse and rider's halo. As they sped toward him, they glimmered, rose and cobalt, red and gold, echoing the earlier sunset.

Eldy shied, as if sensing this unnatural approach. Swan leapt to the ground, snatching up her reins to pull her well away from the forest road. The foreign horse and rider neared. The beast wore neither bridle nor saddle. Its rider moved as one with the steed, lying low over its neck. Black robes and a long scarf streamed out behind, shadowing the horse's mane and tail.

Even in the growing darkness, Swan could see the frenzied whites of the horse's eyes and the flecks of lather on its flanks as they flew past.

Behind them, a storm of pursuers appeared. Dark and ominous, their voices rolled down the road before them, howling their hunting cries. Hoof beats thundered, shaking the road. The Hunt was coming.

Only two of the Dragon-Blooded who sped down the road toward Swan were mounted on horseback. Their heavy destriers' hooves bit brutal chunks from the forest path. The rest drove massive war chariots with cleated wheels that ate up the road, their drivers whipping the harried mounts on to greater speed. Heavily armored and with full weaponry, the Wyld Hunt gleamed serpentine in the wake of its golden quarry. As they neared, Swan realized that less than a double handful of Dragon-Blooded were in pursuit of the rider. He wondered briefly what had happened to the rest of the more than twenty that Marta had described.

The lead rider drew near, piloting a sinister ebon and scarlet chariot drawn by a pair of ferocious bays. A brilliant phoenix flag of spiritual energy burned red and gold behind him. As he gained on the horse and rider, it flared, blazing like a bonfire up into the night sky. Around him, the drifting snow melted, hissing into steam before it could strike the ground. His chariot horses were frothing, flecks of blood coloring the foam that coated their flanks. Swan choked as the air along the road filled with a great foul smoke and the scent of brimstone. The stocky crimson-skinned warrior bellowed to his companions, urging them forward.

"Dalit, take the left! Ciro, the right! Tight now!" The two horsemen moved forward, one on either side, coursing their steeds down the clear cut along the side of the road.

As the hunt leader passed, he lowered a cruel-bladed spear forward. "Anathema!" the red warrior roared. The flames that surrounded him spit forth a bolt of fire that streamed down the road toward the fleeing horse and rider. The burst struck the golden horse with a searing heat that Swan could feel from where he stood. Swan's little brown mare bolted, breaking off into the underbrush with a terrified scream. As he watched in horror, the flame lapped at the golden horse's legs, tangling it in blazing snarls. Unable to slow, the horse's own frantic momentum pitched it forward, shrieking an ethereal death cry that made Swan's skin crawl.

The horse struck the snowy road hard, catapulting its rider ahead of it. As the unnatural flames consumed the horse, it shattered into amber shards, leaving behind the sickly sweet smell of burnt resin.

Swan blinked, unable to believe his eyes.

A victorious howl rose from the Wyld Hunt, who thundered past the fallen rider and turned back for another charge. It seemed the Dragon-Bloods would not be content with a quick death and intended to play with their prey for a while yet. It was hard for Swan to fathom that such feral joy could be inspired by the destruction of a living being. The wanton demolition of the inn replayed through his thoughts, clogging his senses again with the stench of burning flesh. In his mind, he saw Anton's broken body once again, Maressa kneeling in the street and Marta's tears. "*And they just laughed...*" The young girl's voice echoed in his ears. He watched the Hunt prepare its final charge. In the road, the fallen rider lay motionless amid the dusting of snow.

A great cry of triumph struck out from the Wyld Hunt as it thundered down upon its victim. Swan found himself moving before his mind had made the decision to interfere. As he reached the fallen rider, she rose up on her elbows. The scarf she'd been wearing across her face fell, revealing a still-bleeding gash, crimson against the bronze gleam of her skin. He found himself staring down into anguished eyes, pale blue as the summer coastline.

Batilda would kill for those eyes, he thought. The woman's gaze caught at something deep inside him, and he knew, more truly than he had known anything before, that he would help her. He must help her.

Swan gently released the fallen rider. She slumped back to the cold ground. He turned to stand unarmed in the center of the road. Part of his mind screamed for him to reconsider, but it was quickly shut away. "I must," he whispered to himself as the Hunt bore down upon them. Far from slowing, the riders came faster, as if the sight of the unarmed man in the road spurred them on. Their leader whipped his chariot horses, and they screamed in response as his thorny lash tore at their flanks. Relentlessly, he urged them forward, faster still.

Time froze for Swan. One moment, he stood there, unarmed in the road, seconds from death. The next, the world was blazing fire. Around him, there was no longer a forest, no road, no snow. He existed only in the flame, wrapped in a sphere of light that surrounded him completely.

It was not a dream. Not a Dragon-Blooded spell. Never before had anything been so incredibly real. The sun shone around him so true that he could feel it, hear it, smell it, taste it. It passed through him, as if there was no boundary between what was Swan and what was the light.

And then, in an eternity of only brightness surrounding him, the tiniest curve of dark appeared. For what seemed like lifetimes, it slipped slowly across the face of the brightest light, eclipsing it. Inky and opaque, it was the only solid thing in existence. It crept across the sun's surface, growing fat and round, until a full sphere of night rested across the sun's face. All that remained of the sun's true light was a radiant string of celestial pearls, gleaming around the eclipse's blackness. The sun's corona flared, and Swan could feel both heat and cold drive through him, searing his soul. He could see both the light and the dark, and at the same time, he knew he was both of them. He was the flaming sun, and the cold-dark moon. He was shadow and light, day and night, both at once, tied forever to the duality.

All fear was thrust aside as he was filled with a fierce power. He found himself back on the forest road and knew that, here and now, this battle was just and right.

The young woman stood shakily at his side. Swan tried to position himself in front of her to shield her from the oncoming attack, but she pushed him aside, stronger than she looked. "I am not yet finished." Her voice was low and sweet, but it cracked on the last syllable, belying her words.

They stood in the road, watching the Dragon-Blooded assault thunder down upon them. He dropped into a defensive crouch and felt his senses expand around him. It was as if time slowed enough for him to notice every nuance of the night, every flake of snow that drifted around them. The twilight aura emanating from the young woman blazed brighter and melded with the growing sterling flames surrounding him. He could smell the crisp bite of the evergreen trees along the roadway and the rich rot of the earth that had been churned up in the Hunt's passing. The wind against his face was bitter cold, but he felt warm, as if lit from within. He listened as unfathomable words fell from his companion's tongue. They sounded foreign and familiar at the same time, although he could not begin to guess their meaning. She gestured, making a flicking motion with her fingertips and there was a deafening clatter. The night air between them and the charging Hunt shattered into a million obsidian shards. Dazzling blackness drove itself mindlessly toward their oncoming foemen.

Her spell hit the Hunt like a storm of knives. Their horses screamed in agony as the flashing black tempest sliced flesh from bone and severed tendons like butter. Every horse fell, sending their riders spilling onto the frozen ground now slippery with steaming blood. Those pulling the chariots dropped in their traces. The battle carts spun forward, flipping on impact with the horses. Drivers flew through the air and crashed like sacks of grain against the snowy ground. Where the Dragon-Blooded were too slow to raise their shields or weapons against the deadly obsidian storm, their blood joined that of their mounts. Several did not regain their feet. With an exhausted cry, the girl before him slipped to the ground and lay there unmoving before Swan could catch her.

The four Dragon-Blooded who rolled to their feet found Swan waiting. He crouched low in a defensive stance, certain that this particular position had never been taught in his martial training, though it felt extraordinarily correct. Beyond him, like a brilliant war banner, blazing energy streamed white gold across the winter night. The snow continued to drift gently around him, as he stepped forward over the young woman's fallen body, putting himself between her and the Hunt.

"So, the demon has conjured forth another to protect her?" The stocky crimson-skinned warrior bayed his dismay. Sulfurous smoke billowed forth with his words. "Then, share her fate!" He snatched up his spear, gesturing to the nearest hunter who had regained her feet. "To the left, Ciro. We'll take the whelp down."

Beside the Hunt's leader, a female warrior had rolled to her feet. Her eyes glowed an eerie gray in the night air, and her blue-black hair swept madly back from her face in an insane whirlwind. "It'd be my pleasure, Adish," she hissed. "C'mere, boy. I haven't killed nothin' in a week… maybe two. I'm gettin' all rusty at it."

With a blood-curdling howl, Adish lowered his fiery spear, charging Swan as if to spit him upon its length. Ciro leapt to the left at the same time. Her jagged jade daiklave arced up impossibly fast, and she cackled horribly as it descended for a fatal strike.

Swan swept Adish's attack to the left with a gentle motion, ducking to avoid the wind warrior's arcing blow as he did so. He was amazed at how smoothly his body moved, how quick his reactions were. Yesterday, he knew, he was not this fast, not this agile. Yesterday, he would have been dead.

Adish charged ineffectually past, carried on by the ferocity of his own attack. Swan sent him further with a shove, directing him into a tangle of underbrush off the side of the road, hoping to buy some time as the war leader's long spear caught in the bramble.

Swan seized Ciro's weapon arm after her blow fell, continuing her deadly stroke down and around until it would go no further. With an infinitesimal twist, the tendons of her elbow snapped. The bones grated together with a wet crunching sound. The jade sword slipped from her deadened fingers. Ciro fell to her knees on the frozen road, howling in pain and disbelief at the arm hanging uselessly at her side. "You son of a gravehound… You broke my flamin' arm! I'm gonna pull your insides out through your earholes!" Her eyes shined with a hungry light that made Swan shudder.

While the frustrated Adish extracted himself and his weapon from the undergrowth, the other two soldiers of the Hunt now reached the young diplomat. Swan stood calmly, eyes dark and anticipatory. His anima flickered around him, shining with the milky gleam of a solar eclipse. In the dim night, his skin shone slick and cool as snake scales, save for the center of his forehead, which burned with a heat that was both slightly uncomfortable and reassuring at the same time.

At the sight of the glowing gold ring and circle centered on Swan's forehead, Ciro went wild. "Get him! What are you waitin' for? He's one of them!" Ciro screeched, her uninjured arm gesturing with a jade-gauntleted fist at the offensive mark on Swan's forehead. She struggled to her feet, shaking her traitorous limb as if her fury alone was enough to heal the sundered tendons. Her off hand fumbled at her belt for another weapon. The wind rose around her as she circled Swan, gray glowing eyes narrowed with hatred.

"Leave us now, and we have no quarrel," Swan offered, even as she closed to rake a razor-sharp dagger across the young man's outstretched arm. The dragon-headed weapon sliced his silk tunic like butter but barely left a scratch on Swan's skin beneath. He glanced down at the blow's effect and then at his attacker. "I will take that as a refusal."

The Dragon-Blooded's glowing gray eyes widened in surprise. For a moment, her face froze, then an insane expression crept across it, her mouth stretching into a macabre grin. She let out a shriek of mad laughter, diving at Swan, driving the blade forward ahead of her. Swan spun her attack aside, using the momentum of her thrust to whip her into the path of one of the two remaining attackers. The incoming swordsman, half again as tall as Ciro, could not stop his blow. Horror swept across his teal features as his sword's stroke caught her in the shoulder, cleaving deeply into her chest. Bones snapped audibly beneath the blow, her leather shoulder strap parting under the sword's blade. The two warriors twisted together, stumbling for a moment. With a barbarous rip, the jagged jade blade tore from Ciro's shoulder, sending her dark arterial blood fountaining to stain the whitening earth.

The female warrior turned, clutching at her companion's armor for a moment as if to support herself. The eerie glow in her eyes faded. "Dalit?" she said softly, then slumped at her companion's feet and moved no more.

The green-skinned Dragon-Blood looked down at the body before him incredulously. "Ciro?" He stared down, taking in the blood streaks down his breastplate and the blood dripping off of his weapon. His jaw moved as if to say something more, but no words came out. He turned on Swan. With scarlet hatred burning in his eyes, he stepped over Ciro's corpse and swung his still dripping weapon over his head. "Damn you, demon-spawn. I'm going to damn well make you bleed!"

Swan ducked the first swing, stepping forward into Dalit's graceless arm span. Folding his hands together as if in prayer, he jabbed his fingertips into the exposed hollow of the swordsman's under arm. Left unarmored for ease of movement, the nerves there parted under Swan's attack.

Dalit's arm exploded in pain, all control lost. His weapon leaped out of his hands, spinning across the frozen ground toward Arianna's motionless form. Clutching his useless limb, he turned on Swan. "Damn it. Now I'm going to kill you!" A tsunami of spiritual energy rose behind him, and the air was filled with the roar of raging water. Dalit let out a yell that swept out from him like a flash flood. It slammed Swan back onto the ground and lay across him like the entirety of the ocean rested on his chest. For a moment, he could not breathe, could not think. It was as if he were drowning there on the snowy ground.

Dalit moved forward, picking up Ciro's dagger from the ground at his feet. He brought the dragon-headed hilt up in an almost reverent gesture, then moved forward, eyes gleaming a sickly emerald. "That's it. You just lay there."

Swan swept a low kick through the warrior's parted legs. He hooked the warrior's far knee with his foot and then rolled to the side, tangling the heavily armored legs in his. The warrior toppled to the ground, hitting hard, unable to catch himself with his still numb arm. Swan scrambled for the warrior's abandoned weapon. His hand found the hilt, which was wrapped in sharkskin and then a sharp silver wire to hold it better in the Dragon-Blood's armored fist. It burned in Swan's bare hand, and he threw it toward its owner just as the warrior was beginning to rise. The sword buried itself in its owner's back, halfway to the hilt. He slumped forward onto the icy road, pinned like an insect on display.

The crackle of flame alerted Swan to the next attack. Adish had returned, leveling his flame spear for another charge at Swan's back. A deft half step to the side brought the flaming weapon in under Swan's arm rather than piercing him through. Swan twisted, using Adish's weight to splinter the teak shaft into two jagged halves. The crimson warrior growled at the ruin of his weapon.

"Unclean cur, you shall not be victorious! I will scourge you from Creation!" He stepped in to impale Swan on the remaining length of the shaft. Swan flipped the flaming spear half over and twisted in toward the fire warrior. His gaze caught and held that of the Hunt's leader as he drove the spear point like a dagger beneath its owner's chin. Adish crashed to the ground, gurgling on his own blood. The weapon's flames faded, leaving Swan alone once again on the silent road, snow gliding softly to the ground around him.

Swan knelt, feeling the bloody slush on the road's surface soaking through the knee of his pants as he checked the white-haired woman for signs of life. Her skin was now pale as the falling snow, and the drifting flakes no longer melted where they fell against her face. His heart fell, but as he leaned near, her chest stirred with shallow breath.

"I've got to get us out of here," he said to the empty landscape. The rhythmic sound of horse hooves began, so quiet as to barely be heard. Pursuit would not be far behind.

Swan lifted his new companion's frail form into his arms. "Unconquered Sun, protect us both. We're going to need it." With a fervent prayer for aid he carried her deeper into the forest.

Snow continued to fall, beginning to cover the carnage of the scene. The only sound was the growing drum of hooves. The dark watcher assessed the situation carefully from his place deep in the darkness at the edge of the road.

The rest of Adish's Hunt was gone. The few who remained from the other Hunt, approaching from the castle, had little chance of capturing the white-haired woman and her new companion now that he had gone through his transformation. He watched as the falling snow masked their path, shaking his head thoughtfully.

Despite the warnings he'd received, the pale witch's spell had almost done him in when it destroyed his chariot. Only luck placed him beneath its protective shield just before the obsidian onslaught stripped flesh from bone all around him.

Luck, or perhaps fate, he admitted.

From his safe vantage, he'd watched the purple-haired man's transformation and then his devastation of the Wyld Hunt with curiosity but not surprise.

He'd been skeptical that anyone could break the string of successes that Adish's Hunt had held, cutting through emerging Solars like a hawk through a headwind, but these two had indeed done so.

She'll be pleased.

The hoofbeats stirred Otieno from his thoughts, and before the first rider came into view of the battle scene, not even a footprint remained behind as evidence that he had once been there.

CHAPTER SIX

Somewhere, long ago, she'd smelled the pines before. The air was still, but the scent of loam and moss and mostly of pine brought back memories of that trip. She'd been too young to read, barely as tall as his belt and still her father's darling. He'd been a different man back then, his laughter coming more easily. He had taken time for fishing and carving willow whistles and teaching his tow-headed daughter to call birds using blades of grass. She'd gone out with her father as he fished the nearby stream and she'd fallen asleep in the shade of a fallen evergreen and woke to this same scent.

"Papa?"

Gentle fingertips pressed against her lips, quieting her dozing question, and Arianna startled awake. Her eyes flew open in horror as she remembered the Hunt, remembered falling.

Beside her, a violet-haired young man jumped as she sat bolt upright, scattering the blanket of leaves that had been laid over her. He jerked his hand back, but not before her dagger had darted between them.

"Welcome back," the young man said, quietly. He didn't seem at all disturbed to find her blade at his throat. In fact, he looked over at her with a hint of amusement in his amethyst eyes. "There's no need for that. You're safe now."

She frowned, and her blade remained. "Who are you? Where am I?" She frowned down at the leaves still heaped over her legs and then back at the young man who smiled warmly at her.

"My name is Swan. We met last night. You were being chased, and I helped save you from…" He paused, as if uncertain how to go on.

"The Wyld Hunt… I remember now." Arianna frowned as memories came flooding back at her. The Hunt. The horse. The road. And then this one, standing in front of her, putting himself between her and her attackers. The white gold glow that had surrounded him.

She lowered her knife, assessing him with a steely look. "You were Chosen as well." There was no other explanation for either the aura that had surrounded him or their escape from the Hunt.

The young man nodded. "Yes… I guess that's what you'd call it. It came upon me when I saw you. When I saw the… Dynasts attack you…" He seemed to hesitate over what to call the Dragon-Blooded Hunt.

She chuckled wryly, brushing the remaining leaves from her legs. "Dynasts. Yes, you could call them that. Although the Wyld Hunts are more hounds than rulers. Did you feel the noble power of their leadership as they tried to run you down on the road? When they were attempting to sever your head from your body, did you feel honored for the attention of the 'rightful' rulers of all Creation?" She scowled, reaching for the bag that still hung across her shoulder, pulling a clay bottle from it. Unstopping it, she took a drink and then, after a moment, held it out to him. "Water?"

He watched her, confusion dancing across his features. He took the bottle, drank and returned it, then lapsed into thoughtful silence again.

She recorked the bottle and tucked it back into her bag, checking the rest of her meager supplies. Thankfully, the attack had not damaged her books, although the entire bottom of her bag was littered with a thick layer of bread crumbs, all that remained of the loaf she'd tucked in the night before.

She looked up to find violet eyes upon her once more. "What is your name?" Swan asked.

"Arianna." She volleyed a question back at him, unwilling to share more about herself. "The Hunt? What happened to it?"

The young man frowned. "Some, I left back on the road." He seemed indisposed to go on.

"Really? You must handle yourself pretty well then." Months of self-imposed training, and Arianna had barely escaped the first of the attackers. There'd been almost a half dozen behind her on the road and another group further back. "Not bad for your first battle." She smiled, the corner of her lips pulling upward in a gesture that tugged gently at the now-healed scar running down her face. Reaching up, she traced the delicate line with her fingertip and scowled.

He shrugged, bowing his head modestly. "I get by."

"You said you left some back on the road… What about the rest?" A quick glance around the glade revealed no signs of battle here. In fact, all around them, the trees stood almost bole to bole, and in the spaces between, the undergrowth was so thick as to prevent entry. Arianna wondered briefly how they'd gotten in themselves.

"The second group followed quickly after the last of the first group fell. They pursued us…"

A memory slid into Arianna's mind. *The jostling pushed her against something warm and unyielding. Her arms and legs dangled, heavy and limp. Evergreen boughs iced with slush slapped at her face, even as someone bowed protectively over her, accepting the worst of the blows in her place. In the distance, the brassy bay of a hunting horn spurred the jogging gait to a faster pace, and consciousness dipped away again.*

She looked back up at Swan, startled. "You carried me."

He looked down, humbly. "You were in no shape to walk."

"What happened to the ones who pursued us?"

"It turned out that they were not as welcome in the forest as we were." He looked up, glancing around the glade. "The loyal servants of the Forest Lord made that abundantly clear to them, I'd say."

From between the trees, tiny lights slipped into the clearing, glowing cool green. The glade itself was draped in eerie half-light, a murky semidarkness that made it impossible to tell whether it was day or night. The spirits drew nearer, growing as they danced along the edge of the glade like giant fireflies. Watching them, Arianna felt more memories return. *The cool cushion of moss against her back and the forest spirits floating above her like pale green lanterns against the forest canopy, high overhead. The young man speaking words she could not recall, conversing with a spirit of the forest that hovered, pale and glowing, at eye height to him.*

"They chased them off, then?"

Swan watched the swirling spirits around them and then shook his head, looking back at Arianna. "No. The forest took them," he proclaimed solemnly.

Arianna's visage hardened as his words brought back the sounds of flesh being rendered from sinew and bone by sheer brute force. She'd been grateful for the cover of night and the thick wood between them. They filtered the screams of the Dragon-Blooded as the forest consumed the intruders.

A just end, she thought, *to those who had doubtlessly visited such pain and destruction on countless Solars themselves and would have certainly done as much or worse to her and her rescuer, had they had the upper hand last night.* She nodded. "I remember now."

Beyond Swan, there was a quaking in the trees, and a swarm of glowing spirits flew out of the tree line, easily three times as big as those who had been lazily fluttering previously. Behind them, the thick wood parted like a velvet curtain, revealing a wide dark passageway trailing off into the night. From the darkness, the thick scent of evergreens wafted, accompanied by the rich scent of freshly turned loam and the metallic tang of newly spilled blood.

"What the…" Arianna scrambled to her feet, followed quickly by Swan.

The ground began to shake, a rhythmic rumble as if boulder after boulder were being dropped just outside the glade.

Pine needles showered down on them like a fragrant green rain, as wave after wave jolted the clearing.

From out of the darkness, a giant form stepped forward, illuminated by dozens more of the darting, hovering spirits. It was a boar, but a boar so tall that both Swan and Arianna had to crane their necks to look up into its porcine face. It was formed of wood, not of planks and boards, but as if the forest itself had somehow spawned a giant child of living tree and vine. All down its back, thorns as long as Arianna's hand stood upright, adding to the creature's fierce demeanor. Its sides bristled with pine needles, and the massive hooves that carried it into the clearing were covered in oak bark and as big around as a wagon wheel.

Arianna was stunned. She'd read myths of forest spirits such as these, embodiments of the wood and wilderness, but here, with its hot breath filling the air around her, she could not even find enough wit to run.

From beside her, Swan dropped into a deep sweeping obeisance, and Arianna regained her senses enough to follow his lead with a polite gesture that wavered uncertainly between a nod and a bow.

"The trees feed well tonight," the great boar's voice rumbled through the glade. "You are welcome here, Children of the Unconquered Sun. Rest well this night, knowing you are well protected."

"We thank you for your hospitality, most noble Lord of the Forest. We will take nothing that is not offered to us and leave nothing here that is unwanted."

The boar nodded sagely, his immense snout dipping in acknowledgement of the young man's promise. "It has been a long time since any of your kind have visited us here. You will acquaint your companion with the terms of the oath you offered us?"

Arianna scowled as Swan nodded deeply, answering, "I will do so, noble Forest Lord."

"Oath?" Arianna whispered under her breath. *What sort of promise was he making on her behalf?*

"I'll explain soon," he whispered back, eyes lowered as he bowed again to the massive wood spirit. "We thank you again for your hospitality."

With a final snort that sent dry leaves swirling throughout the clearing, the Forest Lord trod heavily back into the darkness, flanked by his swirling spirit servants. The trees sighed at his passing and melded back into a thick grove, leaving no trace of his passing.

"Oath?" Arianna asked again, when she had regained her senses.

"It is nothing to worry about, Arianna."

She frowned at him, hands on her hips. "Call me foolish, but when a primordial forest spirit believes I'm oath-bound to him, I call that something to worry about. I'd at least like to know what you promised him on our behalf!"

Swan shook his head. "Not on our behalf. Only for myself. I would not make a promise for someone who was not present to witness the oath. And while your body was here, you were not truly present."

Arianna calmed, feeling a bit foolish for her outburst. "Oh," she said quietly. "I thought. That is, when he said…"

"I can understand why you thought that. It's all right. I just wanted you to know that I wouldn't speak for you without your permission. Vows are sacred things, and I'd not make one on your behalf without… without you asking me to."

She nodded, frowning uncomfortably. "What did you promise him on your behalf, then?"

"To come if his forest ever needed aid. To enter the depths of his lands only with permission. To raise neither steel nor fire in his wood."

Arianna cringed, remembering her blade against Swan's throat. Silence fell in the glade for a long moment.

"Well, it seems I owe you my life." She hated to acknowledge this debt, but in the face of Swan's oaths, which had protected her as well, there was nothing else to be done. She looked up, and Swan was watching her intently.

"Don't worry," he said with a smile, his gaze not leaving her face. "I'm sure I can find a way for you to repay me."

Arianna's eyes narrowed, glittering as cold and hard as ice. For a long moment, every ribald comment made by every asinine scholar in her years at the library rang in her ears, and she contemplated implanting her dagger haft-deep in his sternum.

He continued to watch her, smiling, then tilting his head in confusion at her reaction before suddenly flushing in embarrassment. *He didn't mean for me to redeem it on my back*, Arianna realized. The sensation crept over her, slowly, working its way at last to her face, where her frown softened almost into a smile.

CHAPTER SEVEN

"Oh, foul..." Samea winced as she removed the oiled rawhide lid from over the top of the bowl. "Must be ready." Sharp and vinegary, the acrid vapors burned at her nose, making her eyes water.

Three nights ago, she'd carefully set twenty-five seeds of ruinweed to soak in just enough soured wine to cover them completely. Tonight, as she'd hoped, they had absorbed enough of the acerbic liquid to soften into an evil-smelling brown paste. Using a carved horn spoon, she measured out the doughy mass into the ritual bowl she'd used for decades.

Thin as porcelain, the bowl appeared quite delicate, but it was actually carved completely from a single block of white stone. She remembered the day she'd found it in an ancient library, sitting as if waiting for her. It had rested on an undisturbed table in the middle of a room that had been thoroughly sacked by looters, alone unbroken among ruin. Since then, it had traveled with her everywhere, and she took great comfort from its presence, solid and delicate, beautiful and functional.

She filled the bowl one quarter full of ruinweed paste, then added enough sweet wine to fill it, stirring them gently. When the mixture cleared, she took the bowl to the center of the circle, moving with precise care despite her anxiety. It had been several years since she'd been able to call upon the power of the plant spirits associated with ruinweed to conjure forth visions of the future. When Yurgen began his campaign, some items had become increasingly difficult to obtain. Ruinweed seed was one of them.

As their name suggested, the plant vines grew only over the remains of long-fallen cities or buildings. And while the Northlands had more than their fair share of ruins, the tropical vine required the warmer temperatures of the more temperate East. Her time spent directing Yurgen's troops in Linowan had allowed her to renew her supply. She'd harvested the gold and purple flowers from the thick hairy vines by hand. They preferred to grow on crumbling structures, where their roots could delve deeply into the cracks and imperfections of the fallen stone. This made harvesting ruinweed seeds risky business. Like gathering the seeds, the ritual itself was also not without risk. Within a nomadic culture such as hers, where day-to-day life was physically taxing, even the three-day fast to prepare for the ritual was difficult and dangerous. She hoped, however, that communing with the plant spirit would allow her greater insight into their near future and perhaps lend some advice on how to proceed. Other plants, skullweed that was made into bright morning or kaempferia galagna, could be used to communicate with the spirit world as well, but most were highly addictive. Samea had seen more than one spiritual seeker find more than they'd bargained for when dabbling in bright morning.

Samea moved to the center of the summoning circle and checked the rings of salt and orichalcum runes that surrounded it, making certain nothing was disturbed. While the security rings were more frequently used to contain summoned spirits, today she intended to use them to keep malevolent beings out while she was vulnerable during her vision ritual.

She set the ritual bowl in front of her and settled herself into a comfortable kneeling position on the stone floor, protected from its inflexible chill by a thick felted mat. She'd made the small rug herself, as a much younger woman, from the wool of a mammoth who'd given itself to the tribe.

Once again, as she had every time she used it, she whispered a soft prayer of thanks to the spirit of the generous mammoth for sharing its strength with her.

The exterior of the thin stone bowl felt warm in her hands. Ruinweed infusion worked with the sweet wine, growing hot after a few moments. Samea knew that, at its warmest, it was ready to imbibe. She brought the bowl to her lips, sipping deeply. Once. Twice. And then, she drained the bowl.

The bitterness of the ruinweed mixture was not quite overcome by the sweet wine. Concentrating on the harsh undertone, Samea set the bowl gently on the stone in front of her. She closed her eyes and breathed deeply, waiting to see if Pegalan, the spirit guide associated with ruinweed, would choose to grace her with visions.

It began gradually, at first. Her fingertips began to tingle where they rested lightly against her thighs. Her face flushed, and her stomach spun slightly, so gently at first that Samea was not certain that it was not simply from hunger. Then came the patterns, green and gold against the inside of her unopened eyelids. Spirals and outlines, animals and abstract shapes danced in and out of her vision. She opened her eyes, and the room around her had changed. No longer was she bound by cold stone on all sides. Instead, it was full night all around her, and she knelt suspended in a starless void. Around her, everything was dark. When she looked in the direction she thought was down, she could not see her own hands. She could not feel her fingers any longer or the reassuring weight of her hands resting on her thighs. It was if she only existed as an idea, a thought within this endless empty space.

Around her, she felt a presence, strong and protective. "Are you there?" she called, gently, surprised at the timbre of her own words.

"Where else would I be?" The thick drawl of the void's voice held amusement. "Am I not always here? The question is, are *you* here?"

Samea tried to follow the sound of the voice, looking left and right, but there was nothing visible to either side. She shut her eyes, although it seemed to make no difference. Breathing in the scentless night, she centered her awareness on a point deep inside herself.

The world around her exploded into a moving mural of sensation. She felt the cold spray of salt water stinging across her cheeks. The wind whipped her hair back from her face, and she could feel the shift and roll of a wooden deck under her bare feet. The low groan of a ship was unmistakable, although a part of her mind knew that she'd never been near an ocean vessel before. As the timbers creaked, she realized it was the sound of her own movement. She had become the ship, the keel, the strength and center of the craft. What she had thought was her hair was actually kelp, caught and carried along as she cut through the waves, foam splashing against her bow.

The world brightened to a painful white. The sea spray changed in a moment to the more familiar bite of snow. Wind drove it hard against her face, and she wondered why she had no scarf to protect her. At a distance out in the storm, she saw a pair of figures, bundled heavily against the weather. They stood, back to back, facing some foe in the white tempest. The wind whisked back the parka hood of one of the figures. His violet hair whipped ferociously in the wind for a moment. Against her tongue, the wind tasted metallic, like steel and blood. The purple tendrils of his hair grew, writhing in the storm. Soon, they were as all-consuming as the wind itself. They blocked everything else from view, and the world was a mass of squirming amethyst vines.

Samea felt herself lifting. The vines shrunk, revealing a circle of gold around them. The golden sun glistened, with the purple filaments at its center, shrinking to become a beautiful jungle blossom. Ruinweed. Its scent was heady, sweet and clear. It smelled of summer, lush and laden with possibility. All around her, Samea felt life and potential. She followed the vine, flying along it like a honeybee following a scent trail. She flew through the thick jungle canopy, darting past birds in brilliant plumage and inquisitive monkeys who stared at her, stunned, as she passed.

The scent trail dropped down out of the canopy and changed. She followed and found herself surrounded by a lush green hollow. The blossom's sweet scent was gone, replaced by the scent of forest and rotting loam. At the center of the greenery sat a woman, cross legged, with a book propped open on her lap. Her hair was so white and fine that Samea thought for a moment she was one of the frost-children, born with no color to their bodies at all. Then, she looked up, directly at Samea. Her eyes were dark and full of pain and her lips red and full of fire. A scar traced its way down her forehead, across the bridge of her nose and down across the opposite cheek, marring the perfection of her features. She seemed about to speak, when the clearing spun again and Samea found herself face to snout with a giant boar made of living wood.

The pig fixed Samea with a sage stare as if it could see her watching it. Within her mind, Samea heard, "Change is coming from far away." The forest spirit exhaled on her. His breath was thick with the scent of blood and rot. He watched her for a long moment with his beady porcine eye and then burst into flames.

The blaze surrounded Samea with smoke so thickly she could barely breathe. It burned into her lungs and stung her eyes until tears were streaming down her face. All around her, the smell of roasting meat and burning wood grew stronger. She could not breathe. Her lungs were filled with fire. Samea found herself stumbling forward on her hands and knees, retching. She had to clear her lungs and rid her nose and mouth of the stench of burning flesh. She stumbled forward, trying to fight her way through the smoke to fresh air.

Her knees struck cold stone, palms slapping painfully against the floor of the ritual circle. Nausea hit, and the sour splash of bile on stone only fueled further spasms. After an eternity, she stopped purging and gasped for breath. Gulp after gulp, she filled her lungs with the cool cavernous air. Samea's arms shook, unable to support her, and she slumped forward into the darkness.

When consciousness returned, it found her cheek numb from the cold stone floor and the oil lamps sputtering their protests at being left lit so long. Samea pushed herself upright and instantly regretted the action. Her brain rattled in her skull like seeds in a pod, almost spilling her to the ground again. "Ruin indeed," she said, softly, wincing at the sound of her own voice.

Great quantities of water helped her recover from her vision quest. Her hair was still wet from bathing when she met with Yurgen in his chambers later that day.

"Samea? What has happened? Did you fall in the river… again?" he said, teasing his Circlemate. Bathing in water was a habit not common in the Far North because of the bitter cold. Samea had developed an affection for it while in the South. Once she'd returned, she'd set up a bathing space in her room and regularly partook of her new fascination. Yurgen took no small amount of pleasure in teasing her about it.

"It was that, or I would have come to talk with you with vomit in my hair, Yurgen. I smell much better now, I assure you."

Yurgen sniffed her direction. "You smell like someone dipped you in sweet wine. Have you given up on water and decided to bathe in akvavit instead?" He raised his cup of honey liquor as if to douse her.

Samea smiled, holding up her hand as if she feared he might indeed pour the liquor on her and then silenced his playful banter with a stern look. "I sought guidance last night. You probably smell the last of the ruinweed on me."

His countenance sobered as well. "Indeed? And were the spirits cooperative?"

She nodded. "Although I am uncertain as to the import of all of it." She recounted her vision to Yurgen as best as she was able. When she was done, she took his cup out of his hand, draining it, as if the memories still left a foul taste in her mouth.

"Well, if the spirits believe these things are of import, we will watch for them. I will alert the patrols to keep a look out for any signs of scarred strangers or wooden pigs." He went to take a sip from his cup and finding it empty, frowned and refilled it. "Our sources say that the Linowan will send word to the Realm, begging them to send aid for Rokan-jin and Talinin. Which means they have finally fully stepped into the war themselves."

Samea nodded, listening to the war leader. "We knew that would happen, when we allowed Chaltra Evamal and her foresters to join our efforts against the Eastern tribes."

The Haltan queen and her people had warred with the Linowan kingdom for more than 500 years. But in the past few hundred, their interactions had devolved into a few border raids. The Haltans did not dare to venture far out of their redwood forests to attack the Linowan cities, nor did the Linowan armies dare venture far into the gigantic Haltan forests. All of that had changed when Yurgen set his sights on the Scavenger Lands to the south of Halta.

Fearing that they would be caught between the Bull of the North's territorial holdings and his new potential conquest of tribal lands in the East, the Linowan had aided the small tribal kingdoms of Rokan-jin and Talinin, effectively pitting themselves directly against Yurgen and his already massive army of Northerners. Queen Chaltra, ruler of Halta, had come to Yurgen, proposing an alliance. Since then, the Haltans had been aiding Yurgen's warriors. They'd not only lent troops to the cause, both warriors and stealthy commando raiders, but the increase in supplies and local transportation had been invaluable. The only downside was Linowan's reaction. But every victory has its price.

Yurgen nodded. "Indeed we did. And it was worth angering Linowan to gain the aid of the Haltans. But this is different. We cannot assume we stopped all of their messengers. Word will eventually reach the Isle of their request. And we must prepare for the worst. The Empress will likely send forces to interfere in Linowan, and we must be ready for it."

Samea watched Yurgen thoughtfully. In his youth, he had been the strongest hunter of the Whistling Plains Elk tribe. Strong beyond his years, he had outlived all three of his wives and many, many of their children. He aged slowly. When his grandchildren had come to marrying age, the only sign of age he showed was a full head of silver-gray hair.

Longevity seems a blessing to those who crave it. Yurgen found it a curse instead. His friends all passed on to the other side before him. His tribe no longer knew what to make of him. All his life, his prowess with a bow and axe had commanded great respect. But now, having appeared to barely age for more years than they could remember, his tribe grew uncomfortable with his presence. They did not know how to treat a man who was not of the shamans, but who clearly was not entirely of man. In their own doubt and uncertainty, the tribe had begun to turn from him. He was no longer asked on their hunts, no longer called out to in welcome. He drifted among them, a ghost who still breathed.

One fateful night, Yurgen had told her, it had finally become painfully obvious that he was no longer welcome. No one dared to actually challenge his right to remain with the tribe, but it was as if he did not exist to them. He had left the tribal camp, skiing out, weaponless and underdressed, into the winter darkness. He was intent on giving his body and spirit to the lethal frosted fog or to the omen dogs lurking around the camp, whichever would take him first.

An ice spirit had attempted to claim his warmth and his soul, luring him into her seductive arctic clutches. The Unconquered Sun, however, had had other plans. Yurgen had told Samea later how he had found his heart and soul filled with living flame and how he had known that the Unconquered Sun had chosen him as his own.

Yurgen caught her watching him. "Samea? Have you heard a word I just said?"

"Yes, of course." She thought for a moment and then repeated a condensed version of his words, with pinpoint accuracy. "The time has come for me to go south again, this time with Florivet and the celestial lions. We're to ascertain that Mors Ialden and the Haltan troops he's leading are prepared for the potentiality of Realm troops becoming involved. We're also to step up the attacks against Linowan targets, and specifically, to make certain that the troops from Ardeleth are being properly recruited and that they're not shorting us on the manpower they agreed to provide." She smiled, sweetly. "Did I miss anything?"

"Yes," Yurgen frowned deeply, and then, his expression softened. "You forgot my order to take care of yourself. We can't do this without you."

Samea smiled, her dark eyes sparkling. "We'll be just fine."

She thought about Yurgen's words again as she reached the small chamber that had been her living quarters off and on for the past few years. Her traveling gear was once again packed, and the sight of the fur-bound bundles made her heart soar. Her time here in the long-abandoned temple that Yurgen had claimed as their base of operations had provided her with shelter from both the weather and the Hunts. In many ways, life had been easier for her and her tribe since Yurgen had led them here, even with the war. In her heart, however, she longed for the sight of the far horizons, the weight of her greatcoat and pack on her shoulders and the fresh scent of the winter wind. The past months, making the jumps back and forth to the Eastern kingdoms, had been a return to those ways, and every time she came back to the Hold, she found herself longing to return to the outside within a few days of arriving.

Despite her joy, she knew that her journey was a serious one. Each journey she had made from this place had been important. She knew she was taking her life into her own hands, leading Yurgen's icewalkers and their allies to the south and to war. The forest folk of Halta were strong allies, and Mors Ialden, the Northern-born Dragon-Blooded outcaste that Yurgen had taken under his wing, led them well. Her own Northern warriors were dedicated and fearless as well, and her spirit allies were powerful, if not completely predictable.

Yet, war was dangerous business. They had lost warriors, both allied and from among those icewalkers who had come with them from the Northlands. Nothing worth gaining was without a cost. The prophecies all had been fortuitous, however. All signs indicated that this path, while not without losses, would lead them to their goal. Thus far, all the preparations had also gone smoothly. The celestial lions had been won to their cause, just as Florivet had, when Samea had called him forth. Their forces were strong, their cause was righteous, and all would be right. She believed that. She had to believe that.

When Samea had discovered Yurgen wandering in the snow after his Exaltation, she could never have guessed that she would walk beside him on a journey that was destined to restore rightness on all of Creation. Who could have seen, even in his flashing eyes and fierce ways, that he was destined to serve the Unconquered Sun in such a fashion? To lead an uprising against the tyrannical Dragon-Blooded who had slaughtered the Chosen of the Sun for centuries to maintain their iron-fisted rule of Creation? To shine the truth of the Unconquered Sun upon the lies told by the Scarlet Empress and her seemingly endless stream of disciples and destructors? To reclaim, at long last, the right of those such as herself to live in Creation without fear of the Wyld Hunts destroying them as soon as the hand of the Unconquered Sun fell upon them? It had been almost too much to consider at first, but Yurgen's role had become clear over the months and years. Now, no doubt remained in Samea's mind as to the correctness of their path.

Linowan and the Eastern tribes were just the first step. A direct attack upon the Blessed Isle, with its First Age defenses and Dragon-Blooded population could not succeed. But, without the support of the rest of the Realm, the Blessed Isle could not hope to maintain itself for long. They relied heavily, too heavily, on the taxes and resources of the rest of the Realm, and without the rest of Creation to bleed dry, the Scarlet Empress' reign would soon tumble into chaos. When Linowan was made to see that the Dragon-Blooded would not supply the safety that they had been paid to provide for centuries, its people would realize that loyalty to the Blessed Isle was futile and unrewarding. They would come to understand the lies they had been blindfolded with, and with a foothold in the rich Eastern lands, Yurgen would be able to begin to carve the genesis of a new Age. The Next Age. The time that portents had foretold, when things would be once again as they should be throughout Creation.

Shouldering the great pack that would reach above her head even when she donned her wool cap and parka hood, Samea took a quick look around her room, making sure that nothing of import had been left behind. Although her spells and the Haltan river barges made travel much quicker than it would otherwise be, she could not count on returning to Yurgen's Hold for many months. Since it was now the coldest time of the year, it would not do to have forgotten the auge root that her troops might need for the unending coughs that Northerners seem prone to in the Eastern climes. Maybe more important was the neem oil needed to help stave off conception among the mixed sex troops when spring was upon them and the blood was flowing high.

Ideally, they would continue to have access to such things through their contacts within the Haltans, and as they pushed back the Linowan resistance, they should have access to a greater supply of food and medicinal herbs than they'd ever had in the North. But one did not succeed by counting on such things. Emergency caches of food, clothing and vital supplies were a way of life in the North, where a blizzard could cut a hunting party off from the rest of the tribe for weeks at a time. She knew travelers who had survived by literally eating the leather of their clothing when stranded by whiteout conditions that even the strongest hunters could not hope to traverse. You did what you must to survive. But she could not keep an army alive and functional under those conditions, and she didn't plan on having to try to do so.

CHAPTER EIGHT

The deep scent of evergreen swelled in the morning air, heralding the return of the forest spirits. Like brilliant floating lanterns, tiny verdant fireflies danced a welcoming pageant in the dawn's glooming.

Taller than the great stone dogs guarding the entrance to the Blessed Isle's Palace Sublime, the colossal boar strode into the glade once more. His heavy hooves sunk deeply into the rich loam with each step. Ancient trees, trunks so wide that three men holding hands could not ring them, bowed out of the boar spirit's path like supple reeds. His hardwood muscles shone as if finely polished, illuminated by the fireflies' glow. Raising his massive oaken muzzle, which bristled with evergreen needles, the Forest Lord inhaled deeply, as if tasting the messages on the winds. His eyes, tiny against the plain of his expansive cheek, squinted smaller still as he exhaled. The scent of rich soil and freshly spilled blood was heavy in the air. Slowly, he lowered his muzzle to lock gazes with the young diplomat.

"You must leave my glade now and return to the road before nightfall," the Forest Lord rumbled. The sound echoed up from deep within the heartwood of his chest. "The dark time will soon be upon us. I can smell it on the winds and hear it in the leaves. Change is coming from far away." The great boar's left ear, fully as large as a warrior's shield, twitched his disturbance. "Soon, there will be no assuring your safety, even with my blessing."

Swan bowed in respect to the enormous wooden boar. "We will do so, noble Forest Lord. Your hospitality has been great, and my companion is now fit for travel."

He glanced across the clearing to where Arianna sat. She'd chosen a place directly in the path of a sunbeam, the only one strong enough to pierce the forest's deep canopy. Her long hair gleamed. The sun's single ray crafted it into a silver plait so fine as to make the greatest moonsilversmith sigh in defeat. Swan once again was taken by the contrast between this mysterious young woman he had rescued and the pampered dolls he had known in Coral.

She seemed to feel his gaze upon her as she pored over the volume in her lap. Frowning, she glanced up to scan the clearing. Her scowl didn't lessen as she caught sight of the violet-haired young man and the forest spirit with whom he spoke. With an abrupt nod, she returned to her studies, turning slightly so that the scar etched down her face was less visible.

"We will make haste at once," the diplomat agreed, turning his attention from the woman back to the great boar before him. "And I will not forget our agreement." Swan's words were a silken vow carried across the glade, witnessed by the myriad woodland spirits present.

The Forest Lord snorted. "So noted." He turned, tromping back into the woods, which swallowed him as if he had never been. A few glittering fireflies swooped in ornate patterns, as if riding the divine eddies left in the wake of their lord's departure. One by one, they flickered out, leaving the two Exalted alone in the clearing.

Arianna looked up at Swan from over her book.

His solemn visage lightened into a smile, violet eyes twinkling. "Well. I guess that's our cue." Looking around the glade, he bent to pick up his traveling cloak, the only possession other than his clothes and belt pouch that he hadn't lost in their flight from the Wyld Hunt the night before. With a grin, he folded it into a tidy bundle. "There. I'm packed."

His pale companion shut her book after placing a scrap of dark cloth as a page marker. She slipped it into the small bundle still slung by her side, carefully adjusting it to assure herself the contents were safe. Solemnly, she looked up at Swan. "Where will you be going?"

Swan unfolded his just-folded cloak and settled it about his shoulders. His demeanor grew more serious, as he realized that his companion was not in the mood for her spirits to be lightened.

"Well, first I need to find Eldy and my gear," he replied, nodding to himself as he pulled his hair loose where the cloak had trapped it against his back. "Then, it's north to RimeHaven. From there, back to the Archipelago. I've been sent to renegotiate the trade treaties between Coral and the merchants' councils here in the North. I'm afraid I've lost the road I was on, but I'm certain I can find another, or the nearest town, and, from there, continue on to RimeHaven."

Arianna frowned. "You're... going on a trade mission? But..." She shook her head, scowling. "You're a Sun-Child. Anathema. Unclean." She spit the last word out as if it fouled her tongue. "The Wyld Hunts will find you." Her pale eyebrows furrowed in confusion.

He thought on her words. "I suppose it will be dangerous. But I have to finish my job. I guess I'll just have to be quick... and careful. But if I..."

Arianna shook her head again, raising a hand to cut off his words. Obviously, the chase last night and his sudden Exaltation had addled this young man's sense of reason. She began again, speaking slowly as if to one who was mentally deficient.

"You do not understand. They'll kill you. That's what they do. Hunt us down one by one and erase the 'Anathema' from Creation. Your only hope is to avoid them, and that means avoiding the big cities and the Dragon-Blooded the Realm has posted in them."

Swan smiled, patronizingly. "I'm not an idiot, Arianna. I grew up in a civilized town. I've seen a fair part of the world. I'm well aware of the Dragon-Blooded and how they hunt down the Anathema," he paused, thoughtfully. "Those they label as Anathema, that is. Like you and I. But I have a duty. I gave my word that I would complete this mission. And while I didn't expect this exact type of challenge…" The ironic understatement there made even Arianna smile briefly.

She shook her head ruefully. "I don't know whether to be pleased or mortified. You'll walk back into the Dragon's maw, simply to keep your word." She turned her icy gaze upon him. "Think on this, Diplomat. What good will come of your trade mission when the Hunt has slain you and tracked your backtrail to the parties you parlay for, destroying them for corroborating with Anathema?"

Her tomes told of a time when an experienced Solar could defeat an entire army of well-trained soldiers or, in the times of chaos, a unit of Dragon-Blooded. Nowadays, however, it was almost unheard of for any Solar to have enough time to learn sufficient defenses to elude the Wyld Hunt, let alone defeat them. Their escape had been a tribute to good fortune more than anything else. It was pure luck that the Wyld Hunt had chased her across Swan's path. Luckier still that something in the conflict had caused his own Exaltation.

Swan tilted his head, watching her change in expression. When she frowned, it emphasized the shallow scar that traced its way down from the right side of her forehead, along the bridge of her nose and across her left cheek. It was amazing to him that this delicate mark was all that remained as proof of the attack that, by all rights, should have killed them both the night before. While his body seemed to have grown infinitely tougher, shrugging aside wounds that would have certainly crippled him before his Exaltation, hers had seemed to knit, mending before his eyes, even after she had fallen into exhaustion. Only the slim scar on her face remained, and far from marring her beauty, it brought out vulnerability in his companion that her chill manner and haughty demeanor could not hide. He found himself wanting to trace its length with a fingertip again, a gesture to which Arianna would doubtless take great offense now that she was awake. With a small shake of his head, he changed the subject. "And you, Arianna? Where will you be going?"

Arianna thought for a long moment. Returning to the library was impossible, of course. Even before her Exaltation, she was a barely tolerated necessity, someone to ignore so long as the chores were done and the male scholars who studied there were not reminded of her presence. Now that she was known as an Anathema, there could be no returning. She'd been at the library since she was a young girl. The idea of being severed from it was at once frightening and exhilarating. Her uncertainty, however, was nothing that needed to be shared.

"Unlike you," she answered frostily, "I am not mindlessly bound to some imagined sense of duty. I will find another place to study. Another library, perhaps." Her cool words lay between them like a dusting of frozen dew across the forest floor.

Swan nodded. "Your studies are as important to you as my duty is to me. We're not so different, Arianna."

"I will not die for my studies, Diplomat," she said. In her own heart, however, she was uncertain if that statement was completely true.

"What happens when they track you down again?" He watched as her cool demeanor faded a bit. The worry was obvious, traced across her face although she tried to hide it.

She stood, turning away. "I will be fine." She began unwinding her scarf, preparing to veil herself again.

Swan cast his gaze upon the glade around them thoughtfully and then turned to address her more fully. "Arianna, I find that I must make a request of you."

She turned toward him, frowning slightly. Releasing her scarf, she nodded for him to continue.

"Last night, you thanked me for saving your life," he said, his tone full of dignified supplication. "And I told you that I was certain you would find a way to repay me. Now, I hope you will return the favor. Your knowledge of what we now are is obviously superior to mine. Your experience with it is far greater than mine as well. You are correct.

Without assistance, I will likely stumble back into the path of one of the Hunts. Would you do me the favor of traveling with me for a short time and teaching me enough of what you know to increase my chances of survival?"

Looking intently into her dark eyes, he allowed her to see the sincerity in his request. And sincere it was, if not solely for the reason he stated. The two newly Exalted Solars had already proven themselves to possess more chance at surviving together than either had on their own. Together, they would have a greater chance of avoiding the Wyld Hunts—or dealing with them should their attempts at evasion fail. And if his new companion's visage was pleasing and her cool nature somehow intriguing, well, that was simply an additional benefit, was it not?

Arianna nodded. "I owe you that much. Let it not be said that the Eclipse Caste are the only Exalted who understand the nature of honor and debt." Standing, she adjusted her scarf circumspectly across her face, shielding her scar from casual examination. "If I cannot dissuade you from traveling to RimeHaven, I will accompany you. And perhaps when you realize the folly of your journey, I will be able to prevent it from being a lethal lesson."

Swan smiled. Maybe he was being overly optimistic, but not wanting him dead was a start, he thought.

"Well then," Swan said, "that's settled." He looked around, but the clearing was bordered thickly on all sides by heavy woods. "Now, if I just knew where RimeHaven was."

Arianna glanced down at the pool of sunlight she had used to illuminate her studies earlier. It had crept slowly across the forest clearing floor, and she used the toe of her boot to draw a line tracing its path. She drew another, perpendicular to it at 90 degrees from the starting point, and then another where 45 degrees would be. Finally she drew a fourth line, halfway between the last two. Looking in that direction, she shrugged.

"RimeHaven is roughly north-northeast from my library. I'm uncertain how far or what direction our flight took us last eve, but if we travel roughly north-northeast, at least we should be proceeding in approximately the correct direction." She looked back up at him. "Unless you have a better idea?"

As if in answer, a trio of the shimmering green firefly spirits zipped back into the glade. Their voices were indecipherable. They were, at one time, the zooming buzz of gnats and the whisper of night winds through the tallest treetops, melded with the chirruping of crickets. But their intent seemed clear, as they swirled first around Swan and then his companion. The flickering lights darted between the Solars and a narrow pathway that, if asked later, both Swan and Arianna would have sworn had not been there moments before.

Swan smiled. "I think I have a better idea." With a grandiose bow, he gestured toward the opening.

Arianna frowned, but the path went in the same general direction her impromptu compass had indicated, and so, she began down the pathway, forest spirits circling as she walked.

They followed the fireflies' light for half the day, down a long dark path where the trees grew so tightly together as to create a hallway of living wood.

"I am beginning to doubt that these 'guides' know where they are going," Arianna stated sullenly, after they had walked for hours.

"The Forest Lord sent them. I'm sure if we only follow them a little further..." Swan looked behind them and noticed the path they'd traveled on all morning now stretched only a short ways behind them, before fading once again into thick woods. He turned, looking back ahead. Quietly he added, "Not like we have a lot of choice at this point."

Before them, the path suddenly made a sharp angle and emerged onto a road. It was narrow and overgrown but a road nonetheless. The sun blazed brightly overhead. Blinded by the sudden brilliance after their long shaded journey, Swan blinked until his vision was restored. He turned to thank the firefly spirits but found them nowhere to be seen. Arianna was looking around, similarly confused at the spirits' disappearance.

"Where did they go?" he asked.

"Perhaps back to the clearing," she offered, turning to look behind her. But the path they had just emerged from was gone as well, nothing but impenetrable forest thicket along the road as far as the eye could see.

CHAPTER NINE

The two primary roads in RimeHaven ran north-south and east-west, crossing in the center of the town to form a cobblestoned square. Many of the city's most prosperous businesses clustered around the edges of the town square, and it had been packed during the middle of the day with such a crowd that Arianna had found herself intimidated by the sheer intensity of it all. While the library's dining room at midday meal might have seemed crowded and chaotic, it was nothing compared to this.

Swan, much more experienced with cities, had taken on the combined role of tour guide and guardian, sweeping through the bustling crowd with expert grace. They'd traveled up and down the lengths of both the main thoroughfares and explored some of the smaller side streets that wound their way less directly through the rest of town.

Originally, she'd been confused at the depth of his concern for his missing horse after they'd left the Forest Lord's haven. She'd managed to call back Swan's frightened little mare and then watched as Swan had pawed frantically through the saddle bags, not relaxing until several sealed scroll tubes and a sheaf of parchment had been carefully laid out on the ground beside them.

"Letters of credit," he had explained. "Without them, we'd have a deuce of a time restocking for the journey, but they're all here." He'd sequestered everything back into the saddlebags, pulling the parchments out as needed to secure lodging for them here in RimeHaven and to fund their shopping that day.

Swan had explained the local money system to her, but while she had memorized the relative values of the jade, gold, silver and copper coins that were most commonly used in this region, she had little practical knowledge of how to apply them to anything more personal than the dishes and daily meals that she'd kept accounts for at the castle. While she recognized that they were beautiful, the idea of a frivolous hand-carved bone comb costing as much as a week's meals for two dozen students or a delicate silver brooch costing more than five replacement settings of plates and bowls was beyond her comprehension.

She'd been fascinated by the apothecary shop, however, and if she'd had coin to spend, she'd have gladly left it all with the bookseller whose mundane wares were intriguing and new to her. Swan had noted what items she seemed to particularly appreciate, and despite her protests, he'd left carrying a bundle of books and papers for which she had no way to repay him.

They'd eaten their midday meal at a small but busy public house called The Heron's Rest, where Swan continued his tutoring over hot beef soup and doughy dumplings that they dipped into the stew with chopsticks. Money was not a matter she'd had to consider before. She had wanted for very little that was not provided by the owners of the castle. Room and board in exchange for her service had been the way of things since she was old enough to fulfill the job duties, and while she understood the intricacies of account keeping and business, she'd had almost no experience with personal finances.

They'd just left The Heron's Rest and were walking past a stone corral of horses, when a commotion drew their attention. A furious whinny cut through the air, and the peal of shod hooves against stone rang out. A gray gelding reared, his front hooves churning the air above the head of a man who scrambled across the wall for safety.

Arianna smiled. The horse screamed his victory, having driven the auctioneer out of the ring, and the crowd around the corral thinned as potential bidders turned their backs on the spirited gelding.

"Ten... ten silver... Five? Come, will no one give five silver cushings for this fine beast?" The auctioneer's sales pitch was half-hearted, and hearing no responses, he signaled for the ropers to begin to attempt to move the gelding out of the stone circle. "Demon horse. To the butcher with it, if he'll have it."

Arianna turned to Swan. "May I have ten silver?"

He blinked. Ten silver cushings was less than their night's lodgings and evening meal cost, a pittance for a riding horse, but far too much for one that was obviously destined for someone's stew pot. "Of course, but you don't want—"

Arianna called out to the auctioneer. "Ten cushings... if you'll include a saddle and tack."

The auctioneer turned. "You drive a hard bargain. Ten is far too inexpensive for this fine horse and a set of gear."

"A moment ago, you would have paid someone to butcher it for you," Swan interrupted. "Sell her the horse."

The auctioneer was a short man with a scraggly fringe of graying hair around his ears, and his bald pate shone with beads of sweat in the afternoon sun. He glanced at Swan and the veiled woman beside him, then at the thinning crowd. "Done. Although I'd be lying if I said I had any idea what you'd want a saddle for. He's pride cut. He'll eat you as soon as let you near him with a bridle."

Arianna merely smiled, as Swan handed his letter of credit to the auctioneer. She leapt nimbly up on the low stone wall, whistling for the horse.

The auctioneer watched first with amusement and then amazement as the silver gelding rushed toward the veiled woman standing on the wall then gently nudged his head against her, as she reached out and gently inspected his eyes and ears. "His name is Mojin," she said, smiling back over her shoulder at Swan and the auctioneer, who both stood mystified at the horse's reaction.

For her, the "demon horse" was as gentle as a child's pony. She couldn't help herself; the expression on the auctioneer's face was priceless. She leapt bareback onto the animal, trotted him around the ring in a prancing gait and then slipped from his back to stand in the stone ring beside him while the ropers and the crowd gawked in amazement. She collected his saddle and tack, and they stabled him next to Eldy, although they quickly discovered that Mojin still was dangerously feisty when he was out of Arianna's control. He nearly kicked the stall in two when a stable boy got too near, but as long as she was present, he was calm as a kitten.

Later, they returned to their shopping, preparing for the next leg of their travels. Swan's employers apparently had recommended which inns could be trusted for safe lodging in the towns he was negotiating with on their behalf. They'd shared a room while in town, him insisting that she take the bed while he claimed to be perfectly comfortable on the floor. It had seemed strange to her for them both to sleep at the same time, rather than in shifts as they had on the road. The first night Arianna had lain awake for what seemed like hours, listening to her companion's deep breathing while he slept. He'd been nothing but a gentleman, but she'd found herself wondering when it would end, when he'd reveal himself to be cut of the same cloth as the rest.

All in all, however, the lodgings were comfortable, even if the knowing grins they'd received when checking in had not been. Swan handled everything with his normal casual aplomb, however, leaving her to remain silent behind her veils. It had been… not unpleasant.

His negotiations here had gone well, better than he'd expected. While Swan said that the council here was as greatly concerned as the one in Glassport with the Bull of the North's war in the East, he'd found himself adroitly addressing the situation with a practiced ease that went far beyond his years of training. The treaty signings had taken only a few days, time that she'd spent in the small rented room studying the few books she'd managed to take away with her from the library. Despite their late arrival, everything Swan needed to accomplish had been completed yesterday. This morning, he'd convinced her to accompany him out into town again, and tomorrow, they planned to head out for Bright Harbor, a small port town north of Glassport. Thankfully, the stores here, supplying travelers and locals alike, were well stocked for such a journey. They were able to purchase thick, fur-lined parkas, warm gloves and boots and even a cunning skin tent that would allow them to find respite out of the weather should it be necessary. They were well provisioned, and Arianna looked forward to leaving RimeHaven behind despite the cold journey ahead of them. Swan had been steadfastly, but unsuccessfully, attempting to convince her to come home with him to Coral for the last few weeks they'd been traveling together. Perhaps, once they were on the road again, he would ease in his pressure.

She wasn't certain exactly why she balked so stridently at the idea of traveling back to his homeland with him. Things were in a mostly comfortable limbo at the moment. The small Northern villages they'd traveled through had no clue that there was anything out of the ordinary about the young couple who passed through, and they'd fallen into a quiet companionship that was not altogether uncomfortable. She had to admit, to herself, if to no one else, that she'd actually come to enjoy traveling with Swan.

But somewhere in the back of her mind, voices whispered that this happiness could not last. It would not last. Something would happen, and they would be revealed and hunted, and it would all end. Surely the family he'd grown up with would recognize something different upon their son's return. It was foolish for him to return there and increase his risk of being unmasked. But it was evident that there would be no dissuading him from his "duty."

Or maybe the end would come from within rather than without. How long, after all, could he continue to offer up only smiles and kindness? She continually expected him to allow his mantle of good nature to slip, revealing his true seeming at last. But it did not. Hour after hour, day after day, he returned her jagged barbs only with kindheartedness and offered compassion and generosity even when met with suspicion and silence. The entire situation was difficult to understand, and it often led to her retreating into silence to contemplate it more deeply. Today, thankfully, he'd left the subject of the ocean travel alone, and they'd enjoyed wandering through the little town.

The streets of RimeHaven were almost empty. They'd been walking since just after dawn and had watched the city swell from nearly deserted to bustling township and back. Night had fallen perhaps an hour ago. Lit haphazardly by the tall lamps set into the street every few blocks, the temporary stalls that had housed merchants and craftsmen now stood empty, like a beggar's gaping grin.

Swan stopped in the middle of the sidewalk, holding out an arm to prevent Arianna from going any further. She looked at him curiously as he tilted his head, ears almost visibly perking to catch some elusive sound.

"What?" she finally whispered, after pausing a long moment.

"Can't you hear it?" He cocked his head again, frowning to himself.

"Hear what? I don't…" she began, but then she too heard the hushed noise that had drawn Swan's attention. The sobs were almost inaudible, but when the wind quieted at just the right moment, they could be heard from the main street. The side road was dark and narrow. Clogged with refuse, it was truly little more than an alley that seemed to end a few blocks back into the darkness.

Swan turned and began to move cautiously down the side street toward the source of the crying.

"What are you doing?" Arianna grabbed his arm, pulling him to a halt.

Swan looked across at her, confused. "I'm going to see what's going on. Are you coming with me?"

Arianna frowned, not loosening her grip. "I really don't think that's a good idea."

"Someone could be hurt. I'll just check."

Shaking her head, Arianna released his arm with a sigh. "Lovely. Don't you think that…"

Swan turned, already taking a few steps into the dark alley. "Hello? Is someone there?"

The sobbing continued as Swan walked past a pile of empty wooden crates stacked higher than his head. Unlike the main roads they'd kept to for most of the day, this side street was unpaved and appeared to be a receptacle for broken and unwanted bits of all shapes and sizes. Some of the piles were too old and decayed to be identified. A three-legged chair leaned crookedly against the wall, with a pile of chipped and broken dishes half-tumbled off its seat, the rest threatening to fall at any moment.

As he continued back, something vaguely rat-shaped skittered just out of sight, trailing a blotchy pink and gray tail the width and length of a small rope behind it. A largish pile of something was heaped a bit further down, reeking with the foul odor of soured milk and long-past-their-prime fruit. A rusted, lidless kettle dripped murky liquid from a small hole in its underside, the drops pinging softly against a jagged shard of broken glass beneath it. The sobbing persisted, and Swan continued slowly, but the further he walked into the alley, the less certain he was that Arianna had been overly cautious in her assessment of the situation.

The stinking bundle of refuse shuddered, startling Swan, who immediately chastised himself for his reaction. He slipped a hand into his pouch, digging for a few of the copper coins commonly traded in this area. "Hello there. I've a few coppers to spare." Swan paused just out of arm's reach as the pile shifted and one skeletally thin arm reached out, grasping at the wall to pull an impossibly thin figure wrapped in rags upright.

Swan stepped forward to assist the starving figure to its feet, offering the coins in his other hand. "Let's get you something to eat, shall we?"

As he reached for the tattered coat, his grasp met only icy cobwebs, passing through the threadbare cloth as if it were a shadow. The coppers dropped forgotten to the dirt at his feet as the ethereal beggar turned toward Swan.

Mismatched eyes, one large and bulbous like that of an ox, the other small and fishy, stared at Swan beseechingly from a face that caved in on itself like a rotted squash. An uneven gash of a mouth produced soft sobs of supplication from just above a tattered paper scarf. Fingers of bare chicken bones reached out toward him, held together with snippets of twine and odd bits of faded yarn.

Swan ducked beneath the bony grasp, stepping quickly away from the creature as it took one shambling step forward, still softly sobbing.

The creature's dilapidated coat hung open, leaving bare its chest, which seemed to be made of a small cask missing half its slats, the hoops rusted almost through. Rotted rope held up trousers of torn silk so old that they were more rip than cloth. Legs of broken broom bits stuck directly into two ill-mated shoes, one a tiny woman's slipper with a broken heel, the other a workman's boot with a large hole worn in the side of the toe. It stepped forward uncertainly, reaching out again.

Swan could not imagine what animated this bizarre creature, but his fingers still ached from the icy brush with its clothing. He could not imagine allowing it to touch him. He backpedaled again out of its pleading grasp, running into the stack of empty crates with a startled shout.

Arianna shook her head, racing into the darkness with her hand on her dagger hilt. "I told you it was…" The construct swiveled its awkward gaze from Swan to Arianna and back. It let out one last plaintive mew, and as the surprised couple watched, it shuddered and grew pale, then transparent and finally faded completely from sight.

Swan stood, blinking at the space where the creature had stood just a moment before. Finally, he pulled Arianna back into the demi-light of the main street. She came along, reluctantly, her curiosity focused on the alley long after she left its dark environ.

"What was that thing?" he asked, after maneuvering her into a brightly lit tavern a bit further down the main street.

"I… I'm not honestly sure." Arianna answered quietly, frowning in thought. "A spirit, obviously. But… nothing I've read about. A product of its environment, most likely— a construct of the tiny spirits in each of the abandoned belongings left in that place, year after year, combining together in despair? I'm not entirely certain… Stranger things have happened."

Swan frowned, shuddering at the thought. He rubbed his fingertips against his thigh as if to clean off the clammy touch he could still feel clinging to them.

After their waitress had taken their order and left them alone again, Arianna tilted her head at him curiously. "I'm confused by something, though. Why did you not fight it? You held your own against the…" She dropped her voice. "Against the others, the night we met. Or I assume you did, since we escaped. And yet, you ran from that thing that was surely no challenge to one such as you."

"It wasn't a threat, Arianna, and it wasn't trying to attack me. It just wanted… something. I'm not sure what. But if I didn't have to hurt it, I didn't want to. It just seemed… sad."

Arianna nodded slowly, watching her companion in silence for a long moment.

Swan returned her gaze, a slow smile spreading across his face.

Arianna frowned, her pale brows furrowing deeply, a gesture that kinked her scar as it ran between her brows, making it stand out a delicate pink against the ivory of her skin. "What?" She blinked, as if she could clear his grin from her sight.

"Your eyes," He answered, slowly tilting his head as he watched her, nonplussed by her reaction. "They're the exact color of the sky just before the sun goes down. They were ice blue the night we met, but now, they're so dark… It's incredible. I think it's possibly the most beautiful color I've ever seen."

Arianna blinked, startled at the compliment, and dropped her gaze to the table, feigning sudden fascination with the grain of the ancient material.

Swan chuckled, softly, then dug into the pouch at his side. "I'm sorry, Arianna. I didn't mean to make you uncomfortable." He deliberately changed the subject. "One good thing came of meeting up with that… thing, though. As I was reaching for some money to give it… I felt this and remembered. Shut your eyes."

She frowned back up at him, arching one snowy eyebrow in suspicion.

"Well… don't you want to know what it is? Put your hand out and close your eyes,"

Reluctantly, she did so, and felt something drop into her palm. When she opened them, she found the delicately carved ivory comb she'd puzzled over earlier in the day resting there. She looked up at Swan in confusion.

"You don't like it?"

"It's… lovely. But…" She traced a finger over the comb's silky surface. The ivory had been painstakingly cut and polished into tiny teeth, each one smoothed to a glassy sheen. The spine itself had been carved with a repeating wave pattern that dipped down onto the teeth of the comb, and a dark-blue dye had been rubbed into the carving, lending depth to the intricate artwork. The caps of the waves had been inlaid with a white shell so artfully that, when Arianna ran her fingertips over them, she could not feel where the ivory ended and the shell began. She frowned softly, placing the comb carefully on the wooden tabletop and slid it back over toward Swan. "I can't accept it."

"Why not?" Swan did not reach for the refused offering.

"I…" Her frown deepened. "I will not be bought."

Now, it was Swan's turn to scowl. "Bought?" His voice rose, and Arianna was surprised to see him angry for the first time since they'd been traveling together. He took a deep breath, staring at her with an intensity that made her regret her hasty words. He lowered his gaze back to the comb, speaking so softly it was barely audible. "There is not enough ivory in all of Creation." He shook his head, solemnly. "And even if there were, I would not. It is a gift. Freely given." He looked up at her once again. "Like my friendship. Accept it as such, or toss it away. It's your choice."

The comb sat between them on the dark wood table, glowing warmly in the tavern's candlelight. At length, Arianna reached slowly for it, hesitating before picking it up again. She did not look up as she slipped it into her pouch.

"Thank you," she said softly.

"No. Thank you."

Their supper arrived, and for a while, they ate without speaking. Little more was said on the way back to their inn, and other than a brief wish of good night, the night passed in uncomfortable silence.

Chapter Ten

The whirling snow was endless.

Bundled so thickly they could barely move, Swan and Arianna carried what remained of their gear with them as they stumbled through the blizzard. They had been struggling to find the road for what seemed like days. Each snow-coated tree looked just like the rest, and the drifts changed bushes to boulders and blew away footprints until they had no idea if they were walking in circles or not. Time passed strangely in the white-dark storm, exhaustion and hunger being no clue to how much time had passed. The winds drove away all sense of measurement.

The ride to Bright Harbor from RimeHaven was supposed to be a simple, if long, one. Five days out of town, however, the snow had begun, and it had not stopped. Heading south as they were, the season for blizzards had passed. Although they were prepared for cold weather, this went beyond their anticipations.

Mojin and Eldy had broken free while they were camped that first night. They'd already been spooked by the storm, and when something foul that smelled of rotten meat passed too near their encampment, it had frightened the pair so deeply that they'd torn their tethers loose and disappeared into the night before either Swan or Arianna could stop them. Even Arianna's skill with summoning the beasts had not been able to call them back. The chilling hyena-like laughter they heard later attested to the horses' probable fate as the supper of one of the legendary Northern titans, although neither Swan nor Arianna ever caught sight of the beast.

They'd returned to their camp after looking for the horses and rested uneasily. One kept watch while the other dozed. Eventually, the blinding snowfall around them became somewhat lighter, and they continued their journey. But the drifts clung to their boots, their pants, the hems of their cloaks, weighing them down. The powdery accumulations were rough, but the ice slicks were worse, making footing dangerous. And still the snow fell.

Travel was slow and tedious, and stories said that these freak blizzards, while infrequent, sometimes raged for weeks. They had counted on their provisions to last them the majority of the journey. The bitter cold and the added exertion of slogging through snow that often came up to their thighs had driven them to eat more than they should have, however, and their supplies were dwindling. They had to keep moving. The infrequently traveled road across the frozen flatlands had been lost under the thick white layer. Neither had been here before, and the instructions that had seemed clear as a bell when they had set out now were ambiguously maddening. At this point, they didn't care much if they were going north or south, only that, if they could find signs of the road, of any road, they could follow it toward civilization.

The frigid wind constantly churned up the gritty layer of new fallen snow, frozen too quickly to develop into full flakes. It hid the terrain, and their feet sometimes punctured through the brittle layer of ice left by a previous storm, leaving them stumbling face first into a drift. Despite their drive to find town, they were forced to proceed slowly or risk breaking a leg.

This morning was just a more brilliantly blinding version of the night before. When the sun rose, it colored the swirling clouds around them blazing silver. It took its toll on their weary vision, and more than once, Arianna had found herself walking with her eyes shut to ease the pain. Now, after what

seemed like hours, the snow seemed almost violet, as if
stealing the color from Swan's hair and eyes. Arianna half
expected to find him as colorless as an albino, when she
turned to him.

She signaled for his attention, shouting to be heard over
the howling wind. "We're not making progress, Swan. We
have to stop. Maybe if we…" Her words dropped off, as
something solid moved past in the swirling storm, just out of
clear sight. She blinked, shaking her head to clear her
eyelashes of the frozen droplets they'd accumulated.

Swan turned to look the direction she was staring, his
heavy hooded parka making turning his head a near impossibility. "I don't see…" At the peripheral of his vision, a dark
shape, vaguely human-sized, melded out of the swirling
snow, but disappeared as he called out to it. "Hey!"

Arianna frowned. She moved until her back was up
against Swan's, warily watching the drifting circle of semi-
clearness that made up the entirety of their world for that
moment. The light distorted, casting blue-black shadows
where lilac luminescence had been a moment before. A
horrible howl tore at their ears as the already unrelenting
wind picked up. It ripped at their clothing like cruel claws,
pulling them away from each other. "Swan, I don't like this."

They came then, soundless but heralded by the screaming gale. They drifted out of the storm, their hair black as
night and whipping in the winter wind like a nest of deadly
vipers. They were naked, their skin pale even against the
glowing snowstorm. But even this was not as disturbing as
their eyes, clear and unblinking.

"The hushed ones…" Arianna said, hardly believing it
even as she spoke the words. She'd read an account of a
survivor of a hushed one attack, years ago. His party had
wandered too far from civilization, and the inhuman hunting pack had descended upon them, killing the only heavily
armed member immediately. The rest of the travelers had
been divided from each other and driven into the blinding
storm. Only two survived out of the party of eighteen. After
falling accidentally into a ravine, they'd been covered over

deeply with a snowdrift. When they dug themselves back to the surface, the snows had passed, and nothing remained to be found of the rest of their party.

Swan frowned in frustration, "The what?" A black arrow with blood-red fletching streaked past his head. The archer's aim had been lost in the raging wind, but it was still close enough for concern. The archer remained hidden from view, veiled by the blinding snow.

"Hushed ones!" she repeated, the words whipped away from her as they left her tongue. "Don't let them separate us!"

Swan crouched in a defensive stance, looking around for cover but finding none. He watched them come forward, sinuous and alien, drifting out of the storm like they were part of it. He didn't know what hushed ones were, but anything that existed in this blizzard without clothing had to be even more inhuman than they appeared.

They moved lightly over the top of the snow, although Arianna and he stood knee deep in it. The one he watched was female, although as slim and curveless as a child. Her eyes were icy blue, a shade not unlike that he'd found when looking down into Arianna's for the first time. But there the similarity ended. In Arianna's face, he always found emotion, even if it was the arrogant wall she used to keep the rest of the world out. Eerie and unblinking, the hushed female approached, icy eyes watching him with cold-blooded blankness from beneath a long mane of night-dark hair. Still-crimson blood smeared around her mouth and down across her bare chest. Swan shuddered, trying not to imagine its source. He prepared himself for her attack, searching her face and body language for some clue that would allow him to gain the upper hand. He'd found, since his Exaltation, a heightened perceptiveness within himself that often allowed him to discern some weakness, some flaw that would put his opponent at a disadvantage. But watching this one, he was surprised to find nothing. This creature was as inhuman as the wind around her, as unfeeling as the storm.

She leapt forward unarmed, still expressionless. The talons at her fingertips reached hungrily for Swan's exposed face. Moving with incredible speed, he intercepted her leap, grasping her naked arm before her claws could reach him. Diverting the momentum of her attack, he sent her soaring past him into a heavy drift of ice and snow. She struck the frozen ground hard, her head slamming against an icy outcropping, and lay there for a moment, dazed. He found himself staring at her, the snowstorm screaming in his ears, and realized suddenly that it was Arianna's voice he was hearing.

Swan backed toward Arianna, finding the pink and lapis shimmer of energy that emanated from her a welcome reassurance against the blinding blizzard. The female he'd been watching regained her feet and slipped to the side, disappearing into a whirl of snow. He turned, confused, to question his companion.

Arianna's skin glinted bronze with her mystical armor, beneath the layer of frozen flakes that had attached themselves to her. As Swan watched, her fingers stretched painfully outward, the tips lengthening into draconian claws of wood. She rubbed the talons together, and they rasped against themselves, as sharp and strong as daggers of oak. Swan swallowed hard, blinking at the transformation as Arianna flexed, the wooden spears of her newly transformed fingers gleaming in the blizzard's strange half-light. She glanced past him, her eyes pale-lit with an inhuman glow.

Around her, a handful of hushed ones struggled silently on the snow, bleeding amid the scattering of obsidian shards she had sent slicing in their direction. Their cold blood did not melt the snow it landed upon, instead pooling on the frozen crust like a crimson lake. As Swan watched, the male who lay closest to them pulled one of the shards from his bare chest, tossing it to skitter across the frozen crust of snow along with his ruined bow. The obsidian blade had struck deeply, but as he rose to his feet, the wound knitted itself closed before their eyes. By the time he took his first step toward them, his skin was as pristine and flawless as if the wound had never existed.

Behind him, the others were on their feet as well, their wounds disappearing from sight. Swan watched in amazement as one female who been struck in the face, her eye sliced from forehead to cheekbone, turned her gaze upon him. Her icy-blue orb began healing itself.

"There's too many of them! We've got to get out of here!" Arianna's attack had taken much out of her. She turned to assess the closing circle, cursing the heavy parka, which prevented her from turning her head easily. Swan pointed to a spot behind her, yelling to be heard above the snow's howl.

"There!" The gap between the closing hushed ones wasn't a large one, but it seemed their best chance. Swan leapt forward, aiming a brutal blow at the only attacker blocking their path to freedom. The hushed one's naked flesh was cold and unresisting, even compared to the icy storm. Swan's hand thrust forward, slamming hard into his opponent's neck, aiming for what he hoped were pressure points similar to those on a human. The hushed one crumpled. Swan reached back for Arianna, whose claws dug into the arm of his heavy coat, as her other hand clenched one of her throwing knives, ready to impale it into whichever of their inhuman hunters might encroach too closely.

The hushed ones warily closed in behind them, as Swan and Arianna rushed forward through the gap in the hunter's circle. Arianna deftly tossed her dagger with what appeared to be a casual gesture. The knife impaled itself to the hilt in the nearest hushed one's throat. The creature did not so much as blink as it crumpled to the icy ground, its weight landing lightly as the swirling snow itself.

As they broke free of the closing ring of attackers and hurried forward, the storm stilled, as if its fury had been egged on by the hushed ones' attack. They raced forward, grateful for the respite. As the snow that had whirled around them so fiercely began to drift gently downward, it revealed stony walls as tall as any tower, to both the left and right of them. Here, the walls were sheer, almost slick. Higher up hung rocky protuberances heavily laden with snow and ice.

The canyon floor was almost clear of snowdrifts, sheltered as it was by the high walls, and the ground was peppered with round gray stones, some as big around as a man's head. The canyon extended quite a ways. Despite the snowfall, a frozen river could be seen on the other side of the gap, open and expansive, with a thick forest beyond.

Swan allowed himself a quick glance behind them, where the hunters followed slowly, their wounds still healing as they came. They filled the gap through which Arianna and he had just escaped, leaving no path save for forward.

Arianna slowed, taking in their surroundings. "I don't like this, Swan. Why are they waiting?" Her claws released his arm, pulling another dagger from her sash, and she picked up her pace again.

Swan nodded, pulling her onward. "I don't like it either," he said, his breath coming in clouded puffs. "But we have little choice…" The hunters continued slowly closing the gap between themselves and their prey, herding them down the canyon. "At least the ground is clear here."

Arianna turned, facing back up the canyon toward their attackers. With a few soft words and an arcane gesture, there was a flash of golden light from behind the hushed ones. The sharp ring of hoof beats on frozen ground echoed directly behind them and then a shrill whinny. The inhuman hunters turned as one, as Arianna's spirit steed galloped out of the swirling snow. Summoned to her side, the horse leapt over the hushed ones' heads, striking one solidly with a heavy hoof as it passed. The hunter crumpled to the frozen ground, its perfect skull crushed like a ripe melon. The others continued forward with no discernable reaction to the loss of their companion, as the steed closed the distance between hunters and prey.

Arianna jammed her knife back into its sheath and leapt onto her mount's back. With a thought, her former claws turned back to bronzed fingers, which tangled deeply into the horse's golden glowing mane. Reaching down to pull Swan up behind her, she urged him to hurry. Together, they shot down the canyon's length at a full gallop. Behind them, the hushed ones broke into a silent loping run, still blocking the upper width of the chasm to prevent the riders from turning back in their path.

The canyon walls led right to the river's edge, preventing escape to the right or left, but the ice looked solid enough to chance an escape across the wide frozen river and into the woods beyond. Swan shouted into Arianna's ear as they dashed onto the unyielding river's surface. "I think we're clear!" He clung tightly to her waist.

As if in answer, the icy river seemed to come to life. Transparent shapes moved on the uneven frozen surface, separating themselves from the thick ice. While Swan and Arianna watched in horror, boulder-sized chunks of frozen river seemed to lift themselves up, unfolding on giant insectoid limbs. The spirit horse screamed in terror, its limbs frantically churning backward against the packed snow in an attempt to avoid the closest beast. Translucent as crystal, the giant insects rose up on long slim legs until their thoraxes were easily even with the height of the horse and riders. A dozen of the monsters formed a rough half-circle around the riders, blocking their escape across or down the ice.

"They were herding us!" Arianna yelled.

Swan took in the ice monster's stance and pulled Arianna off the horse's back. They fell to the ground, and he rolled, catching the brunt of their impact on his shoulder and keeping Arianna from harm.

Opalescent eyes the size of dinner plates came to bear on the horse. The enormous insect in the center, the largest and closest to them, closed in. Swan and Arianna watched in horror as the giant bug's massive mandibles snapped shut on the spirit steed's neck, inches from where they'd previously sat. The mount screamed once more, its spine cracking audibly, before the entire horse dissipated into gold-flecked mist. The creature's mandibles clacked uselessly shut on themselves. Its proboscis darted out, as if unable to sense that its prey was not trapped within its jaws. A clear liquid, thick as honey, dripped from the tip as the insect jabbed the air again and again in search of its missing meal.

Rolling to his feet, Swan quickly assessed the situation. He had no idea what the huge translucent insects were, but they seemed at home on the frozen river, and their powerful jaws made their predatory nature obvious. From up the canyon, the hushed ones were quickly closing in behind them. They were close enough to count now. Only a few of the more than a dozen were armed with more than their bony claws; one held a bow with a quiver of arrows slung over his shoulder, and two more grasped swords. They continued forward, silent even here in the stillness of the canyon, naked and eerie in their onslaught. Arianna struggled to her feet, boots slipping dangerously on the frozen surface.

Swan reached out to steady her. "So... maybe I spoke to soon." He glanced again at the oncoming foes to each side, settling himself into a comfortable defensive stance. "How much longer can you go on?"

Arianna took a deep breath, and Swan recognized her attempt to force her cool demeanor to settle over herself once more as she loosened a pair of richly ornate and razor sharp throwing knives from the sheaths on her sash. Her hands shook, and her attention was failing despite the cool mask. "We'll see."

Beyond Arianna, Swan could see the hushed ones hurried approach. "We've got to go one way or the other. Trapped here, we're helpless."

The hushed ones closed on the riverbank, ranging out to block any possible retreat. Arianna looked from them to the insects.

"Right, then. Forward it is," Swan said as he leapt toward the insect in the center. As he landed, he focused the momentum of his jump to a pinpoint. With hands doubled together, his first strike landed squarely on the only non-armored portion of the creature, its still-probing proboscis. The monster hissed in painful displeasure. Landing in front of the insect with catlike agility, Swan deftly dodged as the thing responded with an icy bite. He could feel the mandibles snap shut just over his head as he crouched, darting under the creature's thorax. Once there, his dagger was out of its sheath in a heartbeat, reassuring in his hand. But he found the underbelly as diamond hard as it appeared when he attempted to thrust his blade home. While the creature hissed and shifted trying to locate its prey, Swan desperately stabbed at different angles, exerting all his strength, but he only succeeded in dislodging a few chips of ice.

"Rock hard all the way around!" he called to Arianna. She breathed deeply, feeling the cold air chill deeply into her lungs as she cleared her mind. Her aura of power gleamed, painting the frozen river path in a brilliant sunset of pinks, gold and blues that seemed to streak up toward the low-hanging clouds. She began to chant, the words rolling forth in a tongue barely remembered in this age, her still-bronzed fingers weaving a complicated gesture in the twilight glow.

Swan darted from beneath the enormous insect. He swept a devastating blow to the lowest joint of its back leg, cracking the fragile limb like glass. The beast spun to turn on its foe, but pitched forward when it put weight on the injured appendage. It crashed to the icy surface of the river in a clattering heap. As Swan watched, deep fissures crisscrossed the beast's carapace, splitting like the river's ice in a spring thaw. A gooey liquid seeped slowly from the cracks. It struggled relentlessly but seemed unable to regain its footing.

As a great howling war cry echoed over the frozen river and through the canyon, Arianna let fly her volley. The black glass shards, summoned from her very will, skittered off of the icy insects with little effect. The river's frozen surface was peppered with chips of obsidian and flecks of icy chitinous shell torn from the creatures, but not a single monster fell under her onslaught. Cursing crisply, Arianna leapt over the fallen body of the insect Swan had downed. As she landed, she pulled her throwing knives, preparing to battle hand to hand. Swan rolled to his feet, looking over her shoulder up the canyon at the oncoming hushed ones. For a moment, his stern countenance grew confused, brow furrowing in concern. Then, as he watched, an arrow bloomed from the joint between his shoulder and neck, just above the neckline of his chain shirt. Blood flowed, fast and red, steaming in the arctic air. Swan's look of surprise and confusion grew, as he craned his neck to stare at the shaft emerging from his body.

Whether drawn to the scent of the blood or its warmth, the effect on the ice insects was immediate. All hesitation was left far behind as the remaining beasts slid like gigantic water striders to close on the wounded man. Growing weaker by the moment, Swan swept a fierce kick at the foreleg of the first arrival. His blow took a lot out of him, but he struck hard, directly on the joint. The knee collapsed backward, sending the beast careening off balance. Its ferocious mandibles snapped shut to his right, missing their intended target. Without the support of its foreleg, the insect crashed viciously into the ice, where its proboscis made contact with the ever-growing crimson pool.

Crooning a hum that sent chills down Arianna's back, the creature began a frenzied lapping to consume Swan's spilled blood. Its probing tongue rasped at the bloodstained ice, over and over. The slippery scratching rasped on Arianna's nerves. "Stop that!" she howled, waving her arms to chase the creature away. "Leave him alone!"

Mindlessly, the insect fed on, seemingly not noticing anything but the nourishment before it. It grew first pink and then red as the blood itself, as the warm fluid filled it. Arianna reached out with her dagger, lightning quick, and the insect's proboscis fell to the ice, writhing. The thing let out a buzzing scream, scuttling backward, its severed tongue dripping ichor and blood as it lamely retreated. "What, no armor there?" she hissed savagely, gore dripping down the length of her blade.

Clumsily preparing for the next attack, Swan felt the world spin, as the wound at his neck and the growing pool of blood at his feet began to sap his strength. He aimed a blow into the tender snout of the nearest insect. The attack landed where he had planned, but even as the creature hissed and backed away, he found his vision narrowing to a pinpoint. He had the brief sensation of falling as his world closed around him.

"No!" Arianna leapt to try to ease Swan slowly to the ground. His body was dead weight in her hands. She stood over his fallen form. The first fallen insect's body was between them and the canyon, and she hoped it would provide some cover from the hushed ones' oncoming attack. Right now, the insects were a more immediate threat. The smell of blood had made them bolder. Darting in, one by one, they tried to reach the pool at her feet. And one by one, she sliced at their probing tongues, sending them hissing away to nurse their wounds. They did not seem to learn from each other's loss, so great was their hunger for Swan's lifeblood.

Arrows arched toward the battle, seemingly from all directions. Thus far they had missed her and Swan's fallen body. Instead, they struck the insects' hard, icy carapaces, skittering away ineffectually. Arianna knew that it was only a matter of time before another shaft found its mark in her own flesh.

One of the few remaining creatures skittered forward. Arianna reached to slice its offending tongue, just as a thick bladed axe whirled out of the air, cleaving into the insect's thorax with enough force to split its carapace asunder. The blow drove the beast over onto its side where it lay, legs wriggling helplessly for a moment.

Arianna swung around, looking in the direction whence the weapon had come. Across the northern length of the river, a dozen strange square-sailed boats rested on the ice. They were raised on sleek runners above the ground and anchored on the ice as if they'd been piloted up the frozen river to arrive there. Near them, a double handful of heavily bundled warriors were making short work of the only creature still on its feet. The impact of their crunching blows carried up the river. They seemed to be taking great joy in breaking the beast's gangly limbs, using heavy axes like the one she'd just seen. As each leg broke, the warriors let out a fierce war cry that Arianna realized she'd been hearing for quite some time. Scattered around them on the ice were the remains of the rest of the insect horde, broken and unmoving. Beside the slaughtered insects lay a single fallen human.

Turning to look up the canyon, Arianna found another gang of warriors heavily dressed against the cold. They fired thick recurve bows down the canyon at the naked forms who were attempting to escape back the way they had come. Four of the hushed ones lay still on the river's frozen surface in pools of cold blood. The shafts that had struck them had sunk almost to the fletching in their naked bodies. The bowmen laughed, firing almost lazily at the fleeing forms, clapping one another on the back solidly with howls of congratulations as the hushed ones fell one by one. Arianna watched as the last one was shot in the upper back. He'd almost reached the far end of the canyon when he fell to his knees, then struggled fiercely to gain his footing again. The bowmen roared in encouragement to him, and he managed to climb to his feet once more. The bowmen gave him a mighty cheer, and then came the thrum of their vicious weapons. The hushed one tumbled face down on the icy ground, pierced deeply by multiple arrows, and moved no more.

Arianna fell to her knees beside Swan's still form. Slipping one hand inside the hood of his parka, she tried to reassure herself that he still lived. His skin was cool. The falling snow no longer melted on contact with it. Yet, his pulse was still present. The arrow still protruded from Swan's neck, and around it, the blood flow had slowed. From the lake of crimson beneath him, Arianna feared his body might simply have little blood left to flow. She weighed her options, quickly. The new arrivals might not be friends, but without someone to remove the arrow and provide healing, Swan would not live long. She couldn't even summon the strength to call a horse to her, were there one in the area, let alone summon her spirit steed. She had little choice.

Standing, Arianna tucked her scarf veil-like across her face, leaving only her eyes uncovered. She called to the closest group of newcomers. They had dispensed with the last of the insects and were now loading their unmoving companion from the ice into one of the strange boats. "Here!" she called.

The men turned toward her and began to approach quickly. Their heavy boots glided across the rough ice, using a strange sliding gait rather than a pounding run. As they approached, she could see they were even more heavily dressed than she'd first thought. Fur-lined leather boots encased their feet, their toes bent up into a blunt point. The leather was so thick that it seemed not to bend at the ankle at all, adding to the strangeness of their gait. From top to toe, the boots were decorated with intricate appliqués of bands of hunting animals and prey, sun signs and other symmetrical patterns. The entire group wore heavy wool caps, pulled firmly down over their ears and foreheads. The caps apparently stretched out into long tails, which were wrapped around their necks and faces like scarves. Brightly colored tassels decorated not only the caps, but the hems of their ponchos and cloaks, as well as their sleeves and the hoods of their parkas. What she could see of their faces were bronzed, with dark eyes. Their builds seemed sturdy, and the majority of their bodies were covered from shoulder to shin in heavy leather parkas that fit loosely. These seemed to allow the men to move much easier in them than she and Swan had in theirs.

"I need a healer," Arianna said when the first was within earshot. The figure nodded, turning to gesture to another of the group and then to Swan's fallen form. The healer's robes were, if anything, more intricately decorated than the rest of the group. Their leather was thickly edged in a fine black fur along the hem, cuffs and collar. A double row of long white feathers fluttered along the underside of each arm. The healer came quickly forward, unwrapping the tail of his cap from around his neck and face. He stripped off his heavy leather mittens, and another layer of woolen ones beneath, kneeling near Swan's head.

Arianna watched as he deftly removed the hushed one's arrow, pressing firmly on the wound with a pad of felted wool from his belt. "Good thing they weren't using our bows," the healer said in a tongue that was understandable but accented in places that were unfamiliar to Arianna. "The wound's shallow, but it nicked the blood canal." He then looked up at the leader. "He'll make it back, but he won't be traveling much further for a while."

Arianna frowned in concern. She turned to address the leader, who was also unwrapping a long scarf. To her surprise, Arianna found herself looking down into the face of a striking woman, rather than the bearded Northman she expected. The dark-haired woman returned her look of surprise with one heavy brow arched in a smirk.

"So," the shorter woman said, brushing the breath frost from her scarf. "As I see it, you have a choice. We can send you on your way from here. RimeHaven's the closest town. You'll find it about six days walk that direction." She pointed up the canyon, past the fallen bodies of the hushed ones, lightly dusted with snow. "You'll probably only have to carry him the first few hours, though. After that, he'll be gone. Or you can leave his body and make better time." She paused a moment, waiting for Arianna to weigh her options. "Or you can come with us, and he'll probably make it. It's up to you."

Arianna looked down at her fallen companion, still being treated by the healer. Without looking back over to the dark woman, she replied solemnly. "We'll go with you."

The woman smiled, broadly. "I thought you might decide that." She called to the rest of her group. "Temur. Ilav. Wait until Noaidi is finished, then move the purple-haired one onto your boat." Turning to Arianna, she extended one hand, encased up to the elbow in a long leather mitten. "I'm Samea. If you want, you can ride in my boat."

Arianna looked down at the extended hand, then back up at Samea coolly. "I'll ride with him."

Samea chuckled, shaking her head as she dropped her hand. She turned to the rest of the group and gave a shrill whistle that cut through the frosty air like a knife. Every person in the party turned immediately to watch her. She gave a circling hand gesture above her head, and they responded without delay, loading quickly back into their iceships. Samea followed the healer and the men who carefully carried Swan between them toward the boats. Within moments, they were seated on benches built into the hull of the strange ships, and the pilots were turning them to glide away from the carnage. Arianna looked back down the frozen river. The warriors had swept the frozen river's surface clean of arrows and thrown axes and taken the few weapons wielded by the hushed ones. Someone had even gathered the shards of obsidian conjured from her spell. All that remained as evidence of the battle were the broken bodies of insects and hushed ones and stains of frozen blood.

The hiss of the barbarians' iceships merged with the whisper of the icy north wind as their sails disappeared up the river. From his sanctuary behind the boulders at the mouth of the canyon, he had watched, wrapped warmly in ermine fur over black silk, as the Anathema were ambushed by the hushed ones and driven toward the ice hollows' trap. They had rushed past him in the storm, and once the winds had dropped, he'd witnessed the entire attack with a detached attention to detail, making mental note of every facet.

When the icewalkers had arrived, they'd driven the hushed ones back with brutal efficiency. The last of the inhuman pack had fallen almost at his feet, skewered deeply by the barbarian's short-shafted arrows. He'd watched the dying creature fall, his eyes locked with the creature's unblinking stare. The creature had reached out toward him before the light went out of its unblinking eyes.

Did you think I was waiting here to help you, hushed one?

With a derisive snort, Otieno stood and settled the ermine hood back around his craggy face. Dark eyes glittering, he stepped over the hushed one's motionless body and away from the battle scene.

CHAPTER ELEVEN

Beyond the heavy curtains, Swan could see the rough-hewn tables fairly creaked from the weight of feast laden there. Roast meats heaped on great platters swam with rich fats and gravies, radiant in the light of the sputtering oil lamps.

Arianna had gone on at length about this great hall and the rest of the Hold that their host, Yurgen, claimed. She'd explored during the time he was still recovering from his wounds, and what she had found had fascinated her. Her studies hinted that once this room had been the largest hall in a great temple to some now-forgotten god. Its lines, she said, suggested that it had been carved long ago, perhaps at the height of the First Age, and certainly, the architecture was unlike anything Swan had ever seen. They'd been kept awaiting an audience with Yurgen for several weeks, consistently put off as he had "matters of import" to attend to, but both he and Arianna had made use of the time exploring what areas they were allowed to investigate and had found the ancient splendor fascinating.

Sweeping arches of gray- and white-veined stone rose up from the night-black floor. Larger around than three men could reach, the base columns had been sculpted with sweeping vines and delicate long-petaled flowers. The arches climbed so steeply that the peaks could not be clearly seen from the ground. Between them were deep empty alcoves where it was easy to imagine priceless statues once rested. Massive wooden beams had been erected to pare the cavernous room into smaller compartments, with ornate woven tapestries hanging as walls. But even these smaller chambers were huge. The largest, where the feast was now being held, would have still taken them a hundred paces or more to cross.

At the head of this large room, with the casual alertness of a snow lion, Yurgen Kaneko watched his clan bustle around him. Swan watched the war leader from his vantage in the hallway behind the heavy tapestry. Yurgen's ice-blue eyes lent to his predatory appearance, as he rested easily in a massive teak chair at the head of the room. In front of him, seated at a long table, his favored associates enjoyed their meal with brutal gusto. Hunting had apparently been good, and the scent of roasted mammoth, venison and boar filled the room.

At long last, Swan stepped forward into the room, and Arianna followed, watching Yurgen as their movement drew his attention. The Northern leader grinned widely, teeth gleaming against the dark gray forest of his mustache and beard. With a deep chuckle, he looked down to catch Samea's eye and then nodded back their direction. One meaty hand reached for a recently filled cup of carved ivory, as the other slid down to the side of his ornate chair.

"It's about time he called for us." Arianna flipped her braid over her shoulder, once again adjusting her veil with a scowl. "We've been waiting for days, while he…" Her frown deepened, words drifting away as she realized her companion was already deeply entrenched in his own thoughts.

With eyes older than his years, Swan scanned the room. Hours of training and experience at reading body language had given him a knack for discerning other's moods and motives, a knack that had only sharpened since his Exaltation. He turned his attention once more to the smiling gray-haired man at the head of the room, and his eyes widened. Abruptly, Swan darted a hand into his companion's, tugging her against her will into a deep bow of deference.

"By the Unconquered Sun! I'll not bow to—" Arianna's irate words were cut off by the whistle of Kaneko's great bladed axe slicing the air just over their heads. There was a resounding *thunk!* as the axe blade bit deeply into the beam behind them.

Arianna snatched her hand back from Swan, rolling from the forced obeisance. Her form caught fire, a blazing banner of blue and gold flames billowing around her, as she glided onto the balls of her feet. Her arms floating with birdlike grace, she cocked her head with a haughty glance and began to gesture lithely, preparing to return the warlord's attack.

Swan stood adroitly from his bow, his violet hair parting like a silken curtain to reveal a self-assured smile. He stilled Arianna's reaction with a minute gesture. "Please, Arianna," he said softly, then transferred his attention to their host, eyes sparkling with energy.

"Well done, honorable Bronze Tiger," the diplomat purred, complimenting Yurgen with one of the ancient names for the warlord's Exalted caste. "Your prowess with an axe is spoken of many days ride from here. It is kind of you to demonstrate it for us upon our arrival. Perhaps now, if your exhibition is completed, we might discuss other matters?"

The room had fallen quiet. Every breath was held in anticipation. Around the Solars, some fifty tribesfolk paused, bits of meat or cups halfway to their mouths. One woman continued to gape at the tense situation at the head of the room, caught in the middle of filling a carafe of dark red wine. While she waited for Yurgen's reaction, the scarlet liquid she was pouring spilled over the lip of the container and across the tabletop. No one moved to stop it.

An eternity of heartbeats passed in silence.

Suddenly, the burly warlord slammed his palm against his thigh with the fleshy smack of a ham striking a tree trunk. His laughter broke the silence, echoing through the timbers and bounced up to be lost in the marble heights of the former temple. Throughout the room, other voices picked up his mirth. Rich echoing laughter filled the great hall.

Gesturing in welcome, he summoned the pair to him, his voice booming out across the marble floor. "Closer, closer. Come closer! Tonight, we drink together. Tomorrow is soon enough for other matters."

Seated at the long table in front of him, Samea grinned broadly, watching Arianna's fury come slowly back under control.

"I'd watch his veiled companion, Yurgen," the dark-haired woman said, in a loud whisper designed to reach Arianna's ears as well as Yurgen's. "She looks like she'd sooner drink your blood than your wine." The dark-haired Northern woman smiled fiercely, raising her cup in a mock toast toward Arianna.

Yurgen studied Swan and Arianna as they drew near. The young man smiled serenely, as if approaching his closest friend, although his eyes darted from Yurgen to scan the room in a cautious manner. His companion, on the other hand, did not bother to hide her fierce glower, evident even behind her veils. Her unnaturally bronzed skin still spoke of her magical protections, and wariness was evident in her body language. Yurgen beamed warmly, welcoming the pair. "I think your companion could use a cool drink, my friend. She seems flushed."

Arianna glared at the Northerner. "Being attacked can have that effect on one," she said, icily. Her anima still fluttered around her, like an ethereal war banner showing her magics to be on the ready should another assault come. Among the tribesfolk, this apparently caused no stir.

Yurgen's laughter boomed throughout the room again, melding with the conversations which had returned around them. "Attacked? Here? No, surely not!" Yurgen took a deep drink from his cup, pausing for effect. "If I had attacked you, you'd be dead now, and from what I can see, you seem very much alive to me." Jovial grins and nods of agreement came from throughout the hall, with more than one lusty comment being tossed in Arianna's direction.

Though not visible beneath her bronze skin, Arianna's face pinked under Yurgen's confident gaze, and she found herself at a loss on how to react. He was not a young man. His hair, though thick and long, was fully gray. Nor was he of striking height. Arianna knew that, if he stood, she likely was much taller than he. But something about him spoke of life and energy in an earthy manner with which she was not certain she was completely comfortable.

Swan stepped forward, diverting Yurgen's attention away from Arianna momentarily and hoping to smooth any ruffled feathers with deftly woven compliments. "Your hospitality has been exceptional, noble Sword of Heaven. Thank you for your gracious care."

Yurgen gestured magnanimously for the pair to join him. Swan slipped onto the bench on the side of the head table nearest to the front of the room, keeping Yurgen in sight. Arianna hesitated, scowling, and said, "I am not hungry."

Swan looked up at her, still smiling. "Would you do us the honor of joining us so that we could share in your radiant company, Arianna?" He gestured to the empty section of bench beside him.

Her scowl deepened as she searched his face and voice for any trace of sarcasm, but she was surprised and relieved to find none. Pulling her robes around her, she made her way to the bench and sat beside him, back to Samea and Yurgen.

"Your woman has the temper of a great-terror with its tail in a knot," Yurgen said, grinning conspiratorially at Swan.

Arianna jerked her head around, leveling an icy glare at Yurgen. "I'm not—"

"Arianna belongs only to herself, honored host," Swan replied. "I'm grateful to find myself as her traveling companion. And I hope, her friend."

Taken aback, Arianna blinked behind her veil, then covered her sudden discomfort with silence, dropping her gaze.

Yurgen called for more food to be brought to the already sagging tables. Swan partook of the offerings with the same gusto that those around him did. He ate with his fingers, dipping the roasted meat slivers into the thick gravy of the serving tray, then sucking his fingers clean with such ease that, to Arianna's eyes, it was as if he'd come home after a long absence, rather than finding himself in an alien culture. And alien it was. Arianna had spent her life near the edge of the Northlands, but these icewalker tribes were a far cry from anything she'd experienced before. Everything they did, they did without hesitation. As she watched the room around her, people laughed, ate, brawled and... shared physical affection... seemingly without concern for the room around them. She turned her attention back to her own table, where it seemed things were a bit more restrained, at least for the moment.

Swan let out a great belch that raised compliments from the rest of the table. Turning his attention from the food to his host, he stood, cup in hand. Saluting Yurgen with the full glass, he drained the cup in one long draught. The room cheered as Swan turned the empty cup over, shaking it to show that not a drop remained. "Yurgen!" he called out, and the room echoed "Yurgen!" in return. A bit wobbly, he sat back down on the wooden bench.

The Bull of the North reached for his own refilled cup and toasted the young man in return. "Kaudara!"

Swan looked confused for a moment, as the tribesfolk around the room hesitated, then shouted back "Kaudara!" He smiled, still bewildered, nodding his appreciation of their gesture.

Yurgen shook his own empty glass, showing it to be drained, and slammed it down on the table with a self-satisfied grin.

Samea leaned over, whispering conspiratorially to Swan. "Consider yourself fortunate, Diplomat."

Swan shook his head, confused. "I don't get it."

She chuckled. "So, you know the toast, but not the naming? Interesting." She scooted over a bit closer to Swan, sparing a quick glance for Arianna as she did so. "Our tribes are eclectic. While many of us were born to the Blackwater Mammoth tribe, as many more were not. Yurgen himself was born to the Whistling Plains Elk tribe, although he does not like to speak of it. It is much smarter, when survival is based on strength, to incorporate strong outsiders rather than keep them out, when possible. It keeps the blood strong."

Swan nodded. "We often marry off-island in my homeland as well, when it can be done. It keeps things from becoming too closely knit." He frowned in concern. "He didn't just propose to me, did he?"

Samea rocked back and forth with laughter, slapping her palm against her thigh. "No! No, no, nothing like that. He *named* you. Kaudara is one of our words for snow swans. He gave you a name among our tribe and basically claimed you as potentially acceptable to be one of us."

Swan looked, if anything, more concerned. "I... That is..."

Shaking her head, Samea went on. "Don't look so worried, Diplomat! We're not outfitting you for boots yet! There is no obligation on your part. It is simply his way, as tribe leader, of saying that he finds you acceptable. And as war leader, that if others do not find you acceptable, they should take it up with him first. It is an honor but not a duty. Not yet, at least."

Samea's words reminded him of how long they'd been "guests" here, and he returned to his feet. He stepped closer to Yurgen, and behind him, he felt Arianna stand as well, watching his back.

"Honorable Bull of the North, we find ourselves once again in your debt. This feast was beyond our dreams, the food worthy of the gods, and the wine..." Swan smacked his lips, loudly. "The wine was... Well, I dare not give its compliments full truth, or I would call the entire rest of the world down upon us, so greatly would they clamor for a taste."

"Let them come!" Yurgen laughed and patted his unstrung bow where it rested beside him. "We would be ready for them!"

"I have no doubt, great warlord, I have no doubt." Swan smiled. "Your hospitality has been more than we could thank you for, but the time has come for us to impose upon you no further. When we were attacked by the hushed ones, we were on a journey to RimeHaven, and while we have certainly missed our transport west, duty requires that we must return posthaste and book another passage."

"Ah... I see." He nodded solemnly. "Duty is, indeed, a harsh master." Yurgen stroked his powerful fingertips along the ebon wood of his bow, as if it were a pet.

"I am grateful that you understand, noble host. If we could impose on you one time further and request supplies to reach RimeHaven, I would gratefully make arrangements for reparations at your convenience."

Yurgen shook his head, solemnly. "I am afraid, Diplomat, that that will not be possible."

"Pardon?" Yurgen's attitude had changed so quickly that even Swan's highly trained senses were having trouble keeping up. One minute, he was being lauded with laughter. Now, Yurgen seemed grimly sober.

"No. You see, while you know some of our traditions, you do not know them all. And it is because of one of these traditions that I must refuse. The tradition of bloodgeld."

"Bloodgeld?" Swan asked, his voice tinged uncertainly. Yurgen was correct. He had only the basic understandings of how not to trip over himself in this culture. Whatever bloodgeld was, he was unfamiliar with it. He hoped it wasn't as potentially fatal as it sounded.

"Bloodgeld." Yurgen nodded gravely. "In saving your life, one of our finest warriors was lost. Guska, brother to Ilav, fell while protecting you and your lovely companion from the ice hollows' attack. He will be sorely missed. And his absence leaves our tribe weaker at an especially bad time. With the war to the south being as it is, we cannot spare a man."

This was the first mention anyone at Yurgen's Hold had made of the war he had been carrying out against Linowan—the war that had inspired Admiral DiBello to send Swan on his long tour so far from home in the first place.

"The life of an icewalker is not an easy one. We do battle daily against the snows that would freeze us solid, against the beasts that would have our flesh for their stomachs and, now, against those who do not have the common sense to know that life under the rule of a fair man is better than death. We cannot afford to be shorthanded. Thus, the bloodgeld. When one of ours falls in protecting an outsider, that outsider is asked to strengthen the weakness that has come to be because of him."

Swan took a deep breath. "While I respect your traditions, gracious host, I regret that…"

From behind him, Arianna interrupted, her clear voice carrying past the veil covering her face and over his words. "It is unfortunate that this noble diplomat is bound to duties that will not allow him to fulfill your tradition. However, on the night of our meeting, my life was saved by his selfless intervention. And to repay that debt to him, I will take on his debt to you, if that will suffice."

Swan all but sputtered as shock swept over him. Arianna had been such an important part of his life in the past months that, despite her protestations, he had not seriously considered that there would be a time when she would choose to walk away from their travels together. "But… Arianna, you don't have to…"

Arianna looked deeply into Swan's eyes. She said solemnly, "Yes. Yes, I do. Just as you have to fulfill your duties. Perhaps our paths will cross again, but there is no place for me traveling across the ocean and sitting idly by while you negotiate the price of chickens and grain. I cannot just wait for the Wyld Hunts to discover us again. There is much for me still to learn, and I must follow the road I am called to, just as you will."

She turned to Yurgen, cutting off any other protestation from Swan. "Yurgen Kaneko, will you accept my offer?"

Yurgen grinned broadly. "I think perhaps that would work. You seem a strong woman, full of fire. I like that. No doubt you would bear strong children to add to our tribe. Your life for his. It is done."

Swan started to protest, but Arianna silenced him with the same minute gesture he had used on her when they first entered. He expected to see her infuriated at Yurgen's personal comments about her, but instead, she seemed almost amused. "There is one further matter to be clarified, just to ascertain that we are all in understanding with each other." She turned back to Yurgen, tilting her head in the manner of a cat studying a songbird.

Yurgen arched one steely eyebrow, amused at this pale woman's impudence. Her fire was unmistakable. She would make an admirable tribeswoman. "Go on."

"Are the members of your tribe held against their will?"

Yurgen frowned. "You think I have to force my tribe against their will? You challenge my ability to lead them?" His countenance darkened, storm clouds moving across his eyes.

Swan smiled inwardly, watching Arianna's body language. She had something up her sleeve, and it wasn't just her arm.

"No. I merely wished to ascertain that my understanding was correct. If a member of your tribe were to decide to walk another path, he would be free to do so, would he not? If he, perhaps, decided to join Whistling Plains Elk tribe… Or if one from that tribe wished to leave it to join yours?"

Swan blanched. Arianna must have overheard his conversation with Samea. He wasn't sure where she was going with this line of questioning, but she was playing a dangerous game.

Arianna just waited for a response, her demeanor as cool and clear as a perfect winter's night.

"Of course. No member of my tribe is held by force. They walk where they will. They are proud to be Blackwater Mammoth!"

A sly smile crept across Arianna's eyes. Swan had seen it before, when she'd relaxed now and then on their journey, at those rare times when the walls were down and she allowed herself to show emotion. Right now, she was showing smug amusement, and he wondered what was coming next.

"Then," she pronounced, "I will walk with your tribe as Guska would have, had he lived. Aiding it with all that is within my power to do so, and for so long as I feel it is the correct path for me to follow. And if, or when, the time comes for me to walk another path, I will be free to leave."

Yurgen sputtered. "But… the bloodgeld!"

Swan could see the smile in Arianna's eyes flare. "A life for a life… but no one is held against her will. Do we have a bargain?"

For a moment, it seemed Yurgen would refuse, but then, a broad smile crossed his face. He laughed again, the sound ringing to the rooftop. "It seems I called the wrong one of you diplomat! A bargain indeed. Let us hope you serve the tribe with as much wit as you've shown tonight!"

Arianna nodded softly and turned to Swan. "And you and I? Our debts are paid as well?"

Swan nodded, unable; for once, to bring forth words.

"Then, I will return to my chamber. Good evening." Arianna turned, walking across the great hall. As she passed, Swan watched members of the tribe greet her as if she'd already been accepted as one of their own. Several of the men watched a bit too eagerly for his tastes as she walked away. Swan waited until she'd disappeared back the way they had entered the room before turning to Yurgen.

Yurgen was watching him with the same studied casualness that Swan knew he himself had used on others. "And so… the swan flies, but the snow cat remains."

Swan ignored the verbal bait. "I will be allowed to go then?"

Yurgen nodded. "Of course! I will see you and your little mare are set with supplies, and Samea will deliver you tomorrow to within a safe walk from RimeHaven."

"Mare? Eldy? But we thought…"

Yurgen shrugged noncommittally. "We found the little brown in the woods not far from where Samea found you two. The gray almost kicked Temur through a snow bank when we tried to bridle him, but he followed the mare when we led her in."

Swan smiled. Loyalties formed in strange places, it seemed.

"Thank you. I will see that you are compensated for whatever supplies I need."

Yurgen shook his head. "No. No, my little diplomat, consider them a gift. I would have us part on good terms. Perhaps, when your duty is finished, you will consider returning. There are few places for the Children of the Sun in Creation these days. Together, perhaps, we can change that. With enough of the Chosen together, we may force the world to see that the murder and tyranny of the Scarlet Empress cannot go on. We may show them that there is another way. The way of right. The way of the Next Age."

Swan watched Yurgen carefully, reading his body just as Arianna would pore over a tome. "I won't help you take over the world, Yurgen. Countless Linowan lives have been lost in your war already. And doubtless many of your own people as well."

Yurgen nodded, solemnly. "Many, indeed. It gives me great sorrow that so much life must be lost. But things must change. For hundreds of years, our kind have been hunted to protect nothing but lies. The change is coming, and we have been killed in the infancy of our power to prevent this change from happening. Now, more of us are being Exalted than ever. The Unconquered Sun grows strong, and the time has come for us to take back what is ours."

"If we declare war on them without trying all other methods, we are as bad as they are. There is a time when one must resort to swords, but not without trying other avenues first."

Yurgen watched the young diplomat, shaking his head, slowly. "There is only one language they will understand. And it is spoken by the voice of sword stroke and bowstring. It is the only way."

"I can't believe that."

Yurgen nodded. "You will. As much as it pains me to say it, Kaudara, you will learn the truth of the matter. And perhaps, then, you will return to us. Until then, I will keep your snow cat safe."

Swan protested. "She's not my—"

Yurgen's voice dropped in volume, his words for Swan's ears alone. "Save your pretty words for her, Diplomat. You deal with the truth from an angle, approaching it from downwind to avoid spooking it. I see things as they are." Yurgen stood, putting his glass down on the table in front of him. "Now, go disturb her reading and say your farewells."

Swan stood, stunned for a moment. Finally, saying nothing, he nodded to Yurgen and turned, walking through the crowded room out into the silent stone hallways that would lead him to Arianna's room.

"Arianna, I don't want you to do this." He'd found her in her chamber, writing. Her brush danced out long rolling characters across the parchment, precise and beautiful.

She looked up, eyes dark. He was fascinated by the way they changed. At rest, they were as dark as the deepest sea. But when she exhausted herself, as she had upon their first meeting, they paled to an ice blue, as if the effort of using her Sun-given sorceries drained her physically as well as spiritually.

"There's nothing to talk about, Diplomat. I'm staying." She set her jaw then, and he knew by the steel in her gesture that there was no way he was going to convince her to change her mind.

"Can you at least tell me why? I… I guess I thought we… I mean… I thought I… and… you… and…" Swan stumbled, finding himself tongue-tied. He waited for the chill of her gaze to descend across her face. He'd seen her icy verbal blade cut through others in their travels, and he'd just left his proverbial shields down to her thrust.

To his surprise and delight, she paused. The expected verbal blow did not come. At least, not right away.

"It is… " She looked back down at her writing, as if hoping to find answers there.

In the glow of the oil lamp on the table, the muscles in her jaw clenched and relaxed, as if she fought back words. Swan watched, fascinated, at this uncustomary indecision in her expression.

Just then, a loud knock on the door interrupted them,. Samea, laden with tomes, had entered without pausing for them to answer. "Oh, sorry. Hope I'm not interrupting. Yurgen thought that Ari might want to take a look at these."

"Arianna," the white-haired woman corrected, standing. She rolled up the parchment she'd been writing on and bound it slowly and deliberately with a knotted cord, saying nothing as her eyes bored into the dark-haired Northerner. When Samea finally took the hint and left, Arianna handed the parchment to Swan. "I hope this will help you on your journey."

Swan accepted the rolled parchment, his fingers working gently over the silken cord's knots.

"Don't undo the knots until you're on board and out of the harbor. They'll assure speed on your journey." Arianna turned away, leaving Swan standing awkwardly between her back and the door that Samea had left standing open.

"I... Arianna... I..."

"If you are going to go, Diplomat, just go. Don't draw this out." Her words were full of ice, and her shoulders stiff as steel. She did not turn to face him.

Swan paused a long moment. Her demeanor was as cold as the night they'd met, and if his duty did not already demand his departure, her chill farewell would encourage it.

"Be well, then, Arianna," he said. And with that, he disappeared down the long, cold hallway.

CHAPTER TWELVE

Two months' journey across the Great Western Ocean found Swan once again in attendance to Admiral DiBello.

"And so, as you'll see, the treaties were renewed with only slight modifications on previous mandates, in Glassport, RimeHaven and Crystal. These modifications, according to our projections, will result in less than a one-percent variation in average revenue, while allowing you to continue in those established markets despite their earlier… concerns." Swan placed the open portfolio in front of the man seated at the head of the long wooden table for his perusal. Seated around the table on long elaborately carved wooden benches, the rest of the council was silent, as if fearing to breathe before hearing their leader's reaction.

DiBello reached over and shut the portfolio, nodding sagely. "Magnificent. Well done, my boy." The rest of the council members mirrored his nod and began talking among themselves, discussing the ramifications of the continuation of their trade with the northernmost cities.

Swan smiled, sinking back into his own chair. Things were going admirably well. The negotiations were done, the journey was safely made, and no one had any idea that Swan was not exactly the same man who had set out on his mission. The only thing that gave him any true concern was the thought of Arianna, halfway across Creation.

He'd had great reservations about leaving her with Yurgen. Allowing her to accept his debt to the Bull of the

North had been a difficult thing, but the idea of leaving her behind when he left was even harder.

He'd left, bearing her gift and a feeling of confusion like none he'd experienced before. Once shipboard, he'd examined the scroll and found the cord tying it contained a charm to grant them fast winds and safe passage over the sea. The captain of his ship to Crystal had been amazed at their "good fortune."

"Forty years on the seas, and I've never seen good winds for two months straight," he'd said. "Day and night, always in the right direction. It's almost spooky." They'd come into port more than a month ahead of schedule, and most of the ship's crew had made right for the wharf's bars, drinking away any lingering concerns about their unprecedented good fortune. The charm had done them well from Crystal down to Wavecrest as well, although its impact had seemed less remarkable on the shorter journey.

Swan would have been more reassured if he hadn't had the niggling feeling that perhaps the gift was less a sign of affection and more a desire to put as much distance as possible between them.

He'd arrived here, where DiBello welcomed him with the fanfare of a returning hero. Now, Swan tore himself from his memories as DiBello pushed his tall chair back away from the table and stood waiting for the conversations around him to end. The council's attention was immediately refocused on him.

"Gentlemen, I think you'll agree with me that the potential loss of the Northern Cities Trade Agreement was a matter of grave import to our economy here in Coral. Without the export income that agreement provides, our lifestyle here would quickly return to the subsistence level shared by the majority of the Western islands." With a charming and conspiratorial smile, he went on. "And, I don't know about you, my friends, but my wife would certainly balk at the idea of giving up her dinner parties for a life of digging clams."

Bawdy laughter filled the room as the Coral tradesmen agreed. In the past, the islands in the Coral Archipelago had suffered from many of the same troubles that faced most small island-based kingdoms. Their economy had been based publicly on shipbuilding. The Azure shipyards at Coral's capital were famous for creating small, swift ships that the people of Coral used to harvest the local waters. Surreptitiously, however, the people of Coral had another industry, perhaps more prosperous than the first. The nimble little ships were also admirably adept at privateering, and fish were not the only harvest that the Coral islanders plucked from the Western Ocean. The Realm, however, was not likely to ignore such a profitable trade, and the Coral islands had been prey to the slow domination of the ships placed there by the Guild and the Realm ostensibly to protect the waters, but that, instead, sucked at the Coral economy like a remora. As the victims of this ever-growing heavy-handed "protection," the Coral islands historically barely supported their populace. Many of the trade council's grandmothers had therefore spent the majority of their years as young women harvesting clams along the coastal beaches to help feed their families.

Thanks in no small part to the leadership of Admiral DiBello, Coral, and especially its capital city of Azure, had stabilized, and its economy had boomed. Under his control, the islands had established a strong traffic with several of the Northern cities, exporting coral, pearls and other precious gems that were highly desired by Northern traders. The wealth that sprang from that trade had catapulted Azure into a city of decadence, with several other Coral cities close behind it.

Admiral DiBello began to pace slowly at the head of the table. His knee-length silk robe swept out regally behind him as he turned almost silently in his flat embroidered slippers. It seemed that DiBello's wife and daughter were not the only members of the family with a penchant for the fashions of the Blessed Isle. Swan watched the Admiral pace back and forth, his short-cropped hair still fully the cobalt blue of his youth, despite him having held dictatorship of the Coral islands since Swan was a small child. Swan recognizing his body language, and he waited for what he knew from past experience would be a controversial announcement. DiBello always paced when putting something before the council that he knew its members wouldn't like.

"As I said, gentlemen, none of us want to return to the way things were. And, if we do not go back, there is only one way to proceed. And that is forward." He paused, stroking his beardless chin. "Grave news has just arrived, gentlemen. News that I think has the potential to change the course of Coral's history forever."

Quiet before, the council fell to complete silence.

"I have just heard from a reputable source that the Lintha Family is planning an attack." Confusion swept across the table. Glances fell upon Swan, the only individual in the room who was not on the council.

Swan did not react to the announcement, his demeanor remaining smooth as he processed the import of this possibility. The Lintha Family was a clan of pirates, ruthless brigands who laid waste to any ships foolish enough to attempt to sail within a hundred miles of their territory. Several of the southernmost Western island kingdoms were within the family's proclaimed boundaries, and rumor had it that, along with their taxes to the Realm each year, they paid what paltry tribute they could to prevent the wholesale pillaging of their underdeveloped towns. Even the southernmost of the Coral islands were well north of the Lintha's territory, however. The trade council's choice to establish trade routes to the North rather than to the Southlands was not in a small part based on its desire to avoid the Lintha's raids.

From the council's confusion, one voice finally dared to speak. "And the sea is wet, Admiral DiBello," a young shipbuilder commented sardonically. "It would be more surprising news to hear that they were *not* planning an attack."

Admiral DiBello turned his attention on the council member who had spoken, leveling a steel-gray stare in his direction. The young man's jaw clapped shut as if on a spring, and he said nothing more as the Admiral continued.

"As I said, gentlemen, the Lintha Family is planning an attack. Not into Abalone or even the Neck." DiBello stroked his chin again. "No. According to my sources, they have become all too aware of our trade to the North and the increased prosperity it has brought to Coral. We are their next target, gentlemen. You and I. Our ships, our homes, our families. The Lintha plan to attack Azure."

A murmur of disbelief ran through the council. "Surely, Admiral, you must be mistaken," one of the eldest members of the council, Harbormaster Ashraf, put forth cautiously. "Azure is the most well-protected city in the Western isles, and we're well out of their normal raiding areas. The Lintha attacking here would be foolishness, pure and simple." Harbormaster Ashraf was a wiry man whose golden skin tone spoke of his childhood in the Far Western islands. He was also in charge of the harbor in Azure, the largest in the Coral islands and a respected member of the trade council.

The Admiral nodded. "I understand your disbelief, gentlemen, but let me assure you that my sources are quite certain." He chose a sharkskin scroll case from a rack that stood not far from the smoothly lacquered council table and drew a large parchment map from it. Unrolling the map out onto the council table, he went on, marking locations with smooth stones from a small dish as he did so.

"Here is, of course, Bluehaven." He placed a stone in the Southwestern sea cove. "It is well known that the Lintha have used this area as their home for generations now. But according to my sources, they have now established outposts here, here and here." He marked one of the small unclaimed islands outside of Wavecrest at the southern tip of the Western kingdoms, as well as two of the smaller islets in the Neck island group, not overfar from Coral to the north.

"Apparently, cowry shells and kelp aren't sating their appetite any longer, and the Lintha are strengthening their hold in the Western islands, in hopes of establishing themselves as a legitimate government here. And, while the Neck and Wavecrest may prove to be the easy target they need for their land grab, neither one has the assets to make it profitable over the long term. Azure, on the other hand, would put up a fight, but it seems that the Lintha have come to believe that the payoff is worth the risk."

Swan listened as the councilmen squabbled among themselves as to the likelihood of various attack scenarios and plans of action on the part of the pirate family. After giving them a few minutes, DiBello spoke again, reclaiming their attention.

"I can tell you gentlemen have already begun to understand the ramifications of this attack. Yes, as Harbormaster Ashraf pointed out, we can likely withstand a direct attack. Here in Azure, our defenses are fairly sound, and we have the majority of the navy at our disposal. But what of Gull's Bay? How long will Perryport stand if their supply route is blocked?" Coral, like all the Western kingdoms, held only a few islands and most of the population of Azure had family in at least one other of the archipelago's major island cities.

"But what can we do?" Ashraf asked, throwing up his hands in dismay. Eschewing the recent trend, Ashraf was dressed in traditional Coral island clothing, his job at the harbors demanding utility that silk robes and slippers did not provide. He'd swept his knit wool cap into a pocket of his faded canvas jacket on arrival, but that was his only concession for the niceties of the council chamber.

"Bluehaven's impenetrable. No one's ever gotten halfway in. We could wipe out their outposts, but they'd just retreat back to their nest like the rats they are. The Red Queen's supposed to be handling this kind of thing, isn't she? Isn't that why we pay tribute? Isn't that why her fleets bleed us dry?"

Swan was amused at the harbormaster's colloquial reference to the Scarlet Empress. At least in the harbor, it seemed, the Realm's influence was not all-pervasive.

Admiral DiBello took a deep breath, pacing again. Swan watched him building anticipation and concern, leaving the council hanging until the room was filled with anxious energy. For a moment, Swan was glad that DiBello and Kallio Johan were several months' travel apart. The two men both seemed to be masters at manipulating the councils they'd created and would likely prove to be either bitter enemies or the best of allies. Possibly both.

"Once again, Harbormaster, you catch the current exactly. This is the type of thing we have paid protection for to the Scarlet Empress and the Realm for generations. Our increase in prosperity, I might add, has also not escaped the attention of the Blessed Isle, as you well know. Our tributes have increased tenfold in the past fifteen years, and yet, when we need the Realm's aid, we receive nothing. In fact, the imperial fleet's numbers have reportedly decreased in our area over the last month. At last report, less than one third its original complement remained in our area."

Every member of the trade council, whether merchant, fisherman or shipwright was well aware of the sharp increase in Realm taxation. Every aspect of the economy had increased, but the more business prospered, the heavier the hand of the taxman dug into every Coral islander's money pouch. But for the fleet to have begun leaving, now, when its presence was actually needed? It was an outrage.

"I've spoken with the Feathered One in Abalone as well as Elder Tasi, spokesman for the Neck's elder council. They've agreed that we will meet in Wavecrest the first week of next month to discuss the matters at hand in the first of what I hope will be many Western Isle Diplomatic Councils." He paused in his pacing, turning away from the council to look out the window at the ocean, as the council burst into an uproar.

"Admiral DiBello!" The young shipwright could no longer remain silent. "For as long as there has been a Coral kingdom, we have been independent. The other islands have no say so in our affairs!"

The Admiral turned from the window. He stood for a long moment, until the council settled back into silence, his face a mask of bronzed stone. "I've also sent messages to the Bodhisattva Anointed by Dark Water." This announcement took the council and Swan by greater surprise than the first. Several of the more superstitious council members made frenetic hand signs to protect against the evil eye, and Harbormaster Ashraf spit over his left shoulder while muttering a warding charm against the unquiet dead. DiBello frowned as he glanced down at the spittle soaking into his imported tapestry carpet.

Swan was once again amazed at DiBello's daring. Few Coral islanders would even acknowledge the Skullstone Archipelago far to the west of Azure even existed, save to threaten wayward children. The Bodhisattva himself was rumored to be anything from a necromancer to an evil spirit to one of the profane Deathlords.

"I'll not be having truck with zombies," Ashraf announced coldly, and the rest of the council nodded anxiously in agreement.

"The Bodhisattva Anointed by Dark Water has not yet seen fit to respond to my messages," Admiral DiBello declared, stepping up to the head of the table and straightening to his full height. "But should he do so, you will interact with him in whatever manner is best for the health and wealth of Coral." He seemed to grow in stature and magnitude as the diplomatic manipulator of a few minutes ago was replaced by the military dictator DiBello was well capable of being. "Is that clearly understood, Master Ashraf?"

Ashraf ducked his head, frowning. "Understood, Admiral." Respect on the council only went so far, Swan noted. When the gloves came off, Coral remained a dictatorship. DiBello had been elected after his successor's death, and he would remain the chosen ruler of this kingdom until his own death, barring political uprising or other of the unpredicted events that sometimes plagued the reigns of unfit rulers.

Swan's mind was reeling from the implications of DiBello's announcement. The Realm's fleet leaving the Western isles was an unknown factor. Was it possible that the Admiral knew more about its departure than he was admitting? For him to break tradition and propose forming a council with the other independent Western island kingdoms led Swan to suspect so. The inclusion of the Bodhisattva Anointed by Dark Water was a bold statement as well.

Most of the Western kingdoms were at least nominally subjects of the Scarlet Empress and the Realm. The Skullstone islands did not pay the Blessed Isle even nominal tribute. In fact, Dragon-Blooded were summarily turned away from Onyx, Skullstone's capital city. For Admiral DiBello to invite the ruler of a rebel kingdom to this proposed diplomatic council indicated at least the possibility of Coral, and perhaps Western isle, independence from the Realm. Whatever was happening here, it might be the opportunity he was looking for. If the Western kingdoms banded together and officially turned away from the Realm's control, if they were willing to include the leader of the Skullstone Archipelago in their alliance, perhaps there was a place for himself and the other Chosen of the Unconquered Sun as well. Perhaps the Western isles could provide both a haven against the Wyld Hunts and a foothold for reclaiming their legitimacy as citizens of Creation.

He had told Yurgen that there had to be another way to bring about change. Perhaps this was it. Perhaps through diplomacy, through alliances, through solidarity, rather than through warfare, change could be brought about.

"Admiral DiBello?" Swan moved forward, and the room turned as one to look at him. "With your permission, sir, I'd like to be included in the council, on behalf of the Coral islands."

The Admiral grinned broadly, crossing the room to clap Swan on the shoulder with a fraternal blow that would have knocked him to the ground before his Exaltation. "Glad to have you, Diplomat. Your presence will certainly be welcome." He turned to face the rest of the council. "Now. Matters are settled. Those of you who have further concerns are welcome to meet with me privately, but for now, I thank you all for your support and cooperation."

Admiral DiBello turned and strode purposefully out of the meeting room, leaving Swan and the trade council standing contemplatively in his masterful wake.

CHAPTER THIRTEEN

The open oil lamps had begun to sputter out, Arianna's first clue that the night had passed. She rose from her seat at the table slowly, stretching muscles that now protested their immobility over the last several days.

The stone room had grown cold while she studied, and she picked up the book she'd been poring over, with the intention of carrying it to a warmer and lighter location.

Her stomach rumbled, growling audibly, and she placed a hand on her flat belly with a quiet chuckle.

"Perhaps some food, too."

She wrapped herself in the heavy fur cloak she'd been given and began the journey from the library to the main room. The cloak was a concession to her strange situation as an outsider who had been accepted into the tribe. Within the tribe, it was considered a sign of insult to wear outer clothing inside a shelter, especially one as permanent and relatively luxurious as the Hold. Strong tribe members took their outer cloaks off in a small foyer just for that purpose before entering a dwelling. To wear more layers was to insult your host's hospitality, basically a complaint that the host had not made the dwelling comfortable or provided enough heat. Even their small nomadic dwellings were built with a tiny chamber just inside the main door where cloaks, ponchos and heavy coats were left before the main room was entered. Arianna had conformed to the tradition until Yurgen had found her early one morning, fingers almost blue despite wearing every piece of indoor clothing she owned. The next evening, he had made a spectacle of presenting her with an "indoor cloak" of heavy felted mammoth's wool, with a collar and hood lined with thick arctic fox. He'd created a tradition to protect her from the cold, and Arianna wasn't at all sure how she felt about it, although it was certainly much more pleasant than freezing over her studies.

When she stepped into the main hall, she found the torches had been extinguished and the fire banked for the night. A few chairs sat near the fireplace, and she curled into one of them, arranging her cloak around her shoulders and down over her feet to keep them warm. The light from the fire was dim, but brighter than the library. Tomorrow, she'd have to ask about oil to refill the lamps there.

She'd just reopened her book and was beginning to lose herself in a text on ancient Hearthstones when a voice came from nowhere.

"And so, Snow Cat, what have you learned?" Yurgen stepped out from behind the tapestry to her left, and she almost bolted from her chair in surprise. She regained her calm, snapping the book on her lap shut with a dull thud.

"I've learned, among other things, that barbarian warlords have very little respect for the wishes of others." She turned back to watch the fire, head held haughty and high.

Yurgen laughed, a great booming sound. "Little respect? Surely you jest, Snow Cat. Have you not been given all you desire here? Good food, good wine. Good books…" He smiled broadly, knowing that she'd have existed on stale crusts and water if forced to make the choice between sustenance and the library. "I have even respected your desires to sleep alone, although I can hardly understand them."

Arianna blushed, keeping her face to the fire. "And yet, you still insist on calling me by that awful name, when I have asked quite politely for months for you to desist."

Appearing in the muted firelight beside her, Yurgen shrugged with an amused grin. "One does not become a warlord by giving in to all demands. Besides, the name suits you.

Arianna sounds like something the wind could tear in two. You, my dear Snow Cat, are made of sterner stuff."

Arianna remembered her own refusal to call Swan by name, the first few months of their travels. He'd taken it as a challenge, striving in his own way to conquer the walls she had put up between them. Eventually, his patience and good nature won her trust. He'd proven himself kind and honorable and had never treated her with the slightest disrespect. She flicked a glance over at Yurgen's broad back as he busied himself stirring up the dwindling fire.

The Northerner looked up at her, catching her glance for a moment before smiling smugly and returning his attention to the fire. "What are you thinking of, Snow Cat?"

"Swan." She blurted out, his name rising on her tongue without thought.

Yurgen nodded, not looking up from the fire. "Ah. Your young diplomat. He has been gone many months."

"It is a very long journey to the Coral Archipelago. And he's not mine."

"What do you suppose he found there, Snow Cat? Did you think, as he did, that he could finish the business he began as a man? That the paths that were once his to tread still remained open to him after being chosen?"

Arianna sighed, softly. "No. I told him as much, but he wouldn't listen. There is no going back. He'll be lucky if he's not discovered as Anathema on his journey, luckier still to complete his mission. But they say luck favors fools and children." She sat, instinctively beginning to pull her light scarf around her face.

Yurgen stood and reached out to still her hand. With a gentleness that seemed alien in a man of his strength, he unwrapped the first layer before she finished it. "There is no need for that, Snow Cat. You are accepted here. You have nothing to hide. Nothing to fear." He rested one hand gently alongside her cheek.

Blood rose hotly to her face, and she pulled away from his hand. She glared into the fire but left her scarf hanging around her shoulders.

"I invited him to stay, you know?" Yurgen pulled up a nearby chair, settling into it without asking permission to join her. "On the evening you volunteered to join the tribe, I told him that he had a place here. That times were changing. Samea has read the portents, and they all indicate that the time when the Unconquered Sun's children are slaughtered in their infancy is drawing to a close. What will come after will be a new Age of peace and rightness."

"And he said?" Arianna held the book on her lap, watching the fire.

"He said that war wasn't the way. That there had to be another option." Yurgen sighed, watching his companion intently. "I wish sometimes that he was right."

Arianna nodded, glancing up at Yurgen. "As do I. But for all of his experience as a diplomat, I think he's failed to realize that things are infinitely different now. The world is a different place. He is a different being. His life cannot remain the same amongst all that change. His nature cannot remain hidden forever."

"Exactly. Things are different now, and we no longer have all of the choices we had while we were human. Some of them were taken by the Unconquered Sun. But at the same time, others were given. We now have the chance to change Creation. To mend it. To force things back to right. We did not have that before. We cannot fail to leap on this chance."

Arianna watched the passion in Yurgen's eyes as he spoke about fixing a world gone wrong. The firelight caught his gray hair, highlighting it with warmth until it looked as if the man had been crowned with orichalcum.

He shook his head, suddenly looking very old. He turned to her. "I ramble. My apologies. How are you finding your books?"

"I'm uncertain I understand all of it… but what I have found has been very interesting." Since Samea's departure for the East again, Arianna had been given full access to what remained of the former temple's library. With the rare exception, she'd not been seen outside that huge stone chamber since, spending night and day absorbing the incredible information contained there. Thus far, she had actually not discovered a tome in the collection she'd been unable to puzzle out, and she was almost finished her first examination of the entire collected works. But there were things contained therein that still seemed to be things she should hold on to, at least for the time being. Sometime, having that one extra spell that no one knew you possessed might be the difference between victory and defeat. Perhaps even between life and death.

"It was very kind of you to allow me access to the information while Samea is gone. The library is very impressive."

Yurgen nodded solemnly. "I have heard from her, this night."

Arianna watched his face in the firelight. He professed to be completely in charge, but she sensed that, beneath it all, Samea often was the deciding factor between them. "How fare your efforts to the south?"

"Good. Good. Things go well. Linowan has thrown more forces against ours, but we have held them off. Even the forces sent by the Realm have not slowed us too greatly." He paused, thoughtfully, stroking his gray beard. "It is unfortunate your studies here keep you so busy."

Tilting her head, she asked with caution, "Why is that?"

Yurgen looked away, up toward the carved chimney of the fireplace where marbled flowers and vines had grown for centuries, conjured by some long-dead sculptor. The petals stretched outward, each more than a hand-span long, and pointed at their tips, exotic blossoms not seen for centuries in the harsh Northlands. He glanced back down at her, eyes guarded.

"I trust that you will keep this to yourself. It would be unfortunate for such information to fall into the hands of those who are not capable of truly appreciating it."

Arianna nodded, solemnly, her curiosity piqued.

"If our reports are correct, there's a Manse of great strength right in the path our troops plan to take north. My scouts found signs of it, just a few days ago. From what they tell me, it looks untouched."

Arianna nodded again. Manses were not entirely rare, although it took a very talented architect with a good working knowledge of the occult to craft one. Built over places of magical power called Demesnes, Manses acted as foci to tap that power, both to benefit the owner of the Manse and to keep the energy from spreading willy-nilly over the landscape. An untamed Demesne was capable of wreaking havoc over great distances, triggering mutations in plants and animals for miles around. Even humans who lived too close were vulnerable to the chaos. But it was rare for one to be discovered uninhabited. Most were claimed by Dragon-Blooded or members of the Immaculate Order, who used them to bolster their own powers. It was not unusual for a powerful Exalt to build his base of operations over a Manse, tapping into the power thereof to supplement his own. They were rarely built and just abandoned.

"I am certain it will aid your efforts in the area, should you take possession of such. But I fail to see how it relates to me."

Yurgen smiled, looking from the ornately embellished fireplace back to Arianna. "Well, Snow Cat, it seems that, within this forgotten Manse, there is a rather extensive library. My scouts brought back word, saying it was ten or twenty times as large as what Samea has here."

Arianna's eyes glittered. She nodded, using an almost tangible effort to force back her sudden greed.

Yurgen smiled, his white teeth gleaming in the firelight. "They brought back a sample." Yurgen pulled a book from his belt pouch. It was tiny, perhaps a hand-span in height and half as wide. What had once been red leather had been worn to a faded raspberry color, and while the deeply tooled pattern was still visible on the cover, if difficult to make out by firelight, any gilt or paint once used to decorate it had long since worn away. The pages rustled together richly, in the way that only ancient vellum will.

Arianna hungered to have the book in her own hands. The longing was painful, a yearning deep inside her that no tempting food or handsome individual had ever come close to inspiring.

Yurgen watched the desire rise in her eyes, chuckling deeply to himself. "It's for you. I think Samea will forgive me. But perhaps you should keep it quiet, just in case."

He held the book out to her, and she snatched it up, eagerly. Her pale fingertips danced sensually over the cover, which had been worn until it was as smooth as silk. In her mind's eye, she could see the hundreds, perhaps thousands, of hands such as hers that had lovingly traced these same faint lines over the centuries.

"It's... beautiful." She delicately held the book up to her face, inhaling the scent of centuries-old knowledge. The soft tang of leather clung to the roof of her mouth, and the sharp scent of ink danced across her tongue, sweeter than ambrosia.

Yurgen watched her, vicariously enjoying the passion with which she embraced the book. "Consider coming with us, Snow Cat. Samea is a witch of the highest caliber, but she does not have your passion for the tomes. It would be a pity to let that knowledge lie unharvested."

Arianna nodded absently, but she had already reverently opened the tome and begun consuming the fluid words inscribed on its pages.

Nodding to himself, Yurgen stood and added more wood to the fire. "I will send some food for you and something warm to drink. You are not used to our clime yet, and it would not do to have you freeze solid as you read."

Already lost in her studies, the white-haired woman made no response.

CHAPTER FOURTEEN

"And so you see, Palani," the Dragon-Blooded magistrate's voice hissed in the night, "Your very best bet for remaining alive and in charge of these islands is to do exactly what I tell you to. You really don't want Wavecrest to be associated with that blowhard from Coral. Especially if he actually does have some foolish notion about turning his back on the benevolence of the Realm. It just… It wouldn't be wise." The Dragon-Blood's gleaming white teeth glowed like foxfire in the shadows of President Palani's room. His dark hair, beard and clothing faded into the shadows around him, leaving only the floating disembodied smile and the barely visible glow of the pendant that hung around his neck.

Shaking like a leaf, Palani Vlori, the Feathered One, President of the Wavecrest Archipelago, nodded, his chubby fingers knotting into his bedclothes. His dislike of being referred to by his given name was totally overcome by his fear of this visitor from the Blessed Isle. Wavecrest was a quiet nation, and it was unspeakably unusual for it to receive anything but the most passing of attention from the Scarlet Empress' emissaries. To wake to find one looming over his bed in the middle of the night had almost given him a heart attack.

"Yes, of course, Magistrate G-Gerik!" The Feathered One's voice shook in the darkness. "We here in Wavecrest have always been loyal to the Realm. If we'd had any idea that this council Admiral DiBello was calling had anything to do with treason, we'd have never agreed. He'd said—"

Magistrate Gerik silenced him, mid-sentence. "I am well aware of what you were told. I'm also well aware that if you'd had the wits of a panic monkey you'd have realized what DiBello had in mind. The pompous spring-belly has been angling to rule the entirety of the Western kingdoms for as long as he's been in charge of Coral. He wants your islands, and he wants you to betray the Empress so he can take them. You're just lucky we got wind of this before your own lack of common sense got you further into this than you already are. You have no idea how truly fortunate you are."

Magistrate Gerik strode across what passed for regal accommodations here in Wavecrest, crossing it in a few long steps. On the Blessed Isle, these rooms wouldn't be considered appropriate to house his scribe, let alone a representative of the Empress' own justice. Here in the Western isles, however, far from true civilization, prosperity worked on an entirely different scale. The Feathered One, his three wives and their entire staff lived in a series of rooms like this one, in a two-story "palace" that was smaller than the Empress' main stables.

Gerik's scribe was seated cross-legged on the floor, keeping an immaculate flow of notes of the conversation, without ever intruding upon it himself. The portable lap desk he carried with him everywhere balanced upon his knees as if it was part of his body, and even in the dark, his pen flowed seamlessly across the parchment, recording his supervisor's words flawlessly.

At the door they'd entered through, Gerik's bodyguard, Markor, stood watchfully, in case someone happened to wander up the hallway during the Magistrate's conversation. It seemed unlikely, however. Palani's security was nonexistent, and they'd slipped in through the front door of the building without so much as encountering another individual. Palani's wives' room was on the lower floor, as were the sleeping chambers of the house staff. Palani was quite alone here on the top floor, an arrangement that suited Gerik and made this conversation a great deal easier. But should they be interrupted, Markor was more than capable of providing enough distraction to allow the Magistrate to finish his duties and slip away. Like most bodyguards who served magistrates, Markor wasn't his employer's equal in the martial arts, but he provided a level of interference that sometimes proved useful. Reaching almost seven feet in height, with a shaved head and eyes so dark they glimmered like coal, Markor was difficult to miss. And more than once, prominent bodyguards such as himself had served as an attractive first target for attackers who might otherwise have surprised the magistrates. By the time the attackers had realized their mistake, it was, most often, a fatal one.

The bed occupied by the Feathered One sagged drastically under Wavecrest's President's notable weight. Its massive beach-tree frame groaned, obviously hard put to support the bulk it was being subjected to, and the gauzy canopy waved back and forth under the effort. He struggled again to get up, the rope-frame creaking noisily. The Magistrate turned, placing his foot up on the seat of the room's single chair. The moonlight streaming through the windows gleamed against the boot and the jade-handled dagger sheathed neatly along it. Palani sunk quietly back against his bed pillows, deflated by the wordless threat.

Gerik rolled his neck, and the vertebrae crunched audibly. He straightened with a wicked smile. Turning to Palani, he continued to speak, his voice a menacing hiss. "You will tell no one of my identity. If they ask, you will tell them that I am a visiting merchant from Eagle's Launch, sent by Orchid Sand to negotiate trade between Wavecrest and the Eagle Prefecture. Considering Coral's new escapades into the Northlands, no one will be surprised that Wavecrest might be increasing its scope a bit as well. Do you understand me?"

"Yes, Magistrate, of course."

"You will also do nothing to reveal your knowledge of DiBello's treason. Not to your closest advisors. Not to your wives. To no one. You will proceed with the council exactly as planned. DiBello will be given precisely enough rope to hang himself."

Gerik's smile cut through the night with a feral gleam. He had anticipated this moment for many years. Few things rankled at him as greatly as did the disloyalty and inattention many of the outlying tributaries seemed to develop when the hand of the Empress was not directly over them. Their affairs were not significant enough to require her direct attention, but without it, the natural greed and laziness of these islanders seemed to run amok. Like DiBello, who seemed to believe that his dictatorship of the Coral Archipelago was a stepping stone to ruling the entire Western kingdoms and to emancipating them from the benevolent protection of the Empress. An unfortunate delusion on his part. Thankfully, there were those, such as himself, to reaffirm such mistaken individuals of their loyalty and to remind them of the debt they truly owed to the Realm.

The Feathered One nodded. "Of course, Magistrate. I will make certain it is so."

"Do not disappoint the Scarlet Empress, Palani. It would be a very poor career move. It would be so terribly upsetting to your wives to have to begin wearing widows-weeds so early in their lives. Not to mention the bother of having to run another election so soon." Palani, Gerik knew, had been raised to the position of Feathered One less than a year ago, and the increased wealth the position afforded him had allowed him to take not one, but two additional wives. Since Westerners married for life, the women's futures would be uncertain if something… unfortunate… were to happen to their noble husband.

As silently as they had arrived, Gerik and his men were gone, leaving no trace of their intrusion into the innermost presidential chambers, save for the faint strengthening of the smell of salt air. Within a heartbeat, the only sound in the room was the distant roar of the ocean coming through the open second-story windows.

Palani Vlori, the Feathered One, just and noble President of the Wavecrest Archipelago, whimpered in his sweat-stained sheets and waited for dawn.

❖ ❖ ❖

The Magistrate and his staff slipped back out to the street and made their way back through the sleepy town of Abalone toward the crowded beach.

At their arrival a few nights past, Gerik had been surprised, an emotion he preferred not to experience. But even his well-paid and normally very accurate network of spies had not been able to keep him adequately informed about the massive changes taking place on the island over the past week.

Even as Wavecrest's largest town, Abalone couldn't hope to begin to provide accommodations for the hundreds of diplomats, councilors, bureaucrats and hangers-on that had been conjured up from across the island kingdoms. The Western Isle Diplomatic Council, as DiBello and his rebellious cronies had named it, had brought entourages from every island, as minor politicos struggled neck and neck with their compatriots, anxious for an opportunity to be in on what DiBello was proposing. Namely, the beginning of a new era for the Western isles.

In the past week, an entire tent city had sprung up on the beach. At its center rose the sweeping wings of the aquamarine pavilion erected by the Feathered One's staff to house the official meetings. Perhaps two hundred feet long and half as wide, the bright blue roof was visible from outside the bay as ships approached. It formed the brilliant center square in the hodgepodge quilt that the beach had become.

Gerik had ordered their small camp set up near the main pavilion, to better observe the preparations for the council meeting. Fortunately, there was so much hustle and bustle throughout the tent city that little attention had been paid to their arrival.

An entire economy of goods and service had grown in response to the temporary city. Wavecrest possessed several islands large enough to grow crops upon, and many Wavecrest women farmed, raised small livestock or tended orchards while their menfolk pursued sea-related occupations. It did not take long for farmers from the main island and beyond to discover that their fresh produce could command garish prices in the temporary kitchens of these visiting dignitaries. Especially in demand were the delicate items, leafy lettuces and easily bruised fruits that were not suited for fresh export. More than one cultivator had been pleasantly surprised as the cooks for rival noble families engaged in a bidding war over her day's harvest. Sometimes, these bidding skirmishes netted the farmer more than a normal season's earnings in one transaction. Likewise, the city's cooks, tinkers, potters, tailors and charcoal sellers found their services in fervent demand, much to their pleased profit.

All of this activity suited Magistrate Gerik admirably. Among all of the minor nobles and backwater political leaders, he and his staff had passed without much notice. Their two small tents, chosen specifically to be unassuming and nondescript, were nothing compared to the sprawling encampments of those around them. In a carnival where everyone else seemed intent on being recognized as much as possible, very little attention was paid to the three of them. Those who guessed at all as to their identities were inevitably far from correct. He'd heard more than one whisper behind his back mistake his precise inflections for the clipped accents of a Darkmister. If they wished to believe he was part of an entourage from the Skullstone Archipelago and ward off the evil eye as he passed, let them. For now, the less interest in his identity, the better.

"Kateb, I'll need full transcripts for my report. Every word that is spoken in that tent tomorrow will need to be sent back home." The dark-eyed scribe nodded. The orders, Gerik knew, were unnecessary. What Kateb didn't write down, he would remember word for word and could recite back along with full details on the speaker at any point.

Gerik stretched, twisting his neck to crack it audibly. He returned to his own small tent, whistling softly to himself. Tomorrow, he thought, DiBello would be his, at last.

Tomorrow was going to be a delightful day.

❖ ❖ ❖

It is good to surprise those who take delight in surprising others. It keeps them off guard. The Magistrate was almost entirely inside his tent before he realized that he wasn't alone. His dagger was in his hand and then sailing across the tent before two heartbeats had passed, but the man dressed all in black silk was out of the dagger's path even quicker.

"Be calm, Magistrate." The intruder's voice, though quiet, was a harsh croak in the night air.

Gerik paused, second dagger still in his hand. "You? What are you doing here? How did you know—"

"I have some information you should know about tomorrow's council." Dark eyes glittered as he glanced down the Magistrate's dagger. "Put that away, and let's talk, shall we?"

With a scowl, Gerik made the knife disappear.

"That's more like it. I'd hate for someone to get hurt." The dark intruder hopped up onto Gerik's favorite chair, perching on the seat like a giant raiton. "Now... let's talk about DiBello. You called him a traitor, but you don't know the half of it."

CHAPTER FIFTEEN

All along the opposite coastline, long silk banners snapped brightly in the crisp ocean breeze. Taller than a man and an arm span in width, these embroidered standards proudly proclaimed a stupendous event. For what might have been the first time in the history of the Western islands, the leaders of the Neck, the Coral isles and the Wavecrest Archipelago were all in one place. Admiral DiBello had ordered the flags specially created from stores of silk he'd imported from the Blessed Isle, much to the chagrin of his wife and daughter. More than three dozen of them greeted the oncoming entourages as they approached the shoreline outside of Abalone.

The same wind that set the banners fluttering majestically also caught at the garish silk walls erected high above the waterline on the main beach. Strung tautly between rigid bamboo poles, these great fabric walls not only provided some diversion from the wind for the sprawling encampments anchored there, but acted as a nominal boundary between the sometimes uneasy makeshift neighborhoods of Western islanders crowded there.

The bay outside of Abalone was crowded with foreign vessels. A sizeable portion of Wavecrest's standing navy patrolled the expansive cove. Fully a dozen of the sixty-foot-long biremes and accompanying smaller ships moved among the myriad foreign vessels, keeping peace as best they could. Outside the bay, half a dozen massive

Wavecrest war galleys stood at the ready, their brass spiked keels gleaming. More than one adventurous Coral privateer had felt the impact of those massive battering rams into their gunwales, and the matched pairs of multi-barreled firewand projectors kept all gathered within the bay on their best behavior. Considering the history between Coral and Wavecrest, the presence of these huge triremes made most of Admiral DiBello's captains edgy. None of DiBello's staff had been welcomed into Abalone Bay before, so it was always possible that the ships' presence was standard procedure for the area. But whether they were there to protect the bay from invasion or to crack down on rebellious guests was anyone's guess.

Swan stood at the bow of the central hull of DiBello's trireme tender. The massive three-hulled ship was designed to act as support for a small fleet of trireme, none of which were small vessels themselves. No room was spared on the standard navy trireme for luxuries such as cargo capacity or even basic bunk space. On long maneuvers away from coastlines, like the trip from the Coral Archipelago at the Western isles' northern tip to Wavecrest at the far south, several of the battle-adept war galleys would be accompanied by one of the gigantic tender vessels. Extra provisions would be stored thereupon, and crewmen could be offered comfortable bunk space on a rotating basis. The tenders were also fully battle-ready in their own right, and they could afford the Coral delegation a hasty withdrawal in a pinch.

Swan watched the sea. Here, just at the mouth to the bay, it was deep and dark, almost inky. But nearer the shore where it was shallow over the white beach, it glowed an icy blue. Like Arianna's eyes. Swan sighed.

Things were, he supposed, going the way they were intended to. He was here, doing what he was meant to be doing. He'd been surprised but pleased to find out that Batilda was engaged to be married to the young aide who Swan had sent to her the night he'd first discussed the Northern trade missions with her father. DiBello was obviously coming into his own right, not only as a political leader for the Corals, but perhaps for all of the Western island kingdoms. Everything, it seemed, was going exactly as it should.

From amidships, heavy boot steps fell behind Swan, drawing him from his reverie. Looking over his shoulder, he saw Admiral DiBello approach. The strong wind that had accompanied them all the way from Coral billowed his distinctive triple-shouldered cape out behind him. Designed to impress, the cape lent his already striking stature an extra degree of grandeur. All of the Coral navy's officers wore similar cloaks, but as Head of the Armada, DiBello reserved the right to wear a crimson version.

He moved to stand beside Swan at the rail, looking out at the chaos in the bay. "Impressive, is it not? I doubt that such a combination of vessels has been present in peace in the Western kingdoms in the past thousand years."

Swan nodded, looking out at the patchwork quilt of triangular, square and oddly shaped sails that filled the natural harbor. "You're likely right, Admiral."

"We're about ready to board the *Amphitrite*. The water's too shallow to take the *Glaucus* closer." Unspoken was the addition that, if there was trouble on shore, the trireme tender and her firedust cannon and light implosion bows would be the Coral islanders' best chance of escape from the bay. Even now, the huge warship was anchored with her bow to the bay's outlet. Her sails could be unfurled at a moment's notice for a speedy departure.

Once ashore, the Coral delegation was swamped in a wave of beggars, peddlers and porters. "Carry your gear, honored sirs, very strong, very affordable!" A black-haired lad still young enough to barely reach Swan's shoulder hopped up and down before them, attempting to gain their attention. Around them, hawkers with woven grass trays strapped around their necks offered, "Turnip cake! Shrimp balls! Hot and crispy! Lotus buns! Best in town!" After weeks of uninspired sea fare consisting predominantly of variations of hardtack, Swan's mouth watered at the tantalizing scents surrounding him.

From out of the chaotic crowd emerged a golden-skinned young woman. She wore her hair cropped in a sleek inky purple bob that fell right at her chin. Her ankle-length court robes were quite striking among the more traditional sturdy clothing of the throng around her. Crafted of a plum silk in a shade that matched the hue of her hair exactly, the dress was embroidered in gold and turquoise with the repeating wave pattern that typified Wavecrest. Clasping one hand over the other, she bowed deeply before the Admiral.

"It is with greatest pleasure that you are welcomed to the humble kingdom of Wavecrest, honored Admiral. I am Kiruska Oki, a humble servant of the Great and Benevolent Feathered One, gracious President of Wavecrest. Please allow me the pleasure of escorting you to the Feathered One's presence. Your arrival has been greatly anticipated." Her words were carefully measured out and pronounced with a minimum of local accent, making them easily understandable to the entire party. With another deep bow, she turned, walking slowly away from the wharf.

The entire entourage followed Oki through the winding streets that had developed on the beach. Here and there, small restaurants and shops could be seen, interspersed between the temporary living structures. After many turns, the group emerged out of the makeshift maze into a courtyard, at the center of which stood the expansive turquoise pavilion Swan had seen from the ship.

Immediately upon their arrival, the majority of the group split off from DiBello and Swan and a few others. Made up of some of the Coral navy's finest marines, they formed an honor guard outside the tent, circling it with military precision. Runners were posted, some remaining at the tent and others returning to the wharf. The Wavecresters looked confused, unaccustomed to the military precision that came with Coral's Admiral's presence. He was a firm advocate of organization and of communication. The runners had been an important part of any ground mission he led and had proved their worth more than once. Not only did they keep DiBello in touch with any changes his ships' crews in the bay might notice, but they would also facilitate shift changes, allowing the honor guard and the diplomatic team to be spelled if necessary. Diplomatic meetings had been known to stretch out for long hours if not days, and no one gathered here knew precisely what to expect from this one.

For privacy and security, the exterior walls of the tent had been firmly staked into the heavy sand of the upper beach. Additional walls had been added on the interior, leaving the pavilion with one large meeting room at its center surrounded by smaller hallways and branching corridors. More of the tall silk walls had been erected outside, allowing only enough breeze to keep the rooms within cool but relatively undisturbed by the often high coastal winds.

Swan accompanied Admiral DiBello and his small assembly of select council members and naval captains into the main room, where they were greeted by more deep bows and officious words. DiBello and Swan, who stood at his right hand, were escorted up onto a low platform. It had been decorated with a long carpet that ran the length of the dais and enough heavy wooden chairs to seat a dozen individuals. At strategic locations, fire pots borne on tall wrought-copper stands rose up halfway to the ceiling. Unlit now, if the conclave stretched out into the evening hours, these lamps would illuminate the proceedings.

All but two of the seats were filled with dignified looking Western islanders. Golden skinned and light eyed, some wore the simple native clothing of their home kingdoms, while others wore the Blessed Isle garb that Batilda and so many of the Westerners had adopted from Dragon-Blood fashions.

The rest of the entourage was encouraged to join the remainder of the crowded room. They were ushered to simple benches that had obviously been quickly constructed to attempt to deal with the massive onslaught of visitors to the island.

At the head of the raised dais sat the Feathered One. The President was a rotund man, almost spherical in shape. This being a formal occasion, he was wearing the sweeping headdress and long cloak of state that gave the office its name. The ebon flight feathers of monstrous grelidaka birds rose in a fan-shaped headdress around his shaved head. Here and there, they were accented with the jeweled plumage of other of the islands' tropical birds, yellow and red against the stark black. Likewise, the length of the cloak was decorated with a rainbow of feathers, seemingly every color imaginable. Most striking was the thick black fringe of twisted plumage around the top that gave the President the appearance of having very shiny curled whiskers which frothed all the way around his neck and under his chin. Under the cloak and headdress, he wore only a brief skirt woven of sea-grass. It hung past his round knees, unadorned in its simplicity. The leader of Wavecrest smiled down at the newcomers like a bronzed statue of some well-fed god of plenty and leisure. But underneath his friendly demeanor, Swan noticed telltale signs of nervousness. The Feathered One's gaze jumped anxiously around the room, and despite being lightly dressed, runnels of moisture rolled down his heavy face. Perhaps a certain amount of anxiety was understandable, in the presence of this massive throng of visitors, Swan thought. Or was there something more?

Oki, their guide from the wharf, bowed low in the direction of the Feathered One. "If it pleases, honored one, may I have the satisfaction of introducing to you the delegation from the Coral Archipelago." She remained bent from the waist for what Swan recognized as the requisite length of obeisance and then rose, gesturing first to the Admiral.

"With greatest honor, do I present DiBello Gerarde, Ruler of the Coral Archipelago, Admiral of the Coral Navy and Head of the Coral Trade Council." DiBello eschewed the bow of respect traditional in Wavecrest, instead offering the Feathered One a nod and brief salute of greeting as he might when being introduced to a new captain in his navy.

The young woman went on, her speech showing no recognition of the impertinence she'd just witnessed. "As well, it is my honor to present to you the honorable diplomat, Swan, also of the Coral Archipelago." Swan bowed deeply, holding the position of respect for a breath longer than strictly necessary. If he had any chance of success today, starting out by insulting the local president was not an option.

The Feathered One swept one thickset arm out, gesturing curtly to a pair of unoccupied bamboo chairs. "Please, do us the kindness of joining our council. Your arrival has been greatly anticipated." Swan frowned, noticing that the President's hand shook as he gestured.

When everyone was seated, the Feathered One heaved himself out of his massive chair like a bull walrus wading to shore. He smoothed his feathered cloak, nervously, and then turned to look over the crowded room. "Honored guests, it is my pleasure to welcome you. While our reasons for gathering may be solemn, it is my hope that our memories of this council, the first assembly of its kind in the history of the Western kingdoms, will be joyous ones. May those memories persevere to be passed on to our children and our children's children. Today, we meet to discuss serious business, but we meet as brothers, and for that, I am thankful."

The tent rang with applause as the Feathered One ended his welcome. "When this assembly was called, each of you was given some information on the current challenges that are facing our kingdoms. Now, to fully acquaint us with the situation at hand, I would like to introduce you to DiBello Gerarde, Ruler of the Coral Archipelago. Admiral DiBello?"

DiBello stood, nodding politely in acknowledgement. "Thank you for the kind introduction." He turned to address the crowded pavilion, and for a few moments, the only sound in the tent was that of his voice.

"Ladies and Gentlemen. We are assembled here today for one reason. No matter where our home port lies, we share one thing in common: Whether we hail from the Coral islands, as I do, or make our home in Wavecrest or dwell within the Neck. Whether we have lived a life of peace or of military skirmish, we are part of these Western kingdoms." As the Admiral continued, he was overcome with a patriotism that was contagious.

"Our hearts, whether we spend our hours working the soil or tending sails, are tied to these lands and these seas. Those who are not a part of our kingdoms cannot truly understand what it is to be one with these islands, the islands that we love."

Swan marveled again at the Admiral's ability to weave the tapestry of reality to fit his needs. In a few sentences, he had bound together nations that had stood fiercely independent for centuries and had labeled all other peoples as "outsiders," and everyone in the room was agreeing.

"Now," DiBello continued, "we find ourselves faced with a threat that is both achingly familiar and, yet, frighteningly new." He frowned, brushing one hand through his cropped cobalt blue hair. "For generations, we have been plagued by the predations of an entire family of rats. These rodents, however, do not limit themselves to the shores. Unlike their terrestrial cousins, these vermin thrive on the sea, scavenging and feasting on anything that is not sufficiently defended from their appetite. We have all, from north to south, from east to west, felt their endless hunger and fallen prey to their ruthless cravings. I am speaking, of course, of the Lintha."

The crowd began murmuring, nodding in agreement. Certainly, the holdings of many of those present may have been obtained through means that outsiders might have considered piracy. Each culture, however, had its own complicated system of legitimacy in regards to privateering, and the Lintha, considering themselves above any one nation's rules, fell outside them all.

"It is not enough," continued DiBello, "for these parasites to prey upon random fleets and shipments that happen to pass too close to the hell-waters they call their own. No, in an act of unrivaled impudence, these fleas, these ticks, these blood-hungry insects have laid their eggs on our good lands. Here, in Wavecrest, to the east in the Neck and, soon, in our northern Coral islands, they have crept ashore, not simply to raid and plunder, but to remain and attempt to establish themselves as legitimate residents! Like the kariba vine that took over the entirety of Blue Island, they will spread onto our lands, squeezing out all native life that belongs there. And once having made an island their home, they will turn it to a barren wasteland where nothing but themselves can survive!"

"I ask you now. Will we let this happen? Can we, the native people of our islands, let this happen? We have so little that is truly ours. Our hard-earned wealth can be stolen from us, even our very lives are ours only by the grace of the fickle fates of the sea. But our native-born birthright, our lands, our homes, our cultures, these are ours to pass on to our children and their children. These, we cannot allow this plague of vermin to pillage from us!"

The cheers from the room carried out of the tent, and a marine poked his head in to see what raised the shouts.

DiBello waited for the crowd to calm, then began again. "I can tell by your reactions that you understand the serious nature of this threat. I had no doubt you would. After all, you are children of these Western kingdoms. You understand what it means to be a part of the sea and our land." He paused, thoughtfully. "What gives me concern is not whether or not each of you will understand the challenge to our way of life. No, what worries me is that our situation is not being understood by the very individuals who supposedly have our best interests in mind—those who are supposed to be watching over us, guarding our good fortune, protecting us from just such a threat!"

The crowd seemed a bit confused, hesitant, but DiBello pulled them along, a charismatic whirlwind that was just building up to full hurricane force.

"Where are the fleets that are supposedly protecting us from these threats? Where are the sailors and soldiers that our taxes are going to feed and arm? Now, when our need is greater than ever before, we look out and find our protection gone! Now, when the sharks are near the beach, we find that we are left to safeguard ourselves! Now, when our coffers are lighter and our taxes are heavier than ever before and when the knife at our throat is sharper than ever before! *Now*, we find ourselves alone!"

The roar of the crowd was deafening. Swan was amazed at how DiBello played them. The crowd was his. Now, he knew, DiBello would go for the kill. He only had to make his demand.

"Brothers and sisters. Western kingdoms. I ask you. Are we going to allow this? Are we going to pay tribute to an uncaring sovereign half Creation away? One who would take our taxes and then sail away? One who would leave us at the mercy of the Lintha? Who would leave us without the resources to protect our selves, our families and our way of life from the scum of the saragasso?"

A tidal wave of refusal filled the room, shaking the tent walls. DiBello stood, center stage, as the Feathered One and the elder spokesman of the Neck sat, gaping in wonder at how they had lost complete control of the proceedings.

CHAPTER SIXTEEN

"You're playing a dangerous game, Yurgen." The dried herbs gave off a pungent tang as she ground them aggressively into a powder. "She's no fool." Samea frowned down into the mortar in her lap, slamming the heavy marble pestle into the mixture with a bit more force than was strictly necessary. Cross-legged on the floor of her tent, she hadn't stopped her preparations when Yurgen had arrived a few minutes ago.

"I know what I'm doing, Samea. She's here, isn't she? She's going with us. What more do you want?"

"I'll tell you what I don't want. What I don't want is for us to count on her and then have her turn tail when we most need her. That could prove disastrous. Better to not count on her at all." Samea rose to her feet, moving to stand next to a small table laden with an assortment of jars, utensils and equipment. Scooping the powder out of the grinding bowl, Samea measured out precise weights using a delicate bronze scale and then packaged the powdered herb into folded paper packets.

Samea's ger had served not only as her home, but as a makeshift still-room since they'd stopped making the regular trips back and forth to their Northern temple. Their camp in the Haltan forest was now their home, and while it was different from what she was accustomed to, it would have to suffice. Almost everything she could do at the Hold, she'd managed to find a way to do here, including the manufacture of fever-drop powder. A sharp bite pinched at her bare leg, and she slapped at the tiny bloodsucking fly there. Now, if she could only perfect a repellant that would fend off these aggravating Eastern pests. They had a tenacity she'd not yet been able to conquer.

Across the room, Yurgen lounged on the thick mountain-sheep hide that covered Samea's pile of bedding, watching her in amusement. "It's those cursed baths you insist on taking, I'm telling you. Look at me… We've been here weeks, and not a single bite." He pulled up the sleeve on his tunic, revealing an arm which bore many scars, but no bug bites.

"Yes, but you also frighten the horses when you cross their path upwind, Yurgen. You smell like badly tanned hides. No wonder they will not bite you."

Her chiding about Arianna left behind, Samea finished her medicinal preparation, putting everything neatly away in a compartmentalized bag she had woven specifically to hold her apothecary paraphernalia. She hung it with care on the woven wall on the eastern side of the tent, before returning her attention to Yurgen.

"So," he said, stretching after getting to his feet. "How are your allies doing? Happy?"

He slowly began pacing the curve of the tent in a gesture Samea was well familiar with. Something had him worried.

"Yes, actually. Amazingly well. Florivet has been a bit petulant, but that is his way. I think he's enjoying this more than he lets on." She paused, frowning slightly. "I had some trepidation, as you know, about the price that the lions demanded to agree to aid us. And then, they'd been so adamant I didn't think I'd ever find someone to meet their specifications. When I finally did…" Samea shook her head. "Nena was a sweet girl. Maybe five. Her mother had died a few years ago, and her father was one of the first Haltans we lost in Rokan-jin. Big dark eyes, green hair. I ended up bringing her to them and expected… well, I expected it not to be pleasant."

Yurgen nodded, continuing to pace. "And she was acceptable?"

Samea chuckled softly, remembering the evening she'd brought the young sacrifice to the celestial lions.

It had been very late, and the child drowsed in the wholesome exhaustion of a creature who still gave every waking moment her all. Samea, fearing the worst, had given her a dose of numbvine to aid her calm, and the child had dozed against Samea's shoulder as she carried her into the clearing the lions claimed as their territory.

The one she'd come to think of as dominant had paused in his grooming, looking over at the witch as she entered. He carefully finished smoothing his shoulder fur and then padded slowly over. His partner, the sly one, had raised one lazy eyelid, regarding Samea for one long moment, and then returned to slumber.

"This is the one you promised?" The lion had drawn near, forcing Samea to crane her neck upward to address him directly.

Samea had nodded slowly, as the child in her arms wriggled sleepily. "She is as you asked, honored guardians. A child of the forest, orphaned, of the right age."

The lion had leaned down then until its shining metal muzzle was nearly touching the child's mossy hair. It drew in a deep breath, inhaling the scent of the ritual herbs Samea had put in the girl's bath that evening and the fresh smell of childhood.

"She will suffice." The lion had stepped back and settled onto his haunches to wait.

Samea had found herself hesitant, now that the time had actually come to give the offering over to the spirits. She paused for a long moment and then steeled herself for what was to come. The lion's cooperation had likely saved the lives of dozens, if not hundreds, in this war already. The sacrifice of one was a small price to pay.

She had stood the young girl onto her feet, gently pushing her toward the spirit that had claimed her.

The girl, dressed only in a sleeveless woven play shift, had wobbled uncertainly, the late hour and numbvine taking away any grace the child possessed.

Unable to bear the waiting any longer, Samea had given the little one a harder push, sending her across the short distance between herself and the lion. "One request, noble spirit. Please, make it quick, please? The child does not deserve to suffer."

The lion had tilted its head curiously. "You are mistaken, witch. On many levels. Do not think you know us so well. This will take a very long time."

Samea had frowned, stiffening as her mind replayed a montage of the horrors she had seen inflicted in the course of her lifetime. Tortures and slaughters, sacrifices and murders ran through her thoughts, leaving her pale and barely suppressing her desire to snatch the child back to safety.

As she'd watched in horror, the lion had lowered its face over the child, stretching wide open it's gleaming metal jaws. Despite herself, Samea had squeezed her eyes shut, preparing for the meaty crunch of the spirit's first bite.

The child's clear laughter rang in the glen.

Samea's eyes had flown open, and she'd been amazed to see the lion standing vigilantly over the girl child while his partner gently held her down with one metal paw. The sly one had softly lapped at the squirming child's face with a golden tongue easily as large as the child's entire head, as the laughing child wriggled to be released.

At the sight of Samea's bewildered stare, the dominant lion had smiled smugly. "Do not think you know more than you do, little witch. A full belly is not the only need we have. When our temple is restored, when you have won this war of yours, we will need one who understand our needs and will serve us diligently. This one will suffice."

Samea had made the trek back through the forest to her own camp that night, pondering the lion's words.

"Acceptable?" Samea said now, answering Yurgen. "Yes. I'd say so. Within minutes, she was crawling all over them, and the pair of them were purring like kittens. When I left, she was feeding them chunks of horse meat the size of my fist, and they were licking her hands clean." She shook her head. "When the war is won, they said. I suppose that's a good sign? They believe we're going to win."

"You had any doubt?" Yurgen paused, leveling a steely stare at her.

"Things are going well, so far. And all the portents indicate they will continue to do so. I don't yet know what to make of the reports that the Scarlet Empress has withdrawn or gone into hiding, but for now, the chaos it seems to have brought serves us well. I haven't heard of a Wyld Hunt being completed in months, and that means more possible allies." She paused, thoughtfully. "But of course I worry."

"Well, don't let it pass these walls." Yurgen gestured around him, returning to his pacing. "The others, they need to see only confidence. We will prevail. We must."

Samea nodded in agreement. "Of course we will." But in her heart, she wondered which of them she was reassuring.

Chapter Seventeen

Midday had fallen before DiBello released the crowd from his charismatic grasp. The applause, when he finally bowed and returned to his seat, shook the ground beneath their feet.

"Well done, Admiral." Swan had rarely heard him speak with such charisma, and for DiBello, that was saying something.

The Admiral's eyes gleamed with a heady fervor. "They're ready now, Diplomat. They're yours. Close this deal." He dabbed at his neck with a clean handkerchief, a slight flush the only sign of his taxing oration.

Swan stood, unconsciously smoothing his tunic as every eye in the crowded pavilion fell upon him.

"Admiral DiBello. Gracious host. Honored elders," he began. "I am—"

"*Infidels!*"

The curtain wall to the left side of the council was split asunder by a flashing jade daiklave, which ripped through the silk with ease.

The entire delegation turned as one, still riding the adrenaline of DiBello's inspiring speech. The warrior who leapt through the cut curtain wore the robes of the Imperial Magistracy, stark and austere, but unmistakable. With one hand, he brandished his sword, and the other clutched a pendant that glowed with a yellow-green light. He thrust the necklace toward the dais, and its beams flared painfully bright, arcing across the room toward Swan.

Where the pendant's rays struck the young diplomat, they crackled with arcane energy. The fiery glow rolled over his form, wrapping him in its sallow aura. He could feel a burning where the beams struck him squarely on the forehead, conjuring forth the mark of his Exaltation. The sight of the golden ring and circle seemed to send the Magistrate into a greater frenzy. He glared at the Feathered One, while continuing across the room.

"Traitorous councils are not a great enough sacrilege, Palani? You now hold court with Anathema?" The Magistrate leapt forward, knocking aside the scribes and minor envoys between himself and the raised dais. An ornately robed woman with upswept hair became tangled when a young man fell on her long skirts. She struggled to back away, but was not able to scramble out of the way quickly enough for the Dragon-Blooded official. The Magistrate's sword swept her aside with a backhand blow, sending her body and head tumbling to the ground in separate directions.

A pair of men slipped in through the gash in the tent wall that the bureaucrat had created. The first, impossibly tall, ducked deeply to pass through the slit. He slowly began to circle the walled room to the left. As Swan watched, more than one fleeing noble deflected off of his chest during their frantic search for an exit and then looked up and up and up in fear until they met the giant's eyes. He glowered down at them without pausing. The sight of his fierce visage drove them out of the tent even faster. Despite the bodily impacts, his smooth movement never wavered.

Dark as a shadow, the giant's companion slipped inside the wounded wall and then settled immediately to the ground, taking out a parchment and brush. He sat, calmly watching the chaos around him, chronicling the entirety. Amid the growing insanity of the room, his writing was a surreal pocket of calm.

Thwarted by the tide of individuals between him and his target, the Magistrate lost his temper. From around him, a banner of spiritual energy flared, a great hissing sea serpent that filled the tent to the topmost peak. The crowd panicked, fleeing for the front and back exits. Delegates trampled each other, pushing and screaming like animals before a forest fire. The smell of panic was as palpable in the room as the growing stench of blood and death.

The Magistrate kept coming, his pendant held forward. Swan didn't know exactly what the artifact was, but it flared brightly every time it neared him, ignoring the rest of the room, and it burned at the ring-and-circle mark on his forehead as if pulling it forcibly into view.

Swan leaped backward, knocking his empty chair off the dais. He landed at the edge nearest to the Feathered One, who almost tipped backward off the edge of the stage in shock. Admiral DiBello looked from the Dragon-Blood to Swan and back, turning his back to neither. "Surely, Magistrate Gerik," he said, gesturing diplomatically holding his hands in front of himself. "There must be some mistake. You and I have known each other for years. Surely we can—"

The Magistrate answered by cleaving in half a round lacquered table full of refreshments, bringing a short-lived scream from some unfortunate scribe who had chosen it as a place to hide from the unexpected arrival of the Realm's representative. "There will be no negotiation with the Anathema. Step aside, traitor, or join in his fate! The Empress may wish to try you for your treason, but there is only one punishment for the demon-tainted!"

Perhaps it was a vestige of loyalty for Swan's years of service to the Coral Archipelago. Perhaps the Admiral just didn't like being told what to do. Swan wasn't sure, but regardless of the motivation, the result was the same.

The Magistrate leapt into the air. His slippers almost scraped the roof of the pavilion as he flipped forward onto the raised platform. The Admiral, never one to be accused of cowardice, did not step back as the Realm official landed, despite his sword or the huge serpent of the seas hissing in the air above him. The bright apparition roared deafeningly, as the Magistrate walked forward toward the Admiral who stood between himself and his prey. Swan lunged to stop the Dragon-Blood's peripheral destruction, and the Admiral stood his ground for a moment too long. As Swan watched in horror, Gerik's blade flashed out, and the back of DiBello's crimson cloak gave birth to the tip of the Magistrate's sword. The Admiral slowly collapsed forward. Gerik roughly jerked the sword from his body and stepped around him to engage Swan. DiBello slumped face first onto the floor, his blood staining the dais around him in a growing crimson pool.

"Get out! Clear the tent!" Swan yelled, sweeping aside the chairs around him to give him room. It was obvious there could be only one outcome from this situation.

Marines from outside rushed to help the few remaining individuals fleeing from the vicinity of the battle. Without orders, they hesitated for a moment until finally one of the senior members of the troop took command. "We're not going to get involved with the imperial justice enforcer. Stay back and keep everyone out of the area." They retreated en force. The Feathered One, glued by cowardice into his chair, remained on the dais, cringing into his seat as if it would somehow hide his massive form.

In the tent, a milky silver aura flared around Swan. It flowed like a silken war banner, leaving no doubt as to his nature. The necklace in Gerik's hand blazed in response, gleaming sun-bright. As Swan concentrated, anticipating Gerik's next assault, his aura began to gently caress his form, slipping around him with sinuous grace.

The Magistrate spun, aiming a low kick at Swan's foremost leg, which was followed by a sweeping sword blow designed to separate the diplomat's head from his neck. Swan leapt over the kick easily. In midair, he bent backward in a fashion which would have broken the spine of any human. His hands found the ground behind him, inches from where his feet had stood seconds before. As the sword swept past, his feet snapped upward into the Magistrate's bearded jaw. The rising kicks were followed by a fierce downward stomp across the bridge of Gerik's nose as Swan sprung from his acrobatic handstand back to his feet. Gerik's howl of pain filled the tent.

Reeling from Swan's attack, the Magistrate stumbled backward toward the Feathered One's chair. His sword swept to the side, sending a small heavily laden table crashing to the floor. The Feathered One paled and tried to sink further back into his throne.

Swan took advantage of his attacker's momentary unbalance. He grabbed the edge of the rug beneath the Magistrate's feet and leapt into the air with it, flicking him backward like a crumb off of a napkin. The unfortunate President chose that moment to struggle to his feet. The rug caught under his bare feet, and he was knocked back into his chair violently. Driven by the great weight, the chair toppled, teetering madly before falling backward off the edge of the dais. Both man and chair went tumbling down onto the rug-covered sand.

Magistrate Gerik growled as he found himself sailing backward off the low platform. He landed heavily, kicking up a great cloud of sand, but managed to remain on his feet. "Feeble tricks will not save you!" His arm lashed out, snapping his jade sword like a javelin toward Swan.

Swan deflected the thrown sword with the heavy carpet still in his hands. The blade sliced into the woven wool, doubtless ruining someone's imported antique. The make-shift shield, however, was enough to send the attack arcing to the side rather than running him through. He was amazed to see the sword circle and return to his attacker's hand like a loyal falcon. "Nice trick."

Gerik snarled as the weapon snapped back into his hand and his target still stood. He glanced at Markor, who was circling behind the dais toward the back entrance.

Swan caught the movement as his attacker's attention flickered briefly away. *Okay, so that's where the big bald guy went*, Swan thought. He didn't relish the idea of being caught between two adversaries. The Magistrate had effec-tively blocked escape through the front.

"Which leaves us with…" Leaping at what might be his only chance, Swan tossed the heavy carpet at his attacker. He spun, darting for the back exit, only to find Markor waiting with a solemn expression and a very large scimitar. Swan ducked low as the giant swiped at his head with the heavy curved blade. He darted past, and the cool breeze from outside the tent caressed his face, cooling the burning on his forehead.

Unfortunately, he hadn't counted on the length of Markor's grasp.

The tall bodyguard stretched with his free hand and grabbed Swan by the neck of his chain mail shirt, tossing him back into the room. As he landed, Swan rolled and narrowly missed being impaled on Gerik's sword. He flipped himself upright, and scrambled for the opposite entryway.

Gerik leaped from the dais, somersaulting through the air to block Swan's path. "There is no escape for you!" He stretched a hand out, and a ripple of energy coursed out of his palm. "Let us see how you fare when severed from your demonic powers!"

The wave struck Swan, sweeping over him like a tidal wave. He felt his knees grow weak, and uncertainty swept across his mind. He had expected pain but felt, instead, confusion, as his limbs no longer answered as readily to his call and his mind clouded with indecision. The flowing opal banner that had flared brightly around him waned. As if feeding off it, the apparition above Gerik brightened, hissing in pleasure as the energy wave rebounded off Swan and rippled back toward the Magistrate. Swan slumped to the ground, drained.

Gerik crowed in delight at his reaction. "I thought as much!" He closed for the kill, eyes awash with glee.

Swan feinted numbly to the left and then rolled to the right, still stunned. His path took him over the beheaded form of one of Gerik's unfortunate victims, and he cringed at the wanton disregard for life, while scrambling to save his own.

Sitting quietly as a statue, the Magistrate's scribe looked up from his recording of the battle just in time to see Swan leap past. The fleeing man snatched up the portable table Kateb had been using to write on, spilling papers and ink everywhere. He held it across his shoulders as a makeshift shield while he dashed for cover behind the raised platform.

Gerik targeted Swan's fleeing back, throwing his sword again like a javelin. He laughed, the smug chortle of one who knows he will be victorious. "The table will not save you, demon-spawn!"

Kateb leapt to his feet, inspired to action by the potential loss of his transcriptions. His timing, however, was less perfect than his penmanship. Gerik's blade skewered him, spearing into his throat with bloody efficiency. The blow knocked him onto his back, where he lay open-eyed, with his beloved papers drifting slowly down around him like snowfall.

"You cost me a scribe, fiend! By the Five Dragons, I'll take it out of your skin before I destroy you!" Gerik wasted no time in calling his blade to him. It leapt from Kateb's corpse and into its owner's hand, trailing a mist of blood through the air.

Behind the dais, Swan panted. The wave that had struck him had left him sapped. He glanced around for an escape route. The Feathered One had managed to extract himself from his fallen chair and was desperately attempting to remain unnoticed as he crawled like a bloated caterpillar for the edge of the tent. He'd almost managed his own escape when he found his passage suddenly blocked by two tree-trunk-tall legs. He looked up and up and up, to where Markor glared darkly down at him. He felt himself grabbed by the ruff of his presidential robe and lifted well off his feet.

"Magistrate, what would you have me do with this one?"

Gerik glanced over and smiled. "Hold him. We'll deal with his part in this when the Deceiver has been dispatched."

Palani paled, dangling like a butchered piglet. "But, Magistrate, surely…" He whined, sweat rolling down his corpulent face as his bladder emptied itself down his grass skirt.

"Let him go, Gerik." Swan's voice was strained. He remained in the cover of the raised dais, trying to whittle out a plan that would free both himself and the helpless President. His wits were failing him. "He's done nothing."

"He has harbored traitors and those who are corrupted by demonic forces. And while he is certainly not of primary import at the moment, it is very likely he will share your fate for his crimes."

This pronouncement was more than Wavecrest's cowardly President could stomach. With a squeal, he shrugged out of his feathered cloak and dashed for the back entrance faster than Swan believed possible for a man of his size to move.

Markor looked down at the now empty cloak and then back up at Gerik. For a long moment, no one moved.

"Get him, you idiot," the Magistrate growled in frustration. "I'll handle this one."

Markor took off after Palani, but fear had lent the Feathered One wings. He had flown from the tent before Markor took his first lanky step after him. The bodyguard turned back to Gerik, questioningly.

"Well? What are you waiting for? Get him!"

Markor nodded, dropping the cloak, and disappeared in pursuit.

Swan used the few seconds of distraction to assess his situation. It was obvious that the Imperial Magistrate intended to kill him. DiBello was dead, and the marines outside would certainly not intercede on his behalf without orders to do so. Whatever that wave Gerik had thrown at him was, it had almost completely sapped his energy. He was no longer moving as quickly or as surely as he had been since his Exaltation. Gerik was armed and seemed fully able. Swan, on the other hand, had no weapon and felt as if a slight breeze could knock him over. His chances of surviving a hand-to-hand melee at this point were slim to none. However, the Magistrate had already proven himself to have no reservations about visiting wholesale random slaughter on innocent bystanders in his path to destroy his target.

If he fled, he was taking responsibility for the fact that there would be more destruction and more innocent lives lost. He couldn't do that. He must stay and destroy Gerik or die trying.

From deep within himself, Swan felt a sudden warming. As if confirming his choice was right, the Unconquered Sun flared through him, renewing him and unfurling his spiritual energy in a radiant opalescent flag. Strength flowed through his muscles as it had on the first night of his Exaltation. In a heartbeat, he found himself leaping to his feet, just as Gerik's sword impaled itself into the beach floor where he'd just been crouching.

Renewed, Swan launched himself up and over Gerik's head, through the serpent banner, which snapped and hissed as he passed, tearing at his clothing. He landed on the stage, looking desperately for a weapon. Miraculously, the tall copper lamps still remained standing amidst the chaos. Swan snatched one of them up, sending the unlit fire pot to the ground. It shattered against the hardwood, oil slipping across the surface in a glistening flood dotted with pottery shards.

"Your demons lend you aid, but it will be to no avail. There is no escape for you, save through the cleansing blow of my sword." Gerik leapt onto the stage, squaring off with his awkwardly armed opponent. He glared at Swan. "You will be my trophy, imp. Your destruction will be the final coup in my exposure of the treason of these islands.

Swan swung the heavy base of the lamp low, forcing Gerik to leap over it. The Magistrate feinted in midair, distracting Swan with a sword blow that was never intended to connect. Gerik's other hand slipped in past Swan's defenses, locking around his throat like a spring-belly's claw. As it made contact, Gerik forced his will through the grasp, calling upon his favored element for aid. "Drown!"

Swan fought for air as the grip tightened, cutting off his breath. He felt a weight across his chest, pressing on his lungs. It was as if he was being dragged to the bottom of the ocean depths. Gerik's eyes lit with savage pleasure, glowing emerald as he watched Swan struggle. Swan knew that he had only moments before the lack of air would rob him of his senses. The copper lamp began to slip from his fingers, but he clenched at it, slamming the heavy base down onto Gerik's foot. The bones crunched beneath the blow, and Gerik's grip loosened just long enough for Swan to slip free.

The lamp dropped from Swan's hands as he gasped for breath. He slumped to his knees, and Gerik was on him again. As the Magistrate slashed at his head, Swan barely slipped under the blow, feeling the deadly breeze swipe just above him. Swan countered with a half-hearted blow to his opponent's middle, which Gerik neatly avoided.

"Enough of this!" Gerik attacked with a spinning fury of blows. His sword work was exquisite, flawless, but as Swan recovered his breath, his defense was its equal. The two men fought with blazing speed, neither able to gain an advantage. Thrust after thrust, Gerik failed to find a path to the target that had seemed open a second before. Again and again, Swan's kicks failed to knock his opponent off balance, his disarming moves failed to strip the vicious sword from Gerik's hands.

Fate, it seemed, would be the final judge in their duel. As he lunged to escape a jab to the face that would have left him blind, Swan's foot landed on an oily shard of pottery from the broken fire pot, and he slipped, momentarily losing his balance. Gerik leapt on the opportunity as Swan spilled to the floor. He flipped his blade point down and thrust with both hands, intent on impaling his prey through the middle.

Swan saw the blow falling and rolled to avoid it. He wasn't quick enough. Gerik's blade flashed like lightning, staking his lower arm to the heavy wooden dais. A jagged bite of intense pain lanced up Swan's limb, as he strained to try to free it. Each movement tore at the wound, until the pain was so great it doubled him up, setting his stomach on fire with his body's need to purge itself of the intrusion. The Magistrate

loomed above him. The gleaming pendant shone so brightly
Swan was almost blinded. A fanatical spark shone in Gerik's
eyes, as he watched Swan struggle to remove the sword blade
pinning his arm to the dais.

"Your powers are nothing, frog-spawn. You are nothing but offal. It will be a pleasure to cleanse Creation of
your taint." He kicked Swan hard in the side, lifting him
off the ground.

Swan's ribs fractured under Gerik's boot with a wet
meaty crack that drove his breath away. The movement
made the sword bite deeper into his flesh, but the blade was
pinned between the bones of his arm and would not tear free,
at least not while his hand remained attached.

"Where are your demon allies now, infidel? Where are
your fiendish companions?" Gerik's smile was feral, as he
relished Swan's ineffective efforts to free himself.

From behind him, a low rumbling voice growled. "I
resent that remark."

Gerik spun around, facing Admiral DiBello, who had
drawn himself up from the floor. The front of his uniform
was stained dark crimson. Just below the medals along his
left breast, a gaping wound bubbled slow pink froth with
every breath.

"I'm not… a fiend. Just… dedicated." Admiral DiBello
drove his ceremonial dagger low into Gerik's gut and then
sliced hard to the left and the right.

Fatally surprised, the Magistrate began to say something, but his words were silenced by the sick slippery sound
of his intestines unfurling themselves from his body. DiBello
pulled the blade from him, and the Magistrate slid to the
floor, slumping into a pile with his own entrails. The stench
of wet offal and blood filled the tent.

DiBello winced, panting softly. He wiped the wet
foulness from his blade on the back of Gerik's shirt.
Stepping over the body, he reached down to wrench the
blade from Swan's arm.

Fire exploded up Swan's limb as the sword was removed. He groaned, curling onto his side, clutching his

arm to his chest. Waves of nausea struck him over and over as his body tried to right itself from the injury.

"You don't have much time, Diplomat." Blood bubbled from DiBello's lips. "Things are going to get insane here very soon." He rocked on his feet.

Seeing his commander upright, one of the marines dashed back inside the tent to help support him.

"Get out of here, before folks realize what's happened." DiBello obviously didn't want to lean against the soldier beside him, but his strength was fading.

"But Admiral, you're hurt."

The Admiral looked down at the wound in his chest. As he watched, the bubbles from his wound grew darker with each shallow breath. "I'm not hurt. He nicked my lung, and from the color the blood's turning, probably my heart. I'm dead. I just haven't decided to fall down yet. Now, you get out of here."

DiBello turned to the soldier supporting him. His roar of a voice had dropped almost to a whisper, and his skin was growing pale, but he issued his last commands with as much authority as he ever had.

"Culin, you're in charge of getting your team back to the fleet. They are to specifically leave this area now." A cough caught him, and his breathing took on a wet rasp. "Tell them I ordered Captain Bargella to get everyone back home. And you tell them how Swan fell trying to save me. You tell them how the Magistrate's magic destroyed his body, leaving nothing behind. You hear?"

The stunned marine nodded. "Yes, Admiral DiBello."

Swan crawled to his feet. His cracked ribs sent sharp stabs of pain with every movement. His arm had stopped bleeding, and he bound the torn flesh with a strip of silk from his ruined shirt.

DiBello motioned for the marine to lower him to the ground. The effort drained the Admiral further, and he paled to a deathly white.

"Admiral?" Culin looked down in concern, unwilling to leave his commander.

"Why are you still here?" DiBello whispered, the sound hardly audible past the flow of blood that now came with every breath. "Go. Now. That's an order."

The marine pulled himself to attention. "Yes, sir, Admiral." He gave DiBello a formal salute of respect, before turning and running out of the tent. Swan could hear him barking orders and the sound of a large group moving from the tent.

"Admiral?"

Swan looked over at DiBello, but a lifeless stare was his only reply. He knelt and, with a gentle touch, closed the dead man's eyes. "Thank you, Admiral. I will not let your sacrifice be in vain." The air shimmered with the strength of the young man's vow.

But how to go about it? A quick glance around the tent revealed nothing but carnage. He tied together a rough bag from a tablecloth, filling it with some of the unruined refreshments. After a moment's thought, he added the pendant that the Magistrate had been carrying. Gerik's sword was too distinctive to risk taking, so he settled for a pair of small serving knives which, lacking a scabbard, he slid into his boot tops. With a last look around, he considered his options. He'd been revealed as no longer human. His mission had failed. His career as a diplomat was over. His ties to his family could only be used against it now. He could not return to Coral, but most immediately, he could not remain here.

"Where am I going to go now?" The enormity of the situation weighed upon him as heavily as Gerik's choking hold had earlier.

"I can't allow you in," the marine's voice said, loudly enough to make Swan jump. "Admiral DiBello's orders."

The debate began, but Swan took his cue to escape out the back and into the chaos of the tent city.

CHAPTER EIGHTEEN

Two guards stood awkwardly outside the Feathered One's bedroom door, their ceremonial spears held in what they hoped was at least close to the proper fashion for such duties. Another pair, spears held uncomfortably over their shoulders, paced an inexpert crisscross patrol around the building's main floor, crossing below the President's open bedroom window.

Palani had listened to them walk for hours. Within the first hour, he had memorized the forty-six steps it took each to cross the courtyard under his window. For a time, he'd stopped listening for the footsteps and tried to decipher the whispered conversation between the sentinels just beyond his door. Now, after an entire jug of imported wine, he just lay in his bed, staring at the gauzy netting above him, wondering if he would ever sleep again. Every time his eyelids began to slip shut, he saw the Magistrate's wicked smile and heard him growling, "Share your fate for his crimes…" and he would startle awake, sweating in fear.

To say that the Feathered One was not a brave man would be an understatement. Bravery had simply never been a necessary attribute for the President of the Wavecrest Archipelago. When DiBello had originally approached him about the conference, his first thought was that it would make a lovely excuse for a feast. Feasting, now, there was something that Palani understood. Although, after today's trials and tribulations, he'd barely been able to consume half his normal evening meal, the rest having been given to feed several large families of beggars.

Palani sighed at the thought of all that wasted food, the sound echoing in the quiet room. For a long moment, there was no sound at all, save for the distant ocean's roar. Palani blinked, straining to hear something. The conversation outside his door had ended, and through his window, there was no sound from the courtyard. Another long moment passed and still no sound came. Where were the guards? A quiet thump came on the second story balcony outside his window, and Palani struggled to sit up, fighting with his sweat-soaked sheets in a growing panic.

The comforting footsteps began from the courtyard below once again, and he sighed in relief. "Getting myself all worked up about nothing."

"There is nothing to be concerned about, gracious Feathered One." The voice from the darkness was softer and somehow kinder than Gerik's, but Palani still nearly fell out of his bed in fright.

"I'm sorry to frighten you, honored President. Please do me the favor of not disturbing your guards? I mean you no harm, I assure you." Swan stepped out of the shadows and into the pale moonlight streaming in through the window, clutching his wounded arm tightly with his other hand.

From his bed, Palani said shakily "Diplomat! Anathema! What do you want of me? How have you come here? We were told you were dead."

Swan ran his good hand through his hair, pushing it back out of his eyes. "And I fear that prediction may still come true very quickly if you do not aid me, sir."

"What do you want?"

"Safe passage away from here, sir. That is all. Once on the mainland, I have some hope of hiding, but here? They will tear your island apart to ferret me out if they believe I am still alive."

Palani imagined a half dozen magistrates, each more fanatical than the next, interrogating him over and over to discover the whereabouts of the Anathema they hunted. "No… no, we can't have that… Can't have them coming again…" he whispered, propping himself up onto one portly elbow as he squinted at Swan in the darkened room. "You must go, now."

"Would that it was in my power to do so, honored President, I would. But I fear that I find myself without the resources to make that happen. It is, after all, a very long swim to the continent, and I am, as you can see, not completely well."

The Feathered One's porcine eyes slipped over the diplomat's disheveled form. He'd obviously been injured, and the diplomat's weakened state gave Palani courage. "Why should I not just call my guards? Why should I not have them seize you and turn you over to the Magistrate's man? You are injured and could hardly defend yourself."

Swan shook his head, slowly. "I fear that I would only cause more destruction to your fair island should you do so, noble one." He paused, looking over the reclining President thoughtfully. "And, should they manage to take me into custody, they would surely confiscate this as well." With his good hand, he placed a cloth-wrapped bundle on the bedside table where it made a dull but heavy metallic clunk.

"What is it?" The greed in the Feathered One's eyes was unmistakable, even in the dim moonlight. He reached for the bundle but pulled his hand back cautiously before touching it.

"An artifact of the First Age, I believe. It belonged to the Magistrate. They surely think it is lost."

Reaching out one pudgy hand, Palani twitched open the cloth and the pendant gleamed brightly, illuminating the room. Quickly, he covered the glowing metal and swept the wrapped necklace onto the bed beside him.

"We must get you away from here. Quickly. No one must know you live." He struggled to pull himself out of his bed, clutching the sweat-stained sheet around him.

"I believe it would be best that way, sir."

Quickly, they wove together a plan. Before the morning sun broke over the eastern horizon, Swan found himself in possession of a full pouch of the President's coins and sequestered aboard the *Swift*, a tiny unmarked ship bound for the North. Ostensibly owned by the family of one of Palani's wives as a courier craft, the *Swift* was a tidy, little three-hulled vessel that had often been employed for covert scouting missions when rumors put the Lintha too close to Abalone Bay for comfort. Swan suspected that it also saw action whenever a merchant ship from one of the other Western islands ventured too close for the Wavecresters to resist a bit of privateering of their eastern shoreline. A single mast towered above the low arch of her three decks, with tiny rooms sequestered below each deck. She was a tricky ship to crew, but the four men assigned to make certain Swan arrived safely at his destination were all experienced with her and handled her with an expert touch.

Days passed into weeks as the *Swift* flew across the Western Ocean. The four crewmembers rarely spoke to Swan, although he did his best to aid where he could, his childhood years in Azure allowing him to gain a fair handiness on shipboard. The last knot of Arianna's sea charm made sure that the winds were with them their entire journey, and they made better time than Swan had imagined possible. But despite his efforts both to aid and to remain out of the crew's way, there was an uneasiness present that made him wonder what they knew or thought they knew about him.

"Dolphins off the starboard bow! We're nearing land!" A few weeks out, they stopped to resupply at one of the tiny islands just off the Blessed Isle. The *Swift* was so small that those on board slept strapped into their tiny sleeping mats, and there was no room allocated for a galley. The crew refilled the water supply and filled the food stores through good-natured negotiation with the Realm shopkeeper who ran the cove. To a man, they returned to the *Swift* with renewed spirits. Swan, however, remained hidden on board the tiny ship, barely breathing until they'd taken to the open sea yet again.

Days passed into weeks that slipped by in relative silence with nothing but the call of sea birds and the clipped orders shared back and forth by the crewmembers to disturb Swan's thoughts. Unlike the larger trireme that cut straight through each wave, the little trimaran dipped deeply in each trough, and her rocking gait lulled Swan into a distracted half-slumber that sometimes lasted for hours. He contemplated what had happened since leaving the mainland, looked for some meaning, some reason behind the chaos into which his life had devolved. Was he supposed to return to Coral and try to help sort out the chaos that DiBello's death would engender? Was he supposed to stay and defend the Western islands against Lintha depredations? Was he supposed to try to find out why the Scarlet Empress' fleets were turning away from their tributary states and returning to their home ports on the Blessed Isle? How would he do any of that? He turned each option over in his mind, examining each choice until he thought he'd drive himself mad with retrospect.

The crew's calls when they finally spotted the White Sea port stirred him from the thoughts that had enveloped him for days. He emerged with only one thing certain. Arianna had been right. Nothing stayed the same. He'd been wrong to think that he could go back to the way things were before he was Chosen.

With the Feathered One's full purse to outfit him for his journey, Swan made preparations to travel north again.

CHAPTER NINETEEN

Ariarina woke as the rising sun heated the dew-damp material of her tent, turning it from comfortable shelter to sauna in moments. She'd situated her cot to remain in the shade as long as possible, but it seemed the slightest touch of sun on the fabric was enough to raise the temperature uncomfortably.

Outside, she could hear the camp bustling. Likely, some of the icewalkers had been awake for hours. She'd been up until the wee hours yet again, trying to make sense of a charm inscribed in the book Yurgen had given her back at the Hold several weeks ago. Chuckling, she looked down at her arm, which had lain across the leather tome while she'd slept and was now marked with the faint pattern from its cover.

Setting the book safely on the small wooden table beside her bed, she fetched her boots from beneath her cot, shaking a shiny black beetle out of one. It was a habit she'd developed after an unpleasant surprise her first morning here. One advantage the colder Northern climes had over the forestlands: far fewer insects.

After dressing quickly, she paused, sitting on the edge of her cot with the carved comb Swan had given her so many months ago held in her hands. As she did every morning when she combed her hair, she cast her thoughts out across Creation, wondering how the young diplomat fared or even if he still lived. As her thoughts wandered, she carefully plaited her hair into the single braid she preferred, tying it off with a bit of wool thread.

Slipping the comb and her red leather book carefully into her traveling bag, along with a wineskin and some dried fruit packaged in an oiled cloth, she stood glancing around for anything she might have forgotten. Today was the day Yurgen had promised to take her to the Manse, and she intended to hold him to his promise. She wrapped her face with the light veils she'd taken to wearing since her arrival here and set out to find him.

Slipping out of the small black silk tent that had been her home since their arrival, Arianna looked around the bustling encampment. Nestled in a wide meadow, the camp was bordered all around by heavy forests and rolling hills and served as the base of operations for all of Yurgen's war efforts. The riding and cavalry horses were corralled at the far end of the long camp, just south of the cooking and dining tents. Both had been set in the area that was most often downwind from the rest of the camp.

Large clusters of round slant-roofed tents had been erected to serve as barracks for those troops who were not currently on patrol or actively fighting on the front lines, as well as the wounded who the healers hoped would return to the front shortly. The portable gers that served the nomadic icewalkers so well in the frozen Northlands had been modified slightly to utilize available materials, but the basic designs had proven as effective against the wind and rain as they had been in fending off the ice and blizzards of their homeland. Only a few high-ranking individuals who desired solitary dwellings used the silk tents with their center pole and staked-out walls. Arianna had opted for one, rather than sharing space with someone else. The silk tents were less sturdy and less spacious, but the privacy they provided was more than worth it.

The smell of breakfast surrounded the encampment. Frying meat, eggs and the thick pine-nut hot cereal popular with the Haltans wafted in the morning air. Yurgen's icewalkers and the other Northern recruits had had to adjust not only to the climate, but also to a substantial change in diet. Northern diets tended to consist almost entirely of meat and milk products, high in fat and protein, with the occasional hardy plant or bark for flavoring. Imported foods were a delicacy, but more often, imports consisted of wines or beers to help while away the long winter nights. Here in the verdant Northeast, plants were everywhere. An astounding variety of fruits and vegetables supplemented the small game, birds and fish to form a more rounded diet. To the icewalkers' tastes, however, the change was not necessarily an improvement.

As Arianna walked across the encampment, a series of hearty squawks filled the air, joined by more human shouts. "Nawt there! No! Nawt like that! Buffoon! You're a waste awf fingers!"

Arianna glanced over to see the cause of the commotion. An ata-heron, almost six feet tall, shifted its weight nervously from one carrot-yellow foot to the other. It ruffled its plumage at the humans around it, obviously irritated. A message harness had been awkwardly placed over the bird's long neck, and one of the men was attempting unsuccessfully to fasten the buckles on it.

"Nawt like that! Under the wing! Nawt over it! The strawp has to go under the wing! How do you expect me to fly with my wing strawpped down?" The bird took a nip at the fumble-fingered man with its long yellow bill, squawking "Imbecile! Hawf-wit!"

Yet another change the Northerners had been faced with were the presence of ata-beasts. Their allied forces had been supplemented by a large number of extremely intelligent animals who could speak as well as most humans. In Halta, these "ata" were treated as citizens. It often took a great deal of effort for the typical Northern tribesman to come to think of a monkey or a bird as an equal, even once the animal had come to trust its new allies enough to begin speaking in their presence. But between the ata-heron's message-carrying and scouting ability and the fighting ability of the allied ata-baboons and ata-tree-pards, soon even the most traditional icewalker had to admit they were a very effective, if disturbing, force to be reckoned with.

A young figure, slight as a boy but with a feminine voice, came running across the camp toward the commotion.

"By Nettie's Needles, man, what are you doing there, trying to maim one of our best scouts?" She pushed the stunned Northerner aside with a strength that was quite out of proportion to her slim build and began twitching the complex harness into place with an expert hand. "Sorry about that, Ardea. You okay? How's that feeling?"

The large bird preened his blue-gray feathers, visibly calming under the handler's skillful care. "It's wawnderful, Ilawni. Thank you. I thawt that brute was going to break my primary shawfts." The heron glared at the man, then nuzzled its long beak against Ilani's arm in a gentle grooming gesture of affection.

Ilani ran a gentle hand down the bird's wing, carefully checking over the large flight feathers nearest the ends. "Everything looks sound. I'll go over the harnessing with him again, Ardea. I'm sorry you got manhandled." She shot a glare at the offending human, who gratefully accepted the gesture as an excuse to slink away.

Harness fitted, the bird took a few ungainly running steps and launched himself into the air, making full use of the open strip of field that had been left unpopulated by tents precisely for this purpose. He made a few lazy circles over the camp then drifted to the north, his huge wingspan slowly growing smaller in the distance until it was almost impossible to see against the clear blue sky.

Arianna watched the ata-heron until she could see him no longer, then returned her attention to the task at hand, namely tracking down Yurgen to make him fulfill his promise.

She found him in the cluster of gers inhabited by his Circle, the group of Solar Exalted who worked as his team and extended family. She was uncertain of the exactly relationship or sleeping arrangements thereof, but it was the most common place to find any of them. Yurgen was currently leaning over a large table outside of the largest ger. The tabletop was thickly scattered with maps and line drawings, and a handful of Haltans were gathered around it, including two human males, a female and a sleek black ata-cat who rested its forepaws on the table to see.

Arianna waited, listening as they discussed the most recent surveillance reports. Yurgen looked up, nodded to her and then returned to his conversation.

"We'rrre expecting rrrreinforcements frrrom the forrrtrrrress at Grrreenhollow to arrrive to supplement ourrr efforrrts herrre within two days." The big cat's growl was difficult to understand at first, but there was no doubt as to the intellect behind it. She gingerly pushed a leaf-shaped block of wood onto the map with her paw, noting the location of the incoming troops. "That should shorrre up any weakness in that flank." Her long tail twitched in thought as she contemplated the maps before her.

Yurgen nodded curtly. "As long as the line holds there until the backup arrives, we should be fine. My main concern is here." He gestured to a small clustering of red cones that drastically outnumbered the green squares in their vicinity. "Linowan has been forcibly conscripting troops in Talinin villages. Reports say some of the villages were entirely emptied of men, women and children alike. We can't keep up with those kind of numbers, even if they do have minimal training."

"Perrrhaps," the ata-cat offered, blinking solemnly. "Perrrhaps we will have to take similarrr actions to maintain ourrr advantage."

Yurgen glanced up at Arianna, running a hand through his gray hair with a frown. "I'll take that under consideration. I don't want our allies in this area to turn against us. At this point, we can't afford to lose their numbers."

He returned his attention to the scattering of blocks and maps before him. "Send Ialden and his units here." He pointed to a small town on the map situated along one of the local rivers. "Have them commandeer what supplies we need, but warn him to not to leave the town without enough to support itself. And not to cause problems with the townsfolk. We may need their assistance soon."

He moved five green wedges into the town area on the map. "Have Ilani coordinate increased aerial scouting in this region." A thick area of forest on the map had several blue threads leading to its edges, but no details on the interior. "I need to know if there are any villages there and where the water's good. If we don't have to pack in water, it will make things that much easier." He regarded the entirety of the tabletop, nodding in satisfaction. "That's all for now. I'll be back by midday tomorrow. Samea will be able to contact me if you need me before then."

The war council broke up, everyone going their own way in ones and twos. Yurgen looked over at Arianna, grinning broadly. "Well, Snow Cat, it's a pleasure to see you here. What's the occasion?"

Arianna nodded, allowing herself a small smile beneath her veils. "I hope I am not interrupting."

"Not at all. Did you have anything to add?" Yurgen looked at her, with such intensity that for a moment Arianna was taken aback.

"I... no. Not really. Other than..."

"Yes?"

"It seems that, if Linowan is conscripting entire villages, if you spoke to the Haltan queen, she might give you permission to do the same in Ardeleth, especially as they aren't technically her people. It may be one of those cases where requesting permission ahead of time may be simpler than seeking forgiveness later."

Yurgen nodded. "You're right. That very well may work. Thank you."

Arianna had prepared herself to be ridiculed for her suggestion. She found Yurgen's complement even more unnerving. She nodded curtly, then turned to look back at the rest of the camp.

"Should we be going then?"

Yurgen seemed confused. "Going?"

Arianna nodded. "Today is the day you promised to take me to the library. Had you forgotten?"

Yurgen's expression slammed closed. "We cannot."

"You promised, Yurgen. You've put me off three times already."

Frowning, the war leader returned his attentions to the maps before him, beginning to roll the first back up into a scroll. "We cannot today. That is all there is to it. I have duties elsewhere."

Arianna's eyes blazed with anger. "I see." Her voice sent a chill dart through the air.

Since their arrival, Yurgen had grown increasingly reluctant to even discuss the library, and today was the final straw. She'd waited for weeks, and she'd wait no longer.

Without another word, she turned on her heel and stalked away.

Being neither icewalker nor Haltan had done much to keep Arianna's status within the camp uncertain. Regardless of whether they understood her relationship to the Bull of the North or not, however, it was obvious he valued her, and no one wanted to upset the white-haired sorceress. This, combined with her own imperious self-confidence, made it a simple matter to demand that Mojin be saddled for her, and within moments of leaving Yurgen's side, she was headed north out of the camp. With a glance over her shoulder, Arianna said a quick prayer of thanks to the Unconquered Sun for the size of the camp and the quick turn in the road that allowed her to be out of sight before anyone could spot her trotting away.

Once around the bend, Arianna set herself to finding the Manse she had heard so much about. While obviously no signs would lead to the building, a tickle began almost imperceptibly on Arianna's skin as she rode. Soft as flower petals, quiet as an insect's hum, Arianna could sense it best when she turned her attention from it, as an elusive star is sometimes best viewed by not looking directly at it. After some moments, a deer track crossed the narrow road, and down its cool depth the gentle charge grew faintly stronger.

The path was narrow and wound around thickets and deadfalls. Arianna was forced to clamber down from her horse and lead it behind her, so thick was the underbrush in places. As they made their way through the undergrowth, Arianna began to notice changes in the woods around them.

At first, the differences were subtle. The trunks on the vine maples along the slim path increased in girth, from as big around as her arm to greater in span than Mojin's chest. Their leaves grew from hand-sized to as big as a parasol. After they'd been walking through the thick wood for quite some time, she looked up and realized that the tent-sized vegetation above her head was another enormous maple leaf. The trees were the same variety as near the road, but here, they grew bigger and broader than she'd ever seen.

"I'm getting close."

On their journey southeast, Yurgen had told her how his scouts had begun to notice changes in the woods around them. "That's how we discovered the Manse," he'd said. "My scouts started noticing something strange in this area. They thought at first they'd stumbled across a Wyld zone, but the changes were too constant. Too regular. I ordered the general patrols to keep an eye on the area but not get too close."

"If the Manse was damaged… or flawed… it might be leaking energy from the Demesne beneath it out into the area around it. There are no villages in the area?" Arianna's research had given her some knowledge of the topic, although she'd never visited a Manse before.

Yurgen had shaken his head. "None. Not for a good day's ride. The closest anyone ever came was to pass by on the road, and it's several miles into the wood from there. Whoever built it valued his privacy."

"That would explain why no one had noticed it before. If it's aligned to wood, rather than one of the other five elements, then it could have literally hidden itself out here with the extra energy it was leaking."

Arianna had little suspected that she'd have to use these few clues to locate the Manse without Yurgen's aid. She paused, looking around. Yurgen had been right. The area wasn't chaotic enough for a Wyld Zone. It didn't have the feeling of insanity and instability that came with brushing against those lands of bedlam. But there was definitely something here. Arianna could feel it tickling stronger at the palms of her hands and down her spine. There was a sparking drive to continue forward, a pining to be united with whatever it was that lay just beyond the next clump of underbrush. She found herself moving forward without realizing it, still deep in thought, urging her reluctant horse through the brush behind her.

A few moments more, and the underbrush opened before her. For a moment, Arianna thought she'd walked out into an open meadow. The floor was shining green, thick with rich grass and scattered with wildflowers. Here and there, verdant shrubs rose up, forming small copses of shelter that fairly begged for one to rest in their shade. The space above her, however, was shining emerald, rather than the blue skies she'd left before entering the wood. The green glow tinted everything in sight, until it was impossible to tell what was stained by lichen and moss and what was merely reflecting the radiance from above.

Arianna craned her neck, seeking the light source, but it seemed to radiate from the entire area overhead. The forest canopy here was so tall that it was impossible to pick out details.

At the center of the vast open area was a tree trunk so broad that it put any of the great redwoods she'd heard of to shame. It stretched up for hundreds of yards, its broad branches seeming to hold aloft the canopy above them.

Around the tree trunk was a curious building, ringing it like a child's fortress built around a giant. It was carved of marble, but rather than shining white, the ornately carved walls glowed with a faintly verdant luminescence.

Several stories tall, the building was constructed not in squares, but in octagons, shapes that were repeated in the open windows and again in the massive front doors. Heavy lichens and mosses grew on the walls, and vines had made their way up many of the vertical surfaces, obscuring some of the angles, but the deliberation put into the architecture was obvious.

As she entered the clearing, she was met by an older man in the green leather uniform of a Haltan soldier. Perhaps a decade past middle age, the soldier's mossy, green-brown hair was held neatly back from his face in a ponytail that trailed halfway down his back. Arianna noted that he wore a talisman against the Fair Folk prominently around his neck. The twisted knot of iron nails hung from a thick leather thong and gleamed as if regularly polished. The soldier approached, warily watching the veiled woman.

"You're not supposed to be here. No one's supposed to be here. Yurgen's orders."

Arianna knew that Yurgen had ordered the core group of scouts who had originally discovered the Manse to remain here on rotating shifts to make certain that no one interfered before he was able to fully explore it. The rest of his men had been told these were guarding a Wyld zone, protecting outsiders from stumbling into it accidentally.

"Yurgen sent me."

The Haltan frowned, uncertain for a moment how to handle this apparent change in orders. Taking advantage of his indecision, Arianna pressed Mojin's reins into his hand. "He'll need water while I'm inside." She breezed past the stunned scout toward the building.

The chittering of squirrels and forest birds that had accompanied her from the road fell silent as she neared the building. The patina-encrusted rings on the front doors held eight angles like the building itself, Arianna noted, rather than being precisely round. She struggled to push open the doors, until, at last, they gave forth. The heavy oak timbers screamed as they grated open on ancient hinges, revealing a foyer that gleamed with a bottle-green phosphorescent glimmer.

The building was only two rooms deep, extending off a corridor that appeared to run the perimeter of the structure. Each room branched off the main hallway, with doorways evenly spaced and alternating, one to the right then another to the left. Straight ahead, the foyer passed through a glassed porch, then opened out into the central courtyard, and even from where she stood, she could see the behemoth roots of the tree that supported the canopy outside.

Once inside with the doors shut behind her, Arianna paused, taking in her surroundings. The floors here were made of the same smooth, greenish marble that the outside of the building was carved from, inlaid with flowers with eight oval petals each. They clustered in groups of two, one of ivory white and one jet black, the stark tones contrasting harshly against the mossy green marble. The vines twined each direction down the hallway, with a set of flowers clustered in front of each doorway. Something about the pattern caught her eye, and she dug out the book Yurgen had given to her weeks before that. The red leather was a dull brown in the greenish light, and she knelt to compare the vines on its cover to the vines on the marble floor, but the patterns were different.

Frowning, Arianna got to her feet and began exploring down the corridor to the left. As she passed, the glow in her area grew slightly brighter, as if sensing her presence. Some of the doors along the hallway stood open. Arianna saw long-abandoned sleeping chambers, washrooms and even a food preparation area, with long tables and a collection of still sharp kitchen implements.

"Curious," she offered to the empty foyer, her voice echoing slightly in the distance. "No fireplaces. Or stoves. Or any sort of heating or cooking devices."

After traveling what seemed to be ten times further than the dimensions of the building should have allowed and finding only sleeping chambers, Arianna found herself at the end of the foyer, facing a pair of great double doors.

"This must be it."

Her hunger for what lay beyond was almost palpable, and it took all her effort to not rush into the room. The door knobs, eight-sided as was the common theme, resisted her effort to turn it for a heartbeat, but as she exerted a bit more leverage on it, it clicked open with a series of mechanical grindings.

The door swung open, revealing a room that had obviously once served as a library or reading room. Across the room, a long-extinguished fireplace took up the entirety of the far wall. Arianna could imagine it, blazing on a winter's night as the room's occupants lounged before it, reading by its light.

Thick carpets covered every inch of the floor and were faded with a layer of dust that dulled their once-brilliant colors. Sofas and chairs clustered in twos and threes but had fared no better in their time of disuse. Arianna took one step into the room, which appeared to have been untouched for perhaps hundreds of years.

Slowly, she turned, taking in the entirety of the room, her eyes growing wider until at last she stood once again facing toward the gaping entrance, shaking with emotion.

The answer struck her as she stared at the doorway, around which twined the same engraved flowers she'd followed up the hallway passage. In that moment of clarity, she'd remembered where she'd seen the pattern decorating the cover of the book in her hand. They were not the eight-petalled Manse-flowers, but the same long-petalled lotus that were carved into the columns and fireplace at Yurgen's hold. She'd been sitting beneath them on the night Yurgen gave her the book and tempted her down here to aid his war efforts. The design on the book's cover was so faint that she hadn't recognized it at the time. The book was not from the Manse at all, but from the Hold library.

Looking around her, she realized why Yurgen had not wanted her to visit the Manse.

"I'll have his hide for this." She turned from the room, leaving in her wake a swirl of dust that settled once again on row after row of empty shelves.

CHAPTER TWENTY

"What do you mean, she's gone?" Swan demanded. "How could she be gone? Where? When?" He couldn't believe what he was hearing. He'd traveled for months, across sea, land and snow, to return to Yurgen's Hold, only to be told that Arianna had left before he'd arrived.

"She's gone with the Bull of the North," came the young woman's cautious reply. She'd answered his pounding on the door a few moments earlier and had had the unfortunate duty of explaining Arianna's absence as they stood in the foyer of Yurgen's great Hold. "They've been gone for... perhaps two weeks."

"No!" Swan slammed a hand against the stone wall in the ornately carved hallway. "No, this is not happening."

Taking a few steps back, the dark-haired woman peered at this young man who had appeared from out of the snow. He had to be Kaudara, the diplomat. His strangely colored eyes and hair were enough to set him apart from the majority of people she'd seen in her lifetime, most of whom possessed darker tones. She'd been informed by Yurgen, as had everyone who remained at the Hold, that it was possible he would arrive searching for Arianna. At the time, he'd sounded as if it were unlikely that the young man would reappear. And yet, here he was.

"If you would like to wait for her return, you are welcome to do so. Yurgen left word that you were to be treated as an honored guest, should you arrive." The young woman gestured to welcome him into the Hold, while staying well out of arm's reach.

Swan shook his head, realizing that his outburst had disturbed his young hostess. He shook his head, apologetically. "I am sorry. You are very kind. It would be good to come in out of the cold." He stepped in through the massive doors, which the young woman pushed shut behind him. She barred them, struggling with a heavy beam of oak. Swan reached out to help her, the bolt swinging easily in his hands.

Swan knew that, during their stay earlier in the year, Yurgen's dark-haired witch had been aiding transport between the Hold and the front line, making sure that troops and supplies were adequately maintained at the main war effort. Journeys of weeks or months were condensed down to a day, with the aid of her magically summoned servant. Its arrival had frightened more than one seasoned warrior, with its lanky clawed legs and bizarre conglomeration of wings. However, the creature proved itself capable of carrying large wagons fully equipped with soldiers, weapons and supplies, and it became clear that it would be invaluable in their efforts in the Northeast. Perhaps, Swan thought, they were still utilizing these methods and would be returning in the near future.

"When will they be back, do you think? Are they expected soon?"

"Not for some time. They took almost everyone with them. All the gliders, most of the supplies. Unless something goes wrong, they said not to expect them until they'd won."

"So you don't have any communication with them?"

"Oh, no... no, we send word by strix every few days, small packages and the like, and they return them about as often. But they go by san-strix, not in great transport wagons like Samea used before they all left."

As a diplomat, Swan had encountered strix before. Larger and more intelligent than their owl cousins, strix could be counted on to deliver small items such as packages and messages over huge distances, flying faster than most courier birds could. They could also be ordered to fly to multiple locations, unlike homing doves and other messenger birds that normally could only be counted on to fly from one set location to another and back.

The next morning he rode out, after having left a message that the young girl promised would go out with the next great owl delivery. The few people still at Yurgen's Hold had attempted to encourage him to stay, but he had not been able to bring himself to wait for what might be months or longer.

The day he left was crisp and clear, cold but bright. As he set out, he found himself filled with a sense of rightness that he had not felt in the months-long sea journey or the several weeks he'd ridden from RimeHaven in search of the former temple in which he'd last seen Arianna. He would find her.

The ride stretched on, days becoming weeks, but the positive feeling never left him. It traveled along with him on his journey, like a comfortable but silent companion, and he found his spirits buoyed by its presence.

His travels took him south and east, out of the stark tundra and through the great grassy plains, rich with flora and fauna. What had looked at first glance to be an endless sea of only grasses revealed itself, as he passed through it, to be home to countless birds and small animals. Once, across the distance, he saw a darkness that he mistook for a large landlocked lake, until it shifted across the horizon, revealing itself to be a herd of plains cattle that must have numbered in the thousands. The ground itself shook with their passing as their massive cloven hooves tore through the grasslands. He instinctively reined in the bay mare who had replaced Eldy upon his return to the mainland, but the placid creature barely looked up from her grazing, unfazed by the moving earthquake. He'd not been able to bring himself to name her. She was a good little mare, but she was not Eldy. He watched the ocean of cattle roll across the plain and thought of the frozen plain outside of RimeHaven, of Eldy and of Arianna.

The grasslands seemed to go on forever, and after several weeks, the advent of the mountains and the great Eastern forests came up almost shockingly quickly, tall and verdant after the golden rolling fields of waist-high prairie grass. Thick groves of ash and oak filled the low mountains like rich green and gold low-hanging clouds, softening the stony heights save for the greatest peaks, which grew bare and snowy. Along the streams, willows and cottonwood stretched their fingerish roots deeply, thirsting for the cool water.

The little bay began to favor one foot late in the afternoon, and they made camp early in a clearing in the center of a massive stand of ancient oaks.

"Easy, girl. We'll get that stone out... just... easy... there!" What appeared to be a small round stone sprung loose from the underside of the horse's dark hoof, landing in Swan's hand. "An acorn. No wonder it hurt." He tossed the nut away, and it bounced a few times before rolling away from the campfire.

Swan swept a few stray bits of debris from the hoof and released the horse's leg, patting her firmly on the withers. "Good girl. I think we got it before it bruised too badly."

A stirring in the air behind him had Swan upright and ready to defend himself before his eyes fully fixed on the cause. What he saw on the other side of the clearing amazed him.

The pesky acorn that had imbedded itself in his mare's hoof had rolled across the small clearing, coming to rest in a small dip in the forest floor. Rootlets and the beginnings of a sapling were extending from it at miraculous speed, questing hungrily for the soil and sky. In heartbeats, the roots had plunged themselves deeply into the thick loam, and the tip of the tiny oak's trunk had stretched as tall as Swan's head. Swan watched in wonder as the tree unfolded, decades of growth passing in seconds. The trunk split, developing a crown of branches, which budded verdantly before his eyes. In moments, the limbs were festooned with vibrant green leaves and then drooped heavily with acorns.

A lively wind picked up through the campsite, feeding the fire, which leapt skyward, sending sparks scattering out into the night sky. Swan snatched up the mare's reins, but she continued cropping a hillock of grass she'd discovered, undisturbed by the unnatural zephyr. Dried leaves separated themselves from the forest floor, dancing on the breeze, which pulled at the new oak tree's branches, summoning a voice from the wood.

"Remember your promise," the tree rumbled, the words sounding as if they came from deep within the earth and up through the ever-expanding trunk. The voice was unmistakably that of the Forest Lord who had aided Arianna and him so many months ago.

"Honored Lord of the Wood. I have not forgotten." Swan bowed low, still clutching his horse's reins.

"Danger comes." The tree shuddered, its limbs convulsing as if in pain. "Peril comes, and all may be lost. You must fulfill your promise. You must prevent the destruction."

"If it is within my power, I will do so. Your debt will be repaid. But whence comes the danger? We are far from the woods in which we met." Swan looked around the clearing, half expecting to see a fleet of axe-wielding warriors emerge from the forest around him.

"Not to my wood comes the menace. Each forest is its own self, and as do your people, we have war between our kinds." The wood thrummed as might an old man, thinking on how to phrase his next sentence. "We also have… alliances… kinships. Once, long ago, all woods were one wood. And then, they were not. The first two forests have warred throughout time, needle against leaf, pine against oak, the Eternal against the Golden Eyed. In time, each has become less, and yet, more. As the forestlands are pierced by road and river, separated by time and distance, the spirits cleave themselves as well. Some are allies. Some are enemies. The Lord of Ironthorn Forest was once a part of this one, or this one was a part of him. Threat comes now. Destruction, down to the roots. It must not happen."

Swan nodded. "A forest fire?" He tried to imagine what could possibly threaten something as massive as the forest he and Arianna had escaped into on their first night.

The tree shook its branches in negation. "Such are a part of the wheel of our lives and not to be feared. Old is made new, seeds are opened by the heat, undergrowth is cleared and new spirits are born from the old. It is not this we dread. The spirit of the forest is only truly lost when all is gone. All life, all spirit, sucked dry like a summer spring that will never run again. It is this we hear on the winds. Change is coming. You must find a way to stop it. The Ironthorn must not die. This I charge you, on your life and your vow."

Swan nodded, although his face was pained. It tore at him, to have traveled halfway across Creation and further to find Arianna and, at the last moment, to be sent off in another direction. But a promise was a promise, and without the aid of the Forest Lord all those months ago, there would no longer be an Arianna for him to seek. He would keep his word. "I will do all within my power, respected Forest Lord. Where will I find the Ironthorn?"

As if in answer, the quaking leaves began to go red, as if autumn had struck them all at once. Gold and russet, they aged on the limb and began separating themselves from the tree. The wind heightened once more, whirling into a small cyclone centered on the forest avatar. The golden leaves danced madly, around and around, as the whirlwind drove them in smaller and smaller spirals. The tree itself began to shrink at the center, until it was once again only a sapling and then little more than a branch erupting from the soil. Even this fell in upon itself until the wind dropped, leaving nothing remaining of the oak at all. Swan walked over to where the tree had stood so briefly and found, on the forest floor, a bronze band forged of linked oak leaves.

Swan lifted it, holding it up to the fire's light. From the center hung a single acorn half the size of his fist. Its cap appeared to be carved of oak heartwood, but the nut itself was shining orichalcum. The gleaming pendant was held fast to the rest of the necklace between two tiny bronze boars' heads. Each eye glittered with a crimson stone, dark and red as a drop of blood.

"Beautiful. But I'm not sure how this will aid me in finding—"

Swan's words cut off as the acorn pulled sharply to the south, tugging in his hands as if it were a bird yearning to take flight.

"Oh. Well, that explains it." Swan looked around at the campsite, and his bedroll laid out enticingly on the soft forest floor. "I don't suppose I could just sleep for a few hours first?"

The pendant almost leapt out of his hands, jerking sharply to the south. "Somehow, I didn't think so." He slipped the necklace over his head, where it rested across his shoulders, the acorn hanging in the middle of his chest.

His gear was packed within moments, and he set out through the dark forest, following the now-gentle draw to the south.

CHAPTER TWENTY-ONE

"This can't wait, Lord Yurgen. It's bad." The messenger looked as if he wanted nothing more than to escape back out of the tent, but he steadfastly remained.

Cursing, Yurgen slapped his hand down on the camp table, which shattered into splinters under his wrath. He frowned and pulled himself to his feet. "This conversation is not over."

Arianna regarded him coolly. "You may continue talking as long as you'd like. My decision will not change." Since returning from the Manse a week ago, Arianna had refused to speak to him. He'd barged into her tent this afternoon, unwilling to be put off any longer. Their conversation had not gone well.

The courier was almost bowled over as Yurgen stormed out of the tent. Separated only by a thin layer of tent silk, Arianna could hear their heated conversation as clearly as if they had remained inside.

"Well?" Yurgen growled. "What is so important that you had to interrupt me against my orders?"

The messenger's voice was a shaking thread. "It's Mors Ialden, sir, and the troops at Krellen Ford."

"And? Don't tell me they encountered much resistance from the Fordfolk? They didn't even have an armory. We had good reports on the entire city."

"Not from the townsfolk, Bull of the North. Realm forces. Four dragons worth, from the reports we've gotten.

Maybe a dozen Dragon-Blooded, including a handful of sorcerers. They caught the troops while they were… resupplying." His voice was grave.

"And?"

"It's not good, sir. The men just weren't ready for that kind of resistance. They'd been expecting the first lance of Realm forces to attack the main body of the army head on, not a resupplying mission. It was chaos for a while. Finally, Ialden ordered the cavalry to stand their ground to cover the retreat. We got most of the footmen out, but we lost all the supplies and most of the cavalry, horses and men both. Maybe a tenth were able to regroup afterward."

"By the Sun's Saber. Where are they now?" Yurgen's gruff growl fairly shook the ground in the area.

"Latest reports say they're heading to rendezvous with Samea's troops. The cavalry stalled the main body of the enemy long enough for them to get a good start. They're hoping to hook up with Samea's group before the imperials are able to catch up."

"Well, that's something. Send word to Samea to move to intercept them, as quickly as possible. Tell her to be discrete. Maybe we can convince the hounds at their heels to come all the way into the snow hunter's den in their hurry to catch the fleeing hare."

Arianna listened to the master tactician in grudging admiration. They'd been anticipating the arrival of Realm troops for several months now. The strong likelihood of the Empress' interference here had been one of the reasons they'd moved the vast majority of their forces here to the front. Or so Yurgen had said. Since she'd discovered the truth about the Manse, she had begun to question both his motives and his word.

"Send a message to Ilani. Let her know that we need to have some of those talking bird folk focus their attention there. The monkeys and cats too. Anything that can get in, get us information and get out without being suspected. Have them keep an eye on the situation and report in frequently with locations, numbers, changes in course.

Anything that might help us get back at those Dragon-Bastards. We will not let this go unanswered."

Murmuring assurances, the courier's footsteps disappeared further into camp. Yurgen paused a long moment before reentering Arianna's tent. His mood had sobered greatly, and his temper appeared at least momentarily under control. He began pacing, studiously avoiding the pile of shattered wood at the center of the tent.

"You heard?"

She nodded. "I did."

"This is why I brought you here, Arianna. Not for personal gain and not for your delightful company."

Arianna frowned, leveling an icy glare his direction.

"If we have any hope of establishing a foothold here, of resisting the destruction they have thrown down on us from that Sun-forsaken Isle for the past seven hundred years, we must overcome them with force. We must speak to them in the only language they understand. Negotiations cannot work. They have established that we have no voice, and who will listen to those with no tongue? Treaties will not work. They do not recognize us as anything but abominations and demon-spawn. They will not make treaties with us until they realize that we are their equals, if not their betters. The only language they will hear is the language of war."

"We were in agreement, Bronze Tiger." The old title sliced through the air, heavy with scorn. "There was no reason for you to deceive me."

Yurgen shook his head and looked away. "Yes, the tome I gave you was from the Hold's library. I admit I had held it back when I gave you access to the rest. Samea wasn't sure she wanted you to have some of the spells in it, until she knew you better and was sure you were on our side."

Arianna frowned, but understood Samea's concern. She'd been amazed at the broad expanse of knowledge held in that single small tome. Spirit-binding, scrying over great distances, summoning elemental forces. She'd learned more from that one tome than any 10 in the rest of the Hold put together. She'd understood the pair not wishing to reveal everything to her. But when she'd seen the empty room at the Manse, the one that supposedly had held hundreds of such books, she'd known the depths of Yurgen's deceit.

Yurgen continued explaining away his misdeed. "And then, when they found the Manse, it seemed like just the tidbit to whet your hunger. Maybe it wasn't right to lead you to believe the book was from the Manse's library. But it was effective. You would not have come on your own. I needed every Child of the Sun here, at the front. If I hadn't tempted you with the possibility of new knowledge, you would have remained in the Hold, studying until you froze to death, while the rest of us sacrificed ourselves. It was necessary."

Arianna considered his words carefully. In her journeys with Swan, she'd become accustomed to the truth, despite a lifetime of expecting only lies and pain from those around her. It should not have surprised her that Yurgen had lied to her. She hadn't realized until just then how much her interactions with Swan had changed the way she saw the world around her.

"I won't be lied to, Yurgen. Not by those who are not my enemy. We can't build a new truth on a foundation of lies. For centuries, the Dragon-Blooded have justified their Hunts with half-truths. We must be better than that if we hope to change things. The light of the Unconquered Sun will shine through, but not if we shade it in lies. Not to them. And certainly not to each other."

"Some things must be done, even if we do not like them, to achieve our goals," Yurgen stated firmly, his jaw set.

"Your goals, Bronze Tiger. I no longer know if yours and mine are the same."

Yurgen glared, his heavy gray eyebrows furrowing together.

"I have much to consider. If you have nothing more to say?" She turned her attention coolly back to the book in her lap.

Yurgen growled and strode to the tent's exit, then turned to glare at her with a ferocity she could feel without looking up.

"Our fates are intertwined, Snow Cat. Not just yours and mine, but all of the Chosen of the Sun. You sit here, with your books to hide in and my warriors around you, and you feel safe to taunt me. But before you decide your goals are no longer ours, think about what it is really like out there. The Empress might have withdrawn and holed up for the moment, but she will be back, and with her, the Wyld Hunts will return in full force. There is no safety for the likes of us. Not until we change things. Remember that."

Yurgen stormed out of the tent with a gesture that said he would have slammed the tent flap had it been possible.

Arianna looked up from her book, watching the tent's sole entry for a long moment. She knew there was truth in Yurgen's words. Things must change. But how much damage and destruction would be necessary to bring those changes about? She glanced at the shattered table, its splinters littering the tent floor. How much indeed?

She waited for a long moment to make certain he was truly gone and then began to pack her gear. She wasn't certain where she would go now. Perhaps she'd try the West. She'd read much about the Western islanders' native magics in the past months. Perhaps she'd even track down Swan.

She paused, cloak in hand. It had been almost half a year since Swan had left the Hold in the Northlands. And she'd been the one who had warned him about how dangerous it was to return to his home. How impossible it was to return to a past that was no longer his. In all likelihood, he'd fallen already, victim of a Wyld Hunt or some fanatical Immaculate monk. And yet, the first place she'd thought to return was to his side. Now, who was unwilling to let go of the past?

"Excuse me please?" A voice came from outside of her tent, stirring her from her morose thoughts.

"Come in." It was late for lunch and early for dinner. Who else would bother her?

The young ata-beast worker, Ilani, stepped in to the tent with a small scroll tube in her hand. "I'm sorry to…" She paused, eyeing Arianna's packing. "Are you leaving, then?

Glad this got to you before you were sent out." She held out the message case.

Arianna took it, asking curiously. "For me?"

The young woman nodded. "It was in with some of the packages in our last strix shipment from the Hold. Sorry I didn't get it to you 'til now. It had gotten wedged between two packages of medicine and didn't get found 'til just now."

Arianna looked down at the case curiously as Ilani slipped back out of the tent.

She broke the seal and stared at the small slip of vellum in amazement.

"Dear Arianna," it read. "I hope this reaches you. I returned to Yurgen's Hold but you had already gone. I am heading southeast. Hope to find you there." It was signed "Swan" but the name had been crossed out, and "Your Diplomat" had been scrawled in its place in the same hand.

Arianna slowly began unpacking.

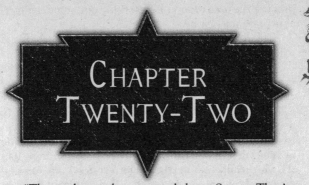

CHAPTER TWENTY-TWO

"The ata-herons have spotted them, Samea. They're less than a mile out, just beyond the pass in the western foothills." The young man was out of breath, and his report came between shallow gasps.

"Will they make it?" The hill he'd found her on protruded above the thick tree line, with only a few sturdy birches enduring at its peak. From here, she'd spent the last few hours scanning the western horizon, looking for some sign of the expected troops and their pursuit. Past the valley, however, Ironthorn Forest obscured everything else from view.

Samea's aide shook his head, frowning. "It's going to be close. They're exhausted, and some of the wounded are slowing them down. I'm not sure they will."

The barbarian witch ran one hand through her dark hair, pulling it back out of her eyes before looking over at her assistant solemnly.

"Send one of the ata-strix to intercept Ialden. Tell him I'm sending him a short cut and to be ready to take it. It won't last long."

The aide looked confused but nodded. "Sending a short cut. Be ready. Won't last long. Got it."

Samea nodded, gesturing for him to hurry back down the heavily forested hill to the valley where the rest of her troops waited for the ambush. Her mind was already probing the area around her, seeking out an uncomfortable presence nearby.

"Florivet, I call thee." She reached out with words and will, summoning the demon to her.

Across the craggy hilltop, the wind picked up briskly. It swirled around her, catching teasingly at her skirt and caressing her skin, sweeping her hair across her face like a lover's caress. The whirlwind carried a scattering of dancing white feathers along with the golden birch leaves that blanketed the peak. One moment she was alone, the next another shared the hill with her. Barely shorter than the white trunks around them, Florivet stood, arms crossed over his broad bare chest and smiled wolfishly down at Samea. He stretched languidly, shaking out his snowy feathered wings.

"I hear your call, little witch, and for the moment, it pleases me to travel here." His voice was rich and slightly raspy, with a predatory edge. He sounded amused.

"My troops were set out to draw in the Realm forces to our ambush. But they may not have sufficient speed remaining to escape being slaughtered before the trap is sprung."

The demon nodded, barely containing his smug pleasure. "So I had noted."

"You will provide them a passage out of harm's way. You will do so only after they are past the bend in the southern road that will hide them from the sight of those who pursue them." Samea's tone was firm.

"Gladly, gladly. It would be my pleasure." The demon's lupine grin broadened, top lip curling up to reveal a muzzle full of gleaming sharp teeth.

"And the passage will take them directly here to this hilltop, where they will depart it as sound and sane as they entered it."

The demon's grin dropped, replaced by an irritable scowl.

"It does me no good for my troops to be whisked out of harm's way only to end up 10 miles out to sea or Elsewhere. They will be taken here, directly and unharmed."

Florivet grimaced again, his plans spoiled. "You are boring me quickly, little witch. Why should I do this for you?"

"It is only by my will you are here, do not forget that. Our bargain stands. You are welcome in Creation at my summoning—and only until your services are no longer necessary."

"Or until I get bored," the winged wolf spirit interrupted.

"You are free to return to Malfeas, should you wish, but you will not find the passage back to Creation so easy without my call." Samea smiled warmly. "And I have reason to believe that the Realm forces carry with them a variety of Blessed Isle wines. But if my men are slaughtered before we can spring the trap, we will never know."

The demon smiled again, ivory fangs gleaming in the afternoon sun. "Very well. For the sake of a new vintage, I will do as you request. But I warn you, little witch: I bore of this petty war."

Wrapping his owl-feathered wings around him like a voluminous cloak, Florivet took a step to the right and passed into nothingness. The swirling wind that had ruffled the hilltop dropped off immediately. Samea had long since ceased to be amazed at his showy entrances and exits, and she turned her attention back to the valley below her, where her troops were arranged.

The horses were corralled against the base of the hill she had climbed earlier that afternoon, with a half-circle of the round nomadic tents scattered around them. The supply wagons and kitchen tent had been set up at the base of the same hill, near the bank of the river that lazily drifted around the northern edge of the hill she was watching. To the idle observer, the valley seemed to be a lazy encampment. Nothing could have been further from the truth. The barracks were empty, save for a few soldiers scattered here and there to preserve the illusion of leisure. The majority of her mortal troops were arranged in the thick woodlands surrounding the meadow, and she was certain that their attention was focused on the southwest corner of the camp where a lone road wound through a narrow pass through the westernmost foothills and on north directly through the meadow.

It was down that road that the small volunteer force had ventured two days ago, and it was from that same road they were returning, albeit a bit more slowly and with worse injuries than she had expected. Reports were that they had encountered almost a dozen of the massive mechanical warstriders, along with half of the human troops remaining from the group that had ambushed Mors Ialden's party in Krellen Ford two weeks before. The other half had apparently pulled back to form a fortified base encampment, reassured by their easy victory at the ford.

But what worried Samea most was not the war machines or the mortal army, but what strengths they might have yet unrevealed. Unless they were foolishly exerting themselves, Exalted individuals often did not look significantly different from their mortal counterparts, especially to avian scouts who were flying hundreds of feet in the air above enemy camps. She knew for a fact that she'd destroyed at least four of them among the full army that had followed Iaden's Haltan forces up from the massacre at Krellen Ford and another pair who had uncharacteristically stayed behind to allow their comrades to escape when the celestial lions and Florivet had proven too strong for them. But she had to assume that the Empress had sent at least a dozen Dragon-Bloods with the troops she'd deployed here, and perhaps five or six could remain with this half of their forces. She feared the number might be significantly higher.

From the southeast, several hundred yards into the wood, a bright white semicircle appeared through the tops of the thick tree canopy. It shimmered, extending down through the branches like the top of a great gleaming stained-glass window.

"Subtlety is not your strong point, Florivet." Samea scowled, shaking her head and scanning the skies over the camp. From just beyond the glowing portal, a white owl winged low over the treetops, starkly contrasting against the deep greens of the forest. The message had been delivered.

To her left, a glowing doorway appeared, twenty feet tall and half as wide. Its top edge was rounded, a twin to the one in the distance. From the swirling luminescent surface of the door stumbled a pair of bewildered looking Haltan soldiers. Both were obviously tired, confused and worse for the wear. Quickly behind them came another pair and then another, until the small hilltop was crowded with warriors, some injured and being supported or carried by their companions. Lastly, Mors Ialden stepped through the portal, frowning. The rogue Dragon-Blood had started as a devoted commander under Yurgen, leading his Haltan forces with great ferocity. Since the rout at Krellen Ford, however, he had grown more and more solemn, and Samea worried that his morale was dropping dangerously low. His white hair had come loose from its customary braid down his back, and his elk-skin shirt and leggings were stained with sweat and blood. Over his shoulder, one of the Haltan soldiers under his command hung limply. Ialden set the unconscious man down carefully, looking around to get his bearings as the gleaming doorway popped shut behind him.

Samea did a quick head count. Out of the fifty fighters they'd sent out, only thirty-eight returned, and of those, seven were being carried or mostly supported by others. None of them were without injury.

"That's everyone?"

Ialden nodded, gravely. "Would have been far fewer if you hadn't sent that short cut. They were almost on us. Powell and Vacco stayed behind to allow the rest of us to get around the bend and through the portal without being spotted."

Samea sighed. "They will be remembered." She turned her attention back to the valley.

Now all there was to do was hope the enemy hadn't noticed their prey was no longer in front of them. They did not have long to wait.

CHAPTER TWENTY-THREE

The acorn was more insistent than ever, and Swan nudged his mare into a trot southward to keep the necklace from pulling him forward over the saddle horn. They'd made good time, thanks in part to the supernatural draw of the pendant. This morning, the urging to leave started before dawn, pulling him out of his bedroll and into the cool morning air, and its tugging had grown only more frantic as the morning passed. They'd been riding through thick woods for several days now, and Swan hoped the increased urgency was a sign that they were nearing Ironthorn Forest.

He heard the battle before he saw it. Or rather, he felt it. The crashing rumble of something immensely heavy impacting repeatedly with the forest floor shook its way up through his mount's legs and almost tossed him from the saddle. He coaxed her a bit faster, with a frantic prayer to the powers that be that he had not arrived too late.

As the road curved, a tall hill emerged, its craggy peak thrusting up out of the heaviest part of the tree line. Along the top, a group of men in forest green gathered among the bare birch trees that stuck out of the rocky crest like sparse hair on a balding monk's head. Their attention was focused on the opposite side of the hill, and the acorn urged Swan onward.

The road opened out onto a wood-bordered meadow. At the edge of the clearing closest to him, a double handful of Northern-style tents were pitched, forming a half-circle that bordered the river beyond on each end. The banners that flapped in the afternoon wind marked them as belonging to Yurgen's army. Within the circle of gers, a corral of irritated horses stomped and nickered their frustration at being penned, although their complaints were barely audible over the rumbling din coming from the valley beyond. Among the stocky Northern browns and bays and the lankier Haltan ponies with their mossy green coats was a singular steed, gleaming silver in the clear sunlight.

"Mojin!" And where Mojin was, Arianna was bound to be near.

Mojin reared up on his hind legs, calling out his challenge to whatever it was that threatened the makeshift herd that he'd obviously claimed as his own. The horses' attention was focused just beyond Swan's range of sight, and he spurred his little mare forward again.

The chaos in the meadow was dumbfounding. As he galloped in seeking Arianna, he was faced with a full force of imperial troops who were charging into the clearing from the opposite end. The imperial soldiers thundered into the clearing through the narrow mountain pass, spreading out into their orderly battle ranks, twenty five to a scale, five scales to a talon, two talons to a wing, two wings to a dragon. A full flight of six dragons arrayed themselves on the field, heavy and medium infantry and a small amount of skirmishers, along with a dozen or more individuals who did not wear the imperial uniform. They settled into the glade with military precision, then paused, seemingly confused at the lack of active targets present.

Beyond them, barely visible around the rolling foothills, a handful of Dynasty warstriders stood like elegant giants in full armor, gleaming in the late morning sun. Armed with swords that stretched more than 10 feet long, the warstriders stood at the ready, prepared to move forward. Swan had never seen more than three of the ancient First Age machines in one place at the same time, and then, only for imperial parades of state. To see this many in battle was heart-stopping. The average Dragon-Blooded warrior might devastate a full scale of human soldiers in a matter of minutes. While harnessed into a warstrider, that devastation could be easily doubled, and Swan could imagine this group destroying Yurgen's entire human army before the night fell. Other than a few workers who scattered at the first arrival of the imperials and the small gathering on the hilltop with Samea, however, Yurgen's army was nowhere to be seen.

From the top of the craggy eastern knoll behind him, a blinding golden flash filled the sky, accompanied by a bone-chilling war whoop that swept down over the wooded forest and across the meadow. The sound dived down the back of Swan's chain mail shirt like an icy serpent. All attention focused on the hilltop.

Highlighted by brilliant gold, Samea stood barefoot on the peak. She wore only a simple wool tunic that did not quite reach her knees, and her hair streamed around her, unbound. At her feet, a gentle whirlwind stirred the fallen birch leaves around her feet, giving her the illusion of being buoyed up on a golden cyclone. She threw back her head and again gave the undulating war cry that had sent shivers down Swan's back.

As if summoned by her call, a host of Samea's army emerged from the thick woodlands surrounding the meadow, heralding their arrival with a volley of thrown weapons and a resounding echo of war howls. Hundreds of the imperial soldiers fell to their missiles, even before the two armies exchanged their first hand-to-hand blow. The remaining forces tightened their ranks, forming up into shield walls that slowed the Northern force's initial impact.

And then, the madness began.

As the mortal armies continued hacking and hewing at each other with dread efficiency, another battle began, over and around them. A force of Terrestrial Exalted entered the glade behind the uniformed army, ranging around the perimeter of the clearing as they came. Dressed in gleaming armor, these elemental warriors did not deign to turn their attentions to the simple human combat before them. Their attention was riveted on the glowing witch on the opposite hill.

Behind them, the first warstrider marched regally into the glade. Three times larger than the tallest warrior in either army, it towered above the combat. Its armor gleamed, inset with verdant jade and inscribed with intricate sigils. The helmet swung from left to right, the thin eye slit offering little in the way of peripheral vision to the Dragon-Blooded warrior inside the great suit. When its search discovered Samea, still glowing on the hilltop, it began to hike the craggy peak, wading through the ancient trees that reached only to its chest.

Swan's pony screamed in fear as the great mechanized suit of armor strode forward up Samea's hill, and for just a moment, he was back in time, his mare protesting as Eldy had so many times, the dangers he put her into. He leapt off the little bay's back, hauling down on her reins to bring her rearing back to earth. Mojin answered that scream with a blown-out snort, and the mare calmed immediately. The gray gelding pranced nervously back and forth along the far wall of the corral, returning his attention back to the forest beyond the western hill.

"She's that way, is she?" Getting closer to Mojin risked a deadly kick from those black hooves, but he seemed Swan's best opportunity to find Arianna. Since the gelding seemed to hate everyone and everything else in Creation, if he wanted to go somewhere, it seemed likely it was to Arianna. Slowly, Swan began making his way around the corral to the gate.

From the hilltop, a ball of molten flame arced over the clearing. It exploded with an echoing boom as it hit the ground just in front of the western road. The fireball impacted directly in front of a second warstrider entering the clearing behind the first. The gigantic set of armor was knocked backward, toppling into the thick forest with a cannon-like boom. The trees beneath it shattered, sending wooden shrapnel in a wave of destruction that paid no heed to which uniforms its victims wore. The screams of anguish were only heightened as the original fireball sprouted ten squirming tentacles and began flailing about itself in a violent frenzy.

Swan reached the gate, leading his little bay by the reins as he slipped up to undo the simple rope binding the corral closed. He'd just begun to lift the latch when the horses, including his own, turned as one, all attention focused on the battle. Swan blinked in momentary confusion, but only for a moment, before the nearest horses began kicking down the lowest spot in the corral and the herd vaulted the ruin. Within moments, the entirety of the herd, including his own docile little bay, were breaking into a full gallop and bearing for the north side of the western foothills.

For an instant, he was dragged in surprise and then remembered to let go of the reins, leaping out of the way to avoid being trampled by the flood of horses that suddenly seemed intent on making their way at full speed to the west.

Nor were they the only animals who had apparently decided to enter the fray. Swallows, herons, owls, ducks and geese filled the sky, swarming in a giant flock over the western hills. Monkeys brachiated through the tree canopy, flooding across the clearing to return to the treetops on the western side, intent on the same destination.

The horses ran directly for the river that curved around the north side of the foothills, and for a moment, Swan feared they would try to ford it and swim upstream en masse. Instead, a narrow deer path revealed itself as they neared the wood and the horses ran single file, never slowing, following the path as if they'd made the trip every day of their lives. Swan watched the little bay disappear along with the others deeper into the forest.

Remembering how Arianna had called Eldy to her on the road to RimeHaven, Swan slowly began to make his way across the clearing in the direction the herd had disappeared, hoping that perhaps she had summoned the entire herd to her. Beyond the scattered cover of the gers, the battle had begun to rage in earnest. As Swan began slipping north after the horses, however, the acorn pendant around his neck protested, physically jerking itself out of his shirt and pulling him toward the warfare at the center of the valley. Swan turned, assessing the battles, trying to envision what exactly he was supposed to be doing there to serve the Forest Lord's purpose.

In the center of the clearing, the phalanxes of imperial soldiers defended themselves against the onslaught of Samea's mixed band of Northern and Haltan warriors. The grass beneath them was churned to gory mud, and the smell of death filled the glade. Blazing missiles volleyed back and forth from the meadow to the craggy hilltop where Samea still stood as Exalted warriors carried out their own battle over the top of the mortal skirmish.

Beside her, a pair of identical golden lions standing at least eight feet tall at the shoulder paced back and forth along the bluff, waiting for the sword-wielding warstrider that was making its way up the hill. As the war machine broke through the last of the forest and quickly climbed the crest of the hill, the lions turned on it in unity. As one, they unleashed a mighty roar that struck the warstrider like a battering ram, shattering its armor and physically knocking the giant backward off the edge of the hilltop. The thunderous crash of the warstrider collapsing into the forested hill shook the entire valley. Unimpressed by the destruction they'd caused, the lions continued their patrol of the craggy hilltop as a squad of Samea's warriors swept down to finish off the warstrider's pilot before he could return the magical machine to its feet.

On the valley floor, a Dragon-Blooded sorcerer wearing armor that seemed to be woven of pure flame turned his attention to the Samea's hill. Shouting incantations that were inaudible over the din of battle, he wove intangible patterns in the air before him and then stepped backward as a trio of sparks winked into being. With an imperious flourish, he gestured to the hilltop where Samea stood.

The witch had not been idly watching the combat below her. At the western road where her first fireball had impacted, a great magma kraken had sprung forth from the ground, its molten tentacles flailing at any Dragon-Blood it could reach with its broad grasp. Her concentration focused its efforts, and as she gestured fluidly, first one tentacle and then another began a more sentient decimation of selected targets in its area. Her silent dance of direction led the lava arms to grasp one armored opponent and throw it into the center of a wing of uniformed Realm soldiers, sending them sprawling like tenpins in a children's game. With another gesture, a centuries-old tree was uprooted and swung like a burning broadsword, clearing a swath around the magma kraken of all foes.

So great was Samea's concentration that she did not notice the approach of the embers that flew swiftly up the hilltop like fiery hummingbirds. The lions snapped at the sparks, which swirled out of their golden jaws before they could be consumed, darting toward Samea.

Swan watched the fire sorcerer's gaze follow his summoned servants' flight, gloating in obvious relish as they eluded the golden spirits. The acorn tugged insistently around Swan's neck, pulling him toward the sorcerer. He crept nearer, staying to the cover of the tents when he could, although there was a great expanse past the cluster of tents where he would be fully exposed to attack.

Over the clamor of warfare, the roar of an inferno belched forth so loudly that Swan paused in his approach. From the craggy hilltop, three pillars of flame exploded skyward, consuming the dry ground cover around them so quickly that the flames barely flickered before the leaves turned to ash. The bare birches began to catch fire like gigantic candles, and within seconds, the entire hilltop was alight.

Samea was pinned between the columns, hair crackling in the fiery updrafts. She looked around frantically, obviously surprised by the appearance of the inferno around her. The lions charged the fire, but their jaws snapped ineffectively through the blazing intangibility, and their gleaming claws had no effect on the flames.

Swan crept nearer as the sorcerer directed the elementals from the valley. The portly sorcerer wore no helmet over his armor, allowing Swan to witness him cackling in glee as Samea's hair and clothing began to char and smolder. She struggled to escape to safety, her magics momentarily forgotten in the panic of the blazing flames.

From behind Samea's attacker, a strange creature stepped out of seeming nothingness. Looming several feet over the Dragon-Blood, the creature wore a feral snarl on its muzzle and ruffled huge white wings in dismay. Its voice carried with unnatural clarity.

"I'm not done with her yet," the demon said petulantly as it reached out and twisted the sorcerer's neck around backward with a meaty snap. The unblinking stare of the Dragon-Blood apparently amused the hound-demon, whose upper lip snarled back into a predatory grin. He looked around, and spying Swan's stealthy approach, chuckled fiendishly.

"Don't make them like they used to, now do they?" With a final glance at the dead sorcerer whose flame armor slowly faded to dull rust, the demon dropped the body and stepped backward, disappearing into nothingness again.

Swan stepped over to the body sprawled at awkward angles on the grass. A gleeful cackle not unlike the dead sorcerer's rolled down from the hilltop. Unfettered by their master's death, the fire spirits had taken a more humanoid form and given up on tormenting the uninteresting woman who had crouched into a tight ball to protect herself from their flames. Fascinated by the tinder-like qualities of the birch trees, the elementals began to consume the trees with a rabid ferocity. Their fire spread to the dry canopy of the tree line lower down the hill, running across the treetops with a speed of which a tree-pard would have been proud.

Samea stood uncertainly, shaking her charred hair back out of her face. Angry blisters pocked her skin with red, and raging sparks filled her eyes as she watched the fire elementals consume the hill and spread out hungrily toward the rest of the forest. Smoky clouds filled the air as the greener wood of trunks and underbrush began to submit to the fiery ministrations of the spirits. She looked down into the valley, eyes drawn to the fallen sorcerer at Swan's feet and frowned, shaking her head. She mouthed inaudible words that surely condemned Swan as a fool, crediting him with the sorcerer's untimely death, before turning her attention back to the battle.

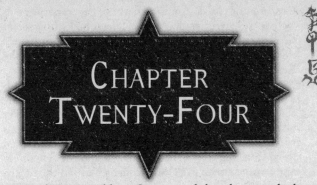

CHAPTER TWENTY-FOUR

Looking around him, Swan noted that the acorn had ceased its insatiable tugging. He stood numbly amid the growing devastation, uncertain how to proceed.

"They're almost here. Ialdens' group is past already. They're on his troop's heels."

The olive-skinned young man called down to Yurgen from where he balanced on what was, to Arianna's eyes, an impossibly thin aspen branch, terrifyingly high up in the tree canopy. The regular rumbling steps of the incoming warstriders caused the branch to swing wildly, but the young man did not appear to be concerned, as much at home in the treetops as the petite green monkey that clung to his shoulder. The Haltans, with their ease in the forest treetops, had proved more valuable than she could have imagined in the past few weeks, but she still wasn't completely comfortable with their agility in the canopy.

It seemed impossible that it was only two weeks ago that they'd set out. Word had come regarding Samea's troops intercepting Mors Ialden's retreating men. Although she'd devastatingly turned the tide of that retreat and sent the imperials that had chased them up from Krellen Ford packing, many losses were taken on both sides. The day, however, was undoubtedly won by Samea's army.

Yurgen, buoyed by the victory, decided to take the battle directly to the Empress' army. Arianna had been against direct confrontation with the Dragon-Blooded foes, arguing the destructive power of the warstriders, as well as the sorcerers that Ialden's men had witnessed at Krellen Ford. Yurgen refused to reconsider until she'd suggested using guile rather than brute force to defeat the Realm army.

With the aid of the ata-herons and ata-tree-pards who served as scouts, they'd laid their ambush in the thickly wooded Ironthorn Forest, sending out two leaves worth of Haltans who volunteered to bait the imperials back into the clearing where Samea's forces would fall on them from the trees. Yurgen, herself and the remaining army would sweep in behind from a chasm in the northern woods, in theory trapping the imperials between the pinchers of their attack. They'd found a small niche in the thick forest, along where the narrow river ran, and they'd been waiting for the enemy to pass so they could slip out and surprise them from behind.

Arianna ticked off the battle plan in her head yet again. Since they'd laid these plans, she'd been studying harder than ever, researching charms and spells that would most help the battle. She didn't trust Yurgen, but he had raised some valid points. There had to be a line, a point at which they, as the Children of the Unconquered Sun, would no longer accept the wanton genocide that had been inflicted upon them for the past centuries. And if she wished to be a part of the future beyond that point, she had to be prepared to shed whatever light she could in the darkness that would surely come when the Scarlet Empress and her Immaculate Order truly realized the threat that an organized force of Solar Exalted could pose to her hierarchy.

Samea's call came over the hill, jostling Arianna from her deep thoughts. She glanced over at Yurgen who grinned ferally and echoed Samea's cry in a voice that sent shivers down Arianna's spine.

Concentrating her power, Arianna called forth to the animals of the area, demanding their aid in the upcoming battle. It was a spell she had found while

studying in Samea's library and one she'd hoped would
prove useful in the fauna-rich forest environment. Her
tongue slipped over the unfamiliar words of the spell
adroitly, and the air around her filled with a howl that
emanated not from her throat but from the power she
called to her. Yurgen and his men looked back at her,
obviously impressed, and then continued forward on
their attack as planned, leaving her to her sorceries.

Within moments, a huge flock of wild birds had lit
in the trees around her. She could hear, in the forest,
animals of all sizes congregating. Green-pelted monkeys
began appearing in the upper branches, chittering nervously as a pair of large tigers prowled silently into the
glade beneath them.

From the other side of the foothills, the battle sounded
as if it had begun in earnest. The steady booming of the
warstrider steps had become a more random syncopation as
the giant war machines entered the fray. Explosions rocked
the ground, again and again, and the smell of smoke began
to filter through the thick forest. Less loud, but perhaps more
distressing, were the occasional screams heard over the din,
often cut off in mid-note.

A thundering of hoof beats cascaded up the narrow deer
track to the southeast of where Arianna stood. Mojin led the
mismatched herd of horses into the small glen. His tall silver
form with dark markings at his feet, neck and tail, stood out
in strong contrast to the stocky little brown Northern ponies
favored by the icewalkers and to the native Haltan horses,
with their silver-green coats and mossy manes and tales.
They filled the glade, stomping and nickering at the sight of
so many forest predators in once place, but there was no
open dissent between the animals.

The time had come. There was no sign of Yurgen's force
on the trail that led toward the road. Arianna swung up onto
Mojin's bare back and adjusted her veils to cover her hair
and face almost completely. Only her bright blue eyes
sparkled clearly beneath the veils as she called out her
orders, using words to focus the mental commands.

"Winged ones! Distract the tall ones!" She envisioned the warstriders, with their vulnerable helmet slits. As fast as thought, the birds took flight in a great cloud of cacophony, heading for the battle.

"Hunters, feast on the prey!" Her thoughts conjured up images of the unarmored monks and sorcerers their scouts had reported. The pair of tigers gave out a blood-chilling roar and, followed by a motley pack of wolves and a few foxes, headed out into the forest surrounding the low foothills. They were followed by a trio of lumbering bears and even a solitary badger that did not so much follow as forge their own path through the wooded hills.

"Scavengers, steal!" Arianna knew there was likely to be a strong force of Dragon-Blooded, and where there were Exalted, there were always artifacts and magical items. She sent mental images of shining rings, talismans, glowing stones and sparkling weapons—and especially of the jade of which the Realm forces were so fond. The small army of raccoons, weasels, opossums and monkeys raced for the war zone, hungry to claim their share of the glittering booty.

That left her with the horses, and she turned, looking over her shoulder at the herd that had finally completely entered the small clearing. With an expressive nod, she gestured for them to follow her and leaned forward over Mojin's neck. The big gray took off down the deer track toward the main road with the rest of the horses trotting behind him as quickly as the thickly wooded path would allow.

As they neared the road, the sounds of battle swelled. The heavy tree cover would not allow her to view the fight itself, but the sounds of sword on sword rang clearly through the heavy wood. Arianna and her band of horses charged forward, and as the deer track opened out on to the road, she saw that their intelligence reports had not been completely accurate.

Yurgen's men, several hundred in number, had hoped to come in behind the entirety of the imperial forces but had, instead, found themselves emerging in a break in the

Realm army, with the warstriders to their left and a dragon's worth of back-up soldiers and skirmishers to their right. Fortunately, the imperial forces seemed to be more surprised to see Yurgen's force charging out of the woods than the Northerners had been to find out that they'd not entirely bracketed in their foes. Many of the fallen bodies on the roadway were imperial bowmen who had not even had time to string their weapons before being struck by the short Northern recurves. Arrows buried to the fletching barely protruded from the Realm corpses, the Northern bows loosing their shafts with devastating effect at this range.

Yurgen was impossible to overlook, despite the complete chaos on the roadway. His anima blazed as clearly as the early morning sunlight, a perfect white and gold. Beneath its gleaming light, the gray-haired warrior was surrounded by a waist-high pile of fallen foes on all sides. His bow still slung on his back, he threw a pair of axes which lashed out, severing limbs with each toss before arcing back to his hands without fail. In the time one of his enemies made a single swipe with their sword, Yurgen's axes had been thrown and returned twice, and four of his enemies lay bleeding on the forest road.

His men were arrayed around him, effectively blocking the imperial forces at the rear of the army from proceeding any further toward the clearing. There were more Realm troops, but the addition of Yurgen to the situation ensured that the Northerners were holding their own, despite the odds.

Arianna turned, focusing her attention on the forces that stood between her and the glade. A handful of warstriders still stood, and Arianna was stunned for a moment at the beauty and ferocity of the giant machines. Standing waist deep in ancient woods, they waded through the trees like men might wade through a field of tall grass, and when one of their immense swords struck, it swept through trees, stones and enemies alike without hesitation. At the moment, they appeared to be attacking something that blocked their entrance to the clearing, orange-glowing lava splattering from their swords as they hacked at it.

As if in response to her appearance, a mixed flock of birds began bombarding the warstriders, darting in and out too quickly for the great armor to respond effectively. They couldn't actually harm the armored war machines, but their attacks distracted the Dragon-Blooded who were piloting them, slowing their assault.

Arianna spurred Mojin lightly with her heels, and he charged forward, slipping adroitly between the warstriders and past the arcing arms of lava that had stopped the giant warriors from entering the meadow. Behind them, the rest of the herd charged into the clearing, nimbly avoiding the magma tentacles, which seemed intent on targeting only their enemies.

Once in the glen, Arianna paused to assess the situation as her animal allies continued their attacks. Near the center of the clearing, the imperial forces skirmished with Samea's warriors. Bloody mud was knee-deep there, churned to a ghastly gray-pink.

The woods were on fire, starting at the eastern foothills, but the blaze was quickly consuming the thick woods in all directions, as well as several of the round nomadic buildings the Northerners had been using as barracks. The sky was orange with soot-filled smoke and growing darker by the minute. Each breath was becoming more bitter as the air grew acrid with fire and death.

Two warstriders had been downed, one with its helmet downhill on the eastern hill and another apparently the victim of a trio of fire spirits that were currently doing their best to melt the giant suit of armor. From the helmet's interior, the fire-tormented pilot's screams stretched out with an eerie round of echoes as she struggled relentlessly to release the harnesses that allowed her to pilot the machine and now held her captive in the impromptu oven.

Samea's hilltop was almost invisible through the growing clouds of angry smoke. What could be seen, however, were flashes of mystical fire as animas and sorcerous attacks flared through the growing clouds of angry smoke. Thunderous explosions rocked the hill, sending boulders as big as men rolling down into the flaming forest below.

Along with the square of mass carnage that surrounded the mortal Realm soldiers, there were other bodies scattered throughout the glade in various stages of destruction. A bald woman who once likely looked quite dashing in her hunter-green robes had found that Haltan swords were not a fashionable accessory. The one that pierced through her abdomen, impaling her to the ground, had strongly clashed with the rest of her ensemble.

Another Dragon-Blood lay further away, head bent backward and his arms and legs at unnatural angles. Over him, a confused-looking young man with hair the color of summer violets stood, clutching something around his throat and looking as if he really had no idea what he was doing in the middle of this battle.

Arianna blinked as her heart leapt.

The young man looked up at her, and from across the glade, she felt his violet eyes widening in recognition.

Mojin was in flight across the clearing before she formed the words to order him there.

CHAPTER TWENTY-FIVE

"There's nothing we can do, Swan. It's out of our hands now. The fire's just too far gone." Arianna's skin was coated in ashes, her hair a dingy gray from the soot. Mojin, snorting his displeasure with the destruction around them, pawed at the burned soil with one hoof.

Swan shook his head, struggling to cover the smoldering stump near him with another layer of ash and dried loam. Acrid dust billowed where the bucketful fell. "I can't give up, Arianna, I promised the Forest Lord." A crazed expression had come over him, the mania only accentuated by the thick layer of black smoke residue across his face. Runnels of sweat had begun to cascade down from his forehead, leaving eerily clean tear stains contrasting down the darker layer.

Arianna stepped forward, physically stopping him from shoveling further. Together they'd been trying to make headway against the destruction here for hours, but it was proving pointless. "You're not making any sense. The Forest Lord you made your promise to is hundreds of miles away from here."

He wrenched the bucket out of her hands, and she grimaced painfully as the wood tore at the blisters across her palms. "Oh, Arianna, I'm so sorry. I didn't mean to hurt you. But you just don't understand."

"Just stop." She wiped her hands on the underside hem of her tunic, the cleanest spot she could find, as he reluctantly stopped shoveling. "Now. Explain it to me. Help me understand why you are killing yourself to fight a forest fire that is beyond stopping to fulfill a promise to the lord of an entirely different wood."

At her words, Swan looked around. Yurgen's men were close to retreat, although the Realm forces were damaged enough to not press the matter. Samea's hilltop was in ruin, and her forces there had already evacuated after she had been gravely injured, pulling her away from the combat to relative safety.

Across the smoke-filled clearing, there was nothing unruined, nothing whole, nothing clean to be seen. Even the river was clogged with mud and blood and bodies, oozing where it had once run swiftly.

He made the mistake of taking a deep breath, and the acrid air burned at his lungs, sending him into a spasm of coughs. When they had ceased, he explained about the encounter he'd had with the Lord of the Forest who had saved them on the night they first met and the vow he'd made to do all in his power to aid this wood.

"But it wasn't the fire he feared?" Arianna asked, brow furrowing in thought.

Swan shook his head, sweat droplets scattering. "No. He said it was—"

Screams filled the meadow, audible even above the roar of the fire and the din of battle. As one, Arianna and Swan looked down the valley in time to see that one of Samea's gigantic magma tendrils still flailed, raining continued destruction on its enemies, despite their summoner's unconscious state. One of the massive warstriders had underestimated the lava-beast's reach, and its legs had become entangled in the molten rock arm. As they watched, the twenty-foot-tall suit of moving armor continued its impossibly slow fall forward, unable to keep its balance as the magma tendril pulled at its feet. Allies and enemies alike scrambled to escape its path, but there were few in the valley who still remained completely able at this point in the battle. As the earth shook at the giant's impact, several were caught completely or

partially beneath the fallen warstrider. The magma tendril pummeled at the screaming wounded, ending their
torment in a crimson blur, as the wind from the impact
only stirred the dancing sparks into greater madness. The
forest was almost as dark as night, canopied in ash and
smoke, lit only by the blaze of burning wood and the
occasional flare of Essence or sorcerous flame, blurred by
the miasma of the battle to an unwholesome glow.

"It's not the fire, Swan," Arianna said in slow realiza-
tion. "It's the death. The destruction. The spirit of this wood
is being desecrated. Carnage on this scale can rend a wound
in Creation all the way to the Underworld." Her voice
dropped to a hoarse whisper. "This place is becoming a
shadowland…" As if to confirm her insight, the sky overhead thundered in an unholy roar, and droplets began to fall
at a fevered pace. Rather than clean water, the rain filled the
air with liquid ash, burning hot, that scalded the skin and
turned the already ash-covered ground to a slick marsh of
pale gray in moments. Blood swirled in the viscous mess, vile
darkness mixing with the deathly pale muck.

"That must have been what the Forest Lord meant!
But what can we do? How can we stop it?" Swan looked
around desperately.

Arianna shook her head. "Nothing, Swan. There is
nothing we can do here and now… If we had… There are
ways… but none that would prevent the change from
happening now."

Swan deflated, leaning against the ruined stump like an
old man against a crutch. "Then we've failed… I've failed.
The Forest Lord here will be destroyed." He tugged the
acorn pendant out of his shirt, wrapping his grimy fingers
around the gleaming metal as he whispered his apologies. "I
am so sorry."

"Wait!" Arianna's eyes lit up at the sight of the
orichalcum in Swan's hands. "What is that?"

"It's the necklace the Forest Lord gave me when he
charged me to save the Wood King here."

"Give it to me."

Swan looked skeptically at Arianna but gingerly pulled the necklace over his head.

She extended her hand for the oak-leaf band and its acorn ornament. Running her blistered fingertips across the sacred metal pendant, she nodded. "He may have sent us the answer. But we'll need something else."

She looked around the meadow, grimacing as a froggish demon leaped across to the fallen warstrider. The Dynast who had piloted the war armor was bleeding from the forehead as she struggled to remove herself from the strider's harness system. The reptilian demon wrapped its prehensile tongue around the head and upper torso of the struggling woman, pulling her into his maw, where he promptly bit her in half at the waist.

"Quickly, before it's too late." Arianna dashed for the woods at the southeastern edge of the meadow, nearest the river where the fire damage had been the least complete. Passing the empty corral and the burned ruins of Yurgen's men's tents, she said a desperate prayer to the Unconquered Sun to find what she sought. She desperately scanned the trees for something, craning her neck as she ran.

Swan followed, confused but desperate. "What are we looking for?" He craned his sights upward as well, hoping to catch a glimpse that would clue him into what it was Arianna sought.

"An oak! There!" Her sprint became a full run as she spotted the rounded foliage of an ancient oak. Its branches were singed, leaves curled and burned, but the tree itself had not yet succumbed to the ravages of the forest fire around it. Arianna knelt in the ashy loam beneath its broad canopy, resting the acorn pendant on the hem of her skirt to keep it free of the pale ash. She dug desperately in the small satchel at her side, pulling out the red leather tome that had caused so much dissention between herself and Yurgen. "If this works, I'm going to have to thank Yurgen for his trick."

Swan stood, confused. "What are you going to do? What can I do?"

"I'll explain later. Just make sure I don't get interrupted. That would be... unfortunate." She flipped madly through the small book, leaving sooty smudges on the pages as she searched for something hidden within.

Nodding, Swan turned to guard the area between Arianna and the rest of the battle.

Their escape had not gone unnoticed. From out of the swirling smoke stepped a beautiful woman dressed in light veils that were caught at her shoulder and waist with long shining black pins. Her hair was dressed immaculately, despite the chaos, as if the ashen clouds that choked everything around her simply could not bring themselves to disturb her beauty. She offered a sweet, tight-lipped smile in Swan's direction, fingertips delicately steepled in front of her.

Swan blinked to clear his eyes, fearing he was hallucinating, then focused his gaze on her, using the insight gifted to him by the Unconquered Sun to determine her intentions. The blankness he found there disturbed and confused him.

"Come no closer!" he ordered, taking up a defensive stance.

The woman's sweet smile became a frown, and she tilted her head in irritation at his words, but she said nothing. She pulled her hands away from each other, and from between her fingertips, shiny black ichor stretched in fragile threads. She continued forward, walking with the same sinuous steps as the strands of dark mucous hardened and then split in half, becoming a set of shining needles, one rising from each fingertip.

Swan blinked in surprise, but reached deep within himself, calling his spiritual power to surround him. His milky anima flared out, and for a moment, the woman paused, watching the dancing flow of opalescent light.

"Don't make me hurt you." Swan wasn't sure what this woman's intentions were, but he could not allow her to interfere with the ritual he could hear Arianna intoning at the base of the great oak behind him. "Leave now, and we have no quarrel."

The intruder's frown deepened still as Swan spoke again, and she continued forward, reaching for him with the strange needlelike claws.

The light from Swan's anima glistened off of them, lending them a venomous gleam, and Swan was suddenly very sure that, unreadable as they might be, the woman's intentions were not good.

He ducked beneath her arm, avoiding her attack. Slipping one foot in front of her ankle, he pulled hard in hopes of tripping her. She remained upright. He turned, reaching to force her off balance and barely jerked his hands back in time to avoid impaling them on the jagged spines protruding from her back. She stumbled to the ground with a muffled outburst, claws digging deeply into the ashy loam. As she struggled to right herself, Swan could tell that her human visage was merely a façade. From the top of her head to the tips of her heels, her back was made entirely of glistening spines identical to the ones she'd spun from her fingertips.

She was almost on her feet again, and Swan looked around, not cherishing the idea of fighting her with his bare hands. A successful attack on his part might still leave him impaled or bleeding, perhaps taking more damage than he could inflict. Of greater concern, however, was that her first charge had taken her past Swan, and she now stood midway between himself and Arianna, who still knelt at the base of the great oak. The inhuman woman stood for a moment, working her talons together, and as he watched, the ten needlelike claws formed into a glistening dagger. She looked from Swan, crouching at the ready, to Arianna's vulnerable back, and turned, charging toward the white-haired woman.

"No!" Swan leapt forward, determined to place himself between his companion and her new attacker. His bound took him over the demon's head, and she stalled her charge in surprise, giving Swan the opportunity he had been looking for.

With one graceful motion, he swept her extruded weapon to the side with his left hand and slammed the heel of the right one up into the woman's perfect face. There was no grinding of bones, no crunching of cartilage—her face simply collapsed in on itself with a shattering sound like the ruin of a plate-glass window. Spines littered the ground behind her as she folded inward with an unintelligible gasp of pain. Her weapon dropped to the ground as she curled into a spiky ball like some obscene hedgehog, leaving no vulnerable locations available for Swan to attack.

Swan looked around for a weapon that would penetrate the spines and turned back to find nothing left of the woman but the remnants of liquid ichor seeping into the ashy forest floor. As he watched, they disappeared completely, leaving only the black glittering dagger and a scattering of shattered spine shards. Hesitant to pick up the offensive weapon, he kicked some loose oak leaves over it and returned to his vigilance.

From behind him, Arianna gave out a gasp that spun Swan around just in time to see her slump limply to the ground.

"Arianna!" He dashed over, cradling her unmoving body in his arms. The necklace was clutched tightly in her hands, and the orichalcum acorn gleamed in defiance of the smoke and ash that filled the air.

Arianna's eyelids stirred, and she looked up at Swan with eyes so light blue they were almost colorless. She smiled, the scar down her face wrinkling softly. "It worked," she whispered.

"What worked? Are you okay? By the Unconquered Sun, I thought for a moment you'd—"

Arianna pressed the ashy fingertips of one hand against his mouth while the other held up the oak-leaf band. "He's here. They can't kill him now."

"Who? Arianna, you're not making any sense." His lips moved against her fingertips, but she did not draw them back.

"The Forest Lord. For a time, at least, he has a new home." Her voice rasped, ravaged by the smoke, which grew thicker by the moment. "We have to get out of here."

Swan nodded, pulling her gently to her feet. She took a step forward, then rocked dangerously back, unable to support her weight. Together, with his arm around her waist, they slipped back toward the clearing.

The chaos had, if anything, magnified since their departure. It was no longer possible to see even halfway across the once-verdant meadow, and even after they left the thick forest canopy, the smoke hung over their heads in a tangible layer, blocking out the sun. Ashes and embers swirled madly in the air, and the fire leapt like a sentient beast, consuming everything in its path. Mojin stood, as they had left him, and they hurried their pace.

"We have to get the spirit out of here," Arianna repeated, quietly, almost falling yet again. Swan held her up, striding forward with strength enough for both of them, pulling her toward her steed and escape. Mojin turned as they approached, and his eyes rolled up in anger. The huge gray reared, a scream of anger cutting through the polluted air as his dark hooves churned in the air above them.

Swan pushed Arianna to the muddy ground beneath him, throwing himself over her to protect her from the angry gelding's attack. The horse dropped forward, screaming his ire, his hooves barely missing the crouched couple before he leapt into the air again.

There was a sickening crunch, and the smell of fresh blood overpowered the smoke-filled haze around them. Swan looked up to see the crumpled form of Arianna's faithful gray lying with legs askew. Crimson fountained from a black ichorous dagger that was deeply buried in the horse's neck. Beneath the horse's fallen body, a pair of deceptively delicate bare legs still struggled, pinned only by the beast's great weight. Black spines tore at the muddy ground as the demi-woman from the glade fought to free herself from her muddy prison.

Swan pulled Arianna to her feet, tugging her along as she stared with empty eyes at her fallen mount. "We have to get out of here. Come on."

Ahead, the empty corral mocked them, its inhabitants long scattered save for those whose burnt or half-eaten carcasses still littered the ground within. The oven of the glade blazed around them, fire on every side.

"Stop." Swan looked confused as Arianna dug her heels into the slick ground with strength he doubted she could spare. She refused to go further.

"But we have to get out of here."

Arianna shook her head, the damp tendrils of her hair clinging to her soot-stained face. The air surrounding them was searing and growing hotter by the moment. "You have to get it out of here, Swan. I can't do it." She broke into a rasping cough. "I don't even have enough strength left to walk out of the fire. You have to go. You have to get the spirit out of here." She handed the pendant to him, pressing his fingers painfully tightly around it.

"But…" Swan shook his head. "I can't leave you here."

"You have to, Swan. You promised. You gave your word." Sweat no longer gathered on her brow, evaporating before it could form beads. Ash began to gather there instead, a deathly snowfall dusting her skin. She began to slump slowly, unable to support her own weight.

"No… I… Not again. Not here! There has to be another way!" Swan's anima flared to life with such brilliance that, for the briefest moment, the illness in the air was burned away, leaving the pair of them surrounded in clean white light. It wrapped itself around them, twining them together with pearly strands of pure radiance. Swan looked down into her pale eyes.

"The first night we met, the Unconquered Sun put me in your path, Arianna. Since then, everything has drawn me to you, to here, to now. I cannot believe that the only choice we have now is to… I will not leave you!"

His vow filled the space between them, pushing outward with a force that even the destruction around them could not smother immediately. As Swan stared deeply into her eyes, a voice echoed in his head so loudly that he could not stop himself from mouthing the words that filled his mind.

We are one.

As the soundless phrase slipped between them, Arianna's eyes brightened. From the colorless ice they had been, Swan watched them grow first to a pale blue and then deeper, until they glowed like the summer seas. His breath caught in his throat.

She straightened then, standing on her own, although she did not pull away. A wave of confusion slipped across her face, then a grimace of concentration.

From out of the burning smoke, a flash of golden light struck forth, accompanied by a screaming whinny. Arianna's spirit steed leapt out of the blaze, slowing only long enough for them to scramble aboard before racing east out of the tormented valley.

Swan slumped forward, arms wrapped tightly around Arianna's waist as they fled, leaving the burgeoning shadowland in their wake. Within moments, the air, while still filled with smoke and ash, had cooled perceptibly, and Swan shuddered, leaning his cheek against his companion's soot-stained back. The steed continued on, tirelessly, and behind them, the din of battle and the roar of the forest fire grew quiet, leaving his ears ringing in the silence.

With tears streaming down his face, he whispered a prayer to the heavens. It was only two words.

"Thank you."

CHAPTER TWENTY-SIX

"I wanted you to know, you were right."

Swan broke the silence that had hovered over them for the past few hours.

Arianna nodded, continuing to watch the stars above them. On her spirit steed's back, they'd left the war zone far behind them, pausing only long enough to wash the stains of death and fire from their skin and clothing before continuing on through the night. Ragged and drained, they'd dozed in exhaustion as the golden steed ran through forests and over foothills, stopping only when the spell that called it was spent. Here, far away from the forest fire, the night sky was clear and the grass was sweet and green. With no shelter or steed, no food or supplies, it still seemed to her that there was no place as perfect as this in all of Creation.

"I understand now, what you meant. That we can't ever go back to the way things were. I mean, don't get me wrong, I'm glad to be back traveling with you." Swan's understatement hung in the air, glaring in the light of what they'd just been through. "I... I rather missed you while we were apart. It's just... " He frowned, turning to face her, frustrated at finding himself short for words.

Arianna's nod was so subtle that it might have merely been lost had he not been watching her so intently.

Swan looked down at the pendant hanging around his neck, tracing his fingers over the rough texture of the cap and the silken smoothness of the acorn itself.

He frowned, suddenly uncertain how to speak to her of what he was truly feeling.

At last, Arianna glanced over at him. "You are very distracted this evening. What is it that is truly bothering you?"

Shrugging, Swan shook his head. "I don't know… I've just been thinking about… about all of it. Have you thought about what would have happened if the Wyld Hunt hadn't attacked when they did, that first night? Or if someone else had been chosen to go on the treaty mission? Or if we hadn't been found by Yurgen's men when we were, that day on the ice? So many coincidences, putting us in the right places at the right times for something to happen."

Arianna lay back, shaking her head. Her silver-white hair rippled in contrast to the dark grass beneath her. "Existence is a series of coincidences, Swan. Any two people meeting at any time is just that. Call it fate, or call it destiny. It is what it is. Some would say the gods are playing games with our lives, twisting the threads into a tapestry that pleases only their eyes." She paused, thoughtfully. "I prefer to think that we create our own paths, through our strength of will and our own choices. We are here because, in spite of the challenges we have faced, it is where we have chosen to be. We are the masters of our own fates."

He smiled, reveling for a moment in the sound of his name on her lips. With a chuckle, he shook his head, clearing his thoughts before returning his attention to the skies over head. "Perhaps you're right."

EPILOGUE

Like a raiton coming to light on a delicate branch, Otieno landed on the stone windowsill with hardly a sound. The scent of burning incense tickled at his pointed nose, and he rubbed it absently with the back of one hand as he waited.

Admon Mada did not bother to look up from her scribal work. Her ebon hair was swept into a tight chignon into which golden hairpins had been expertly skewered. From the ends of the pins dangled fine gold chains that suspended brilliant crimson garnets as big around as a man's thumb. Her gown was of yellow silk brocade, embroidered with ornate jungles of monkeys, parrots and butterflies in fine silk thread. At the outer corner of each eye, a facetted amber teardrop glistened against her snow-pale skin.

Across the parchment, a delicate pattern of solar symbols and elements intertwined. Layer upon layer of carefully drafted ciphers were added until the original information was lost in the intricate art.

A long moment passed.

"Well?" Her voice cut through the silence like a razor.

"They've decided to make their way to Nexus. They should arrive within two weeks." Otieno's voice was a harsh croak, quite a contrast to his petite form.

"Both of them?"

Otieno nodded, stripping the black leather gloves from his hands and tucking them into his belt.

"Excellent."

A long silence fell upon the room, where the only sound was the gentle whisper of the sable brush upon the parchment.

"Immaculate One? May I ask a question?" His voice rasped, tearing the sweet silence asunder.

"You just have."

Another long silence. Finally, Otieno decided that his curiosity was great enough to risk his mistress' displeasure.

"Why send the Wyld Hunt against them if you wanted them alive? It would have been just as easy to have me switch those orders out for ones that sent us off on another quarry, rather than meeting up with that other group and going out against the woman."

The dark-haired woman delicately laid her brush against its rest and then turned a serene expression upon her servant.

"For the same reason, my dear dark one, that the hushed ones were sent to try them in the blizzard. And the same reason Magistrate Gerik was ready to meet the diplomat in Wavecrest and cut short his career. One cannot craft a strong weapon from untempered steel. These two would be no good to me untested. To serve their purpose, they had to look beyond the paths they were born to, to separate their past from what will come and to choose correctly the road they would travel into the future."

Otieno nodded uncertainly, more out of habit than understanding. As often happened, he was now more confused by Mada's answer than he had been before he asked the question.

"But, I don't understand, Mistress. Why them? Why—" His questions were cut off by the tiniest gesture from Mada's hand.

With the elegance of a willow in the wind, Admon Mada slipped out of her chair, her silken robes rustling softly. She glided toward the window, looking out into the night sky past Otieno's slight form. With one delicate hand she gestured toward something just above the horizon, her movement as graceful as if it had been choreographed for the stage.

"Look there," she said softly, her voice silken against his ear. "The Maiden of Journeys rises."

Otieno shuddered softly at the whisper of breath against his skin and then obediently gazed out toward the horizon, taking in the radiant yellow star that glittered in the velvet sky.

He never felt the stiletto-sharp golden hairpin enter at the base of his skull. With an almost loving gesture, Mada slipped the delicate pin in, flicked it to the left and right to deftly sever his spinal cord, wiped it across his silk sleeve and returned the jewelry back to her flawless coif. The entire gesture was over in a heartbeat and might have been mistaken for a loving caress had she been careless enough to allow it to be observed. With a final exhalation, the petite man in black slipped lifelessly from the window-sill to the floor.

"Good journey, faithful servant." She reached down and gently stroked his face, running a gold-lacquered finger-nail across his cooling lips. "Do not carry your questions with you to the next lifetime. There are things you will not comprehend, not in this existence or the next."

By the next morning, all trace of the woman's occupancy was gone, save for the single dark corpse with a knowing smile upon its craggy face.

About the Author

Jess Hartley is a housewife doing her part to dispel the myth that anime-inspired fantasy is only for those under 30. She lives in the Pacific Northwest, where she gives constant thanks for her fabulous family, a constant source of support, as well as her former desk job that inspired her to write professionally, out of desperation to escape. **In Northern Twilight** is her first, but hopefully not her last, novel.

Acknowledgements

I would like to thank my family for their support; to my parents and sister for the encouragement to follow a dream, to my children, Nathan, Nicole and Autumn for keeping me young enough to write and to my friends, who promised to buy my first book, even if it was awful.

In Northern Twilight is dedicated to my husband, Patrick, without whom I would not be the person I am today. Without his hours of patience and prodding, this book would have never been started, let alone finished.

Thank you, Bear.